Animal Crackers

ANIMAL CRACKERS

WRITTEN BY
SCOTT CHRISTIAN SAVA

ILLUSTRATED BY
ALISON ACTON

X
GN

:01

First Second
New York

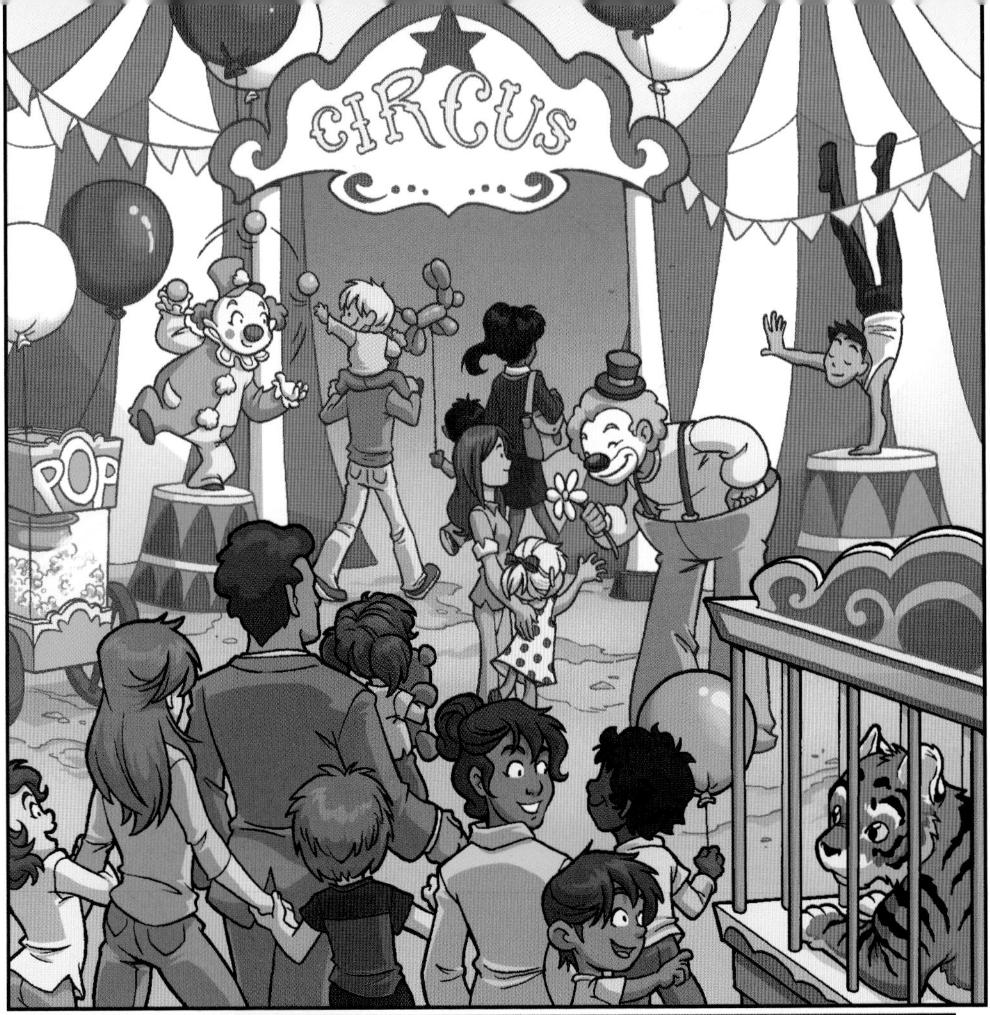
CIRCUS
POP

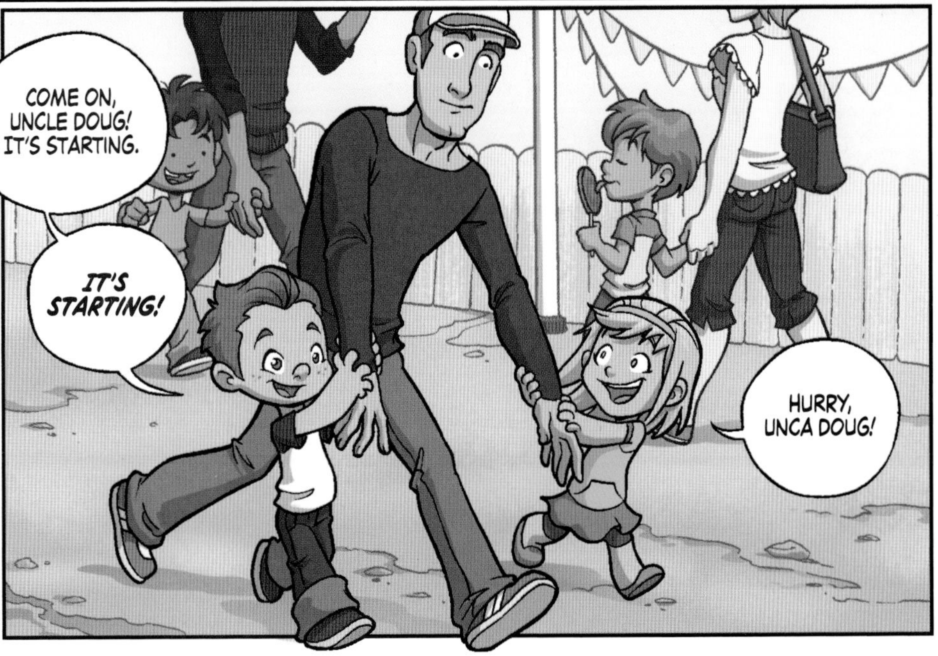
COME ON, UNCLE DOUG! IT'S STARTING.
IT'S STARTING!
HURRY, UNCA DOUG!

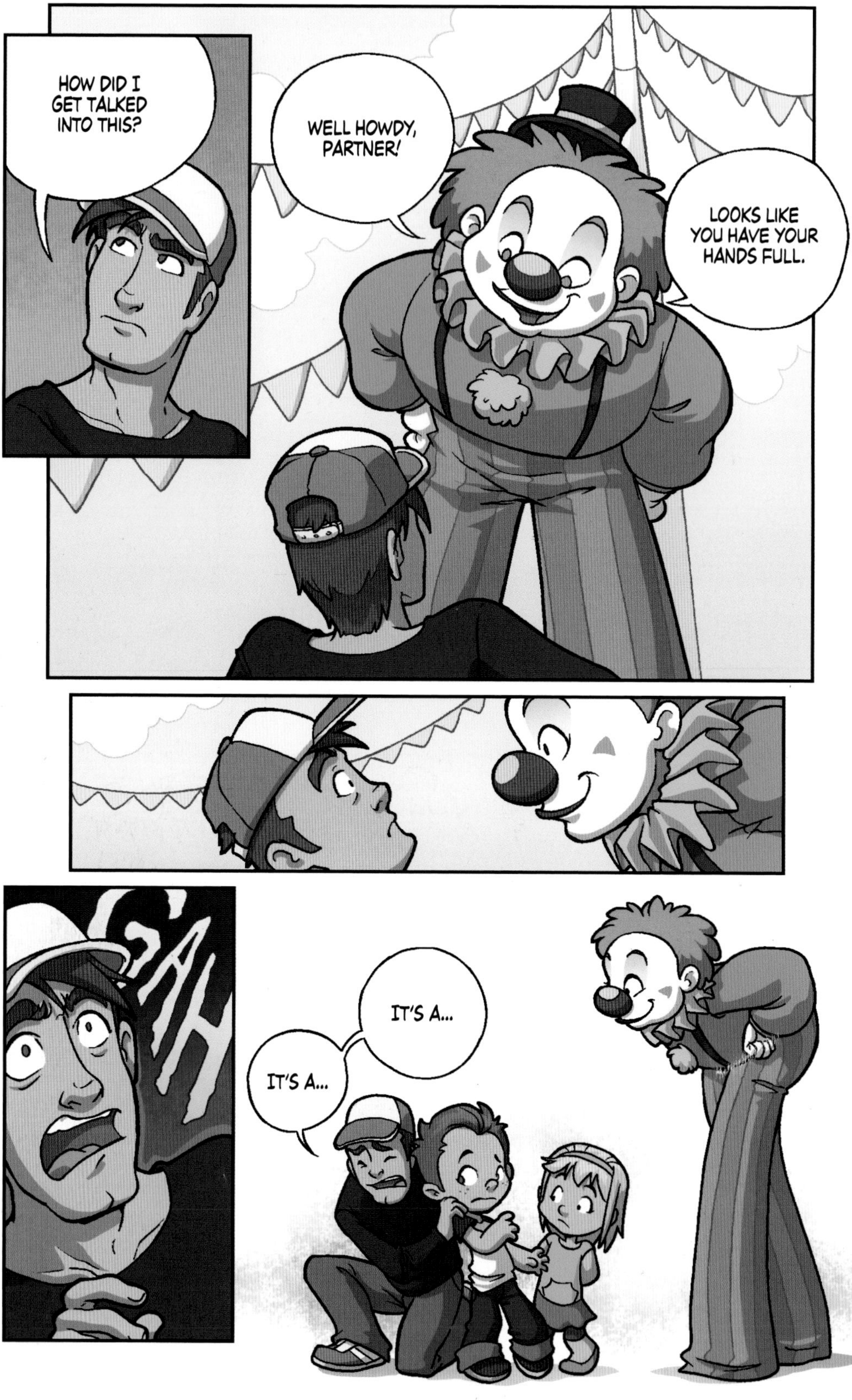
HOW DID I GET TALKED INTO THIS?
WELL HOWDY, PARTNER!
LOOKS LIKE YOU HAVE YOUR HANDS FULL.
IT'S A...
IT'S A...

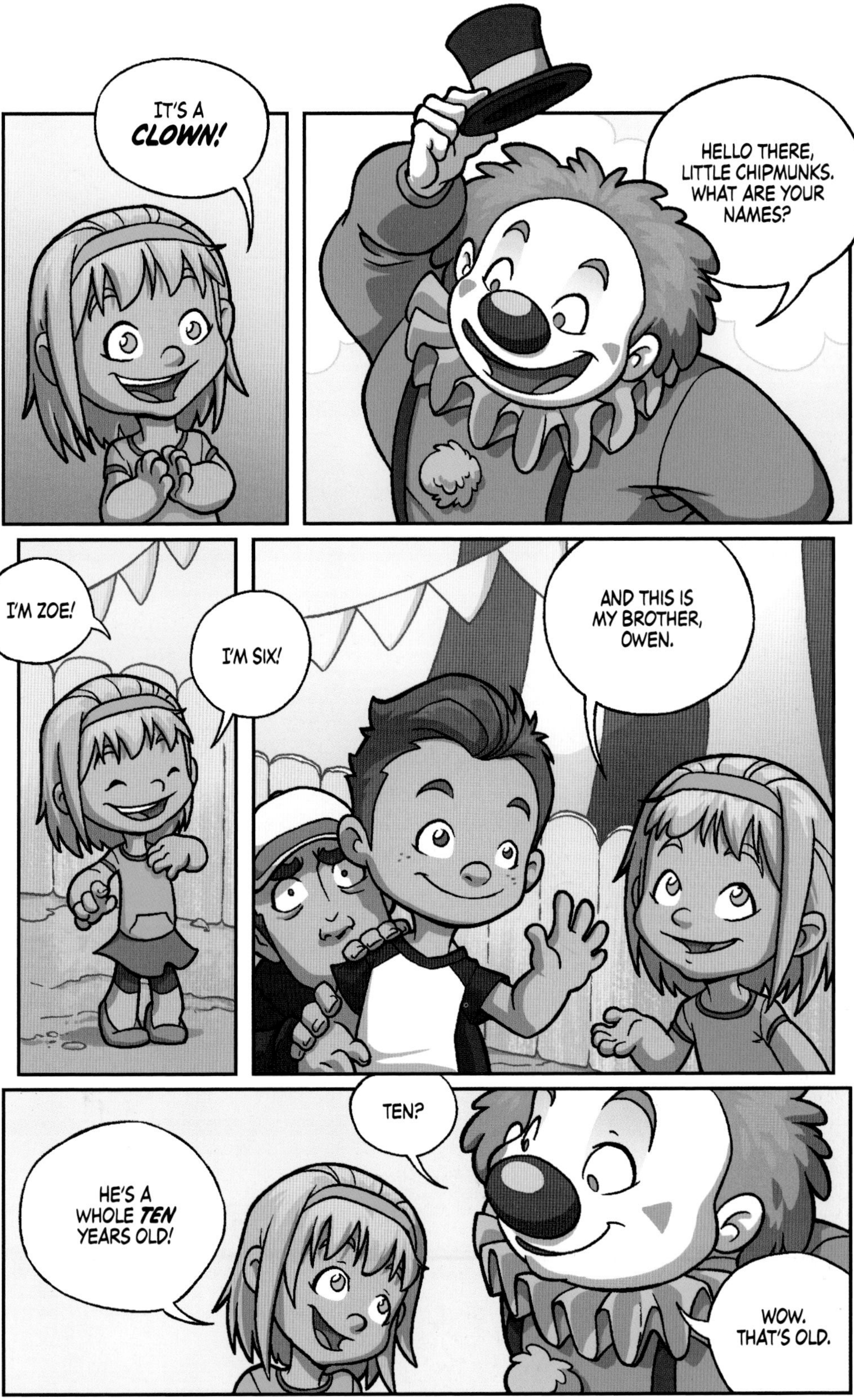
IT'S A CLOWN!
HELLO THERE, LITTLE CHIPMUNKS. WHAT ARE YOUR NAMES?
I'M ZOE!
I'M SIX!
AND THIS IS MY BROTHER, OWEN.
HE'S A WHOLE TEN YEARS OLD!
TEN?
WOW. THAT'S OLD.

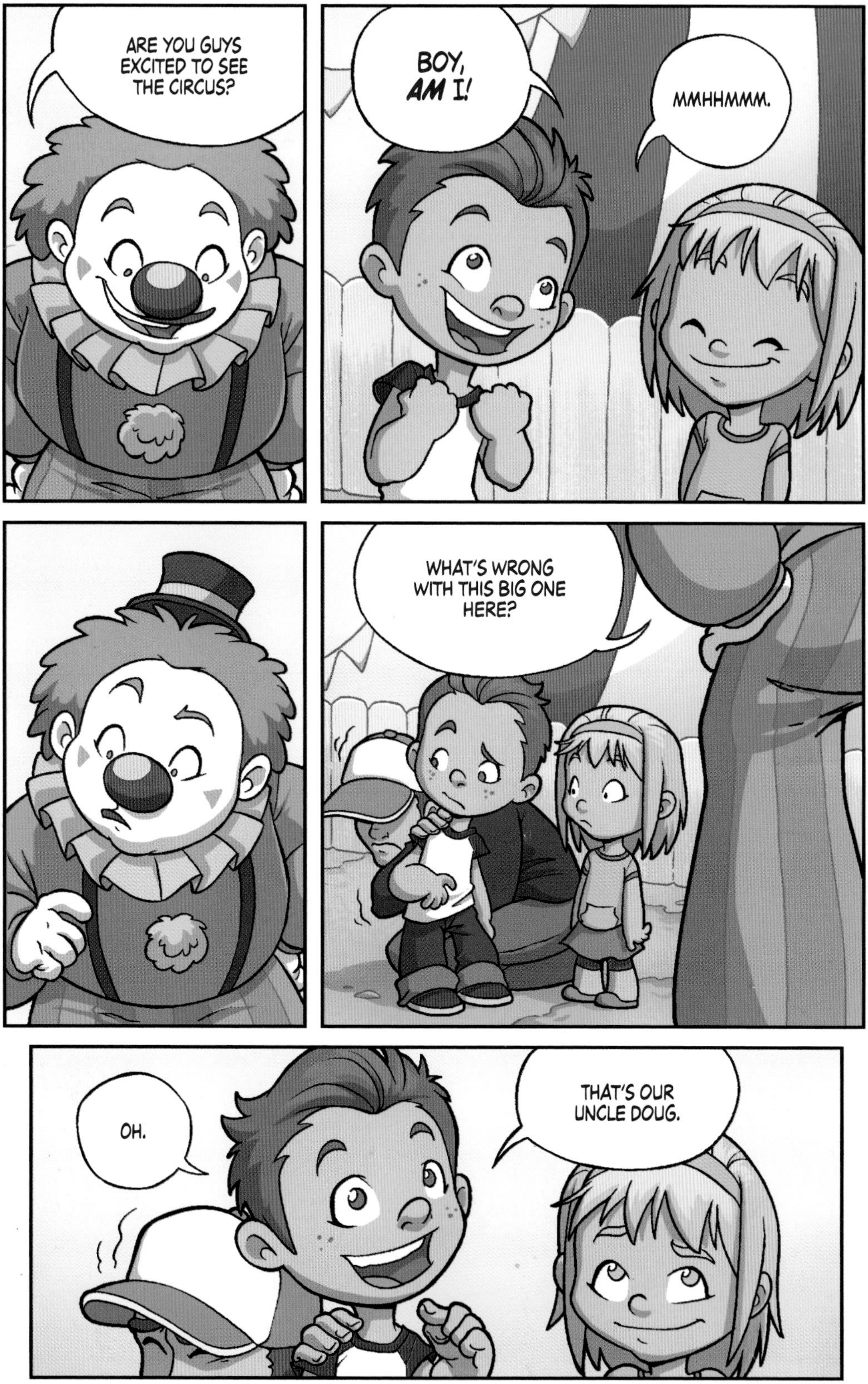
ARE YOU GUYS EXCITED TO SEE THE CIRCUS?
BOY, *AM* I!
MMHHMMM.
WHAT'S WRONG WITH THIS BIG ONE HERE?
OH.
THAT'S OUR UNCLE DOUG.

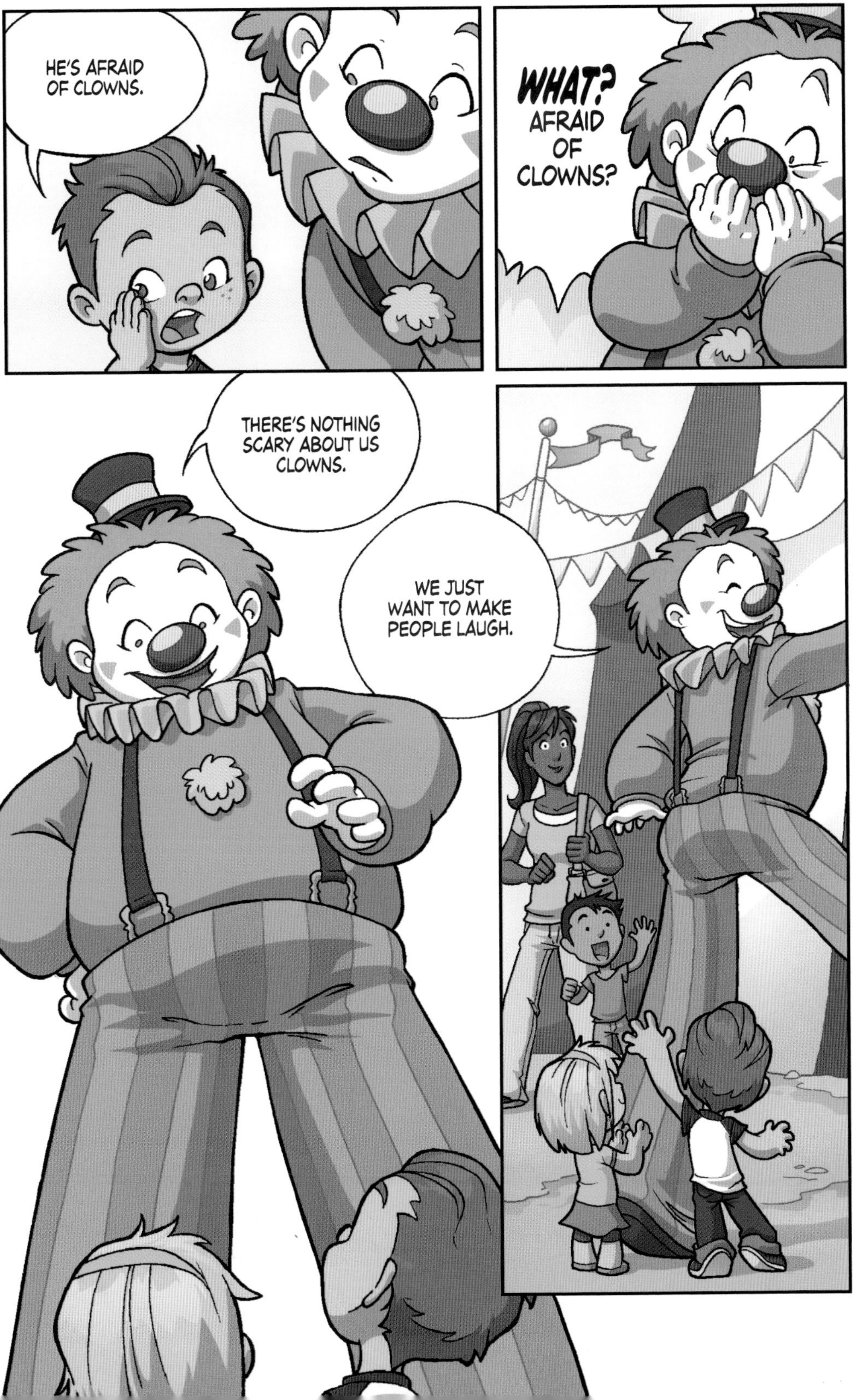
HE'S AFRAID OF CLOWNS.
WHAT? AFRAID OF CLOWNS?
THERE'S NOTHING SCARY ABOUT US CLOWNS.
WE JUST WANT TO MAKE PEOPLE LAUGH.

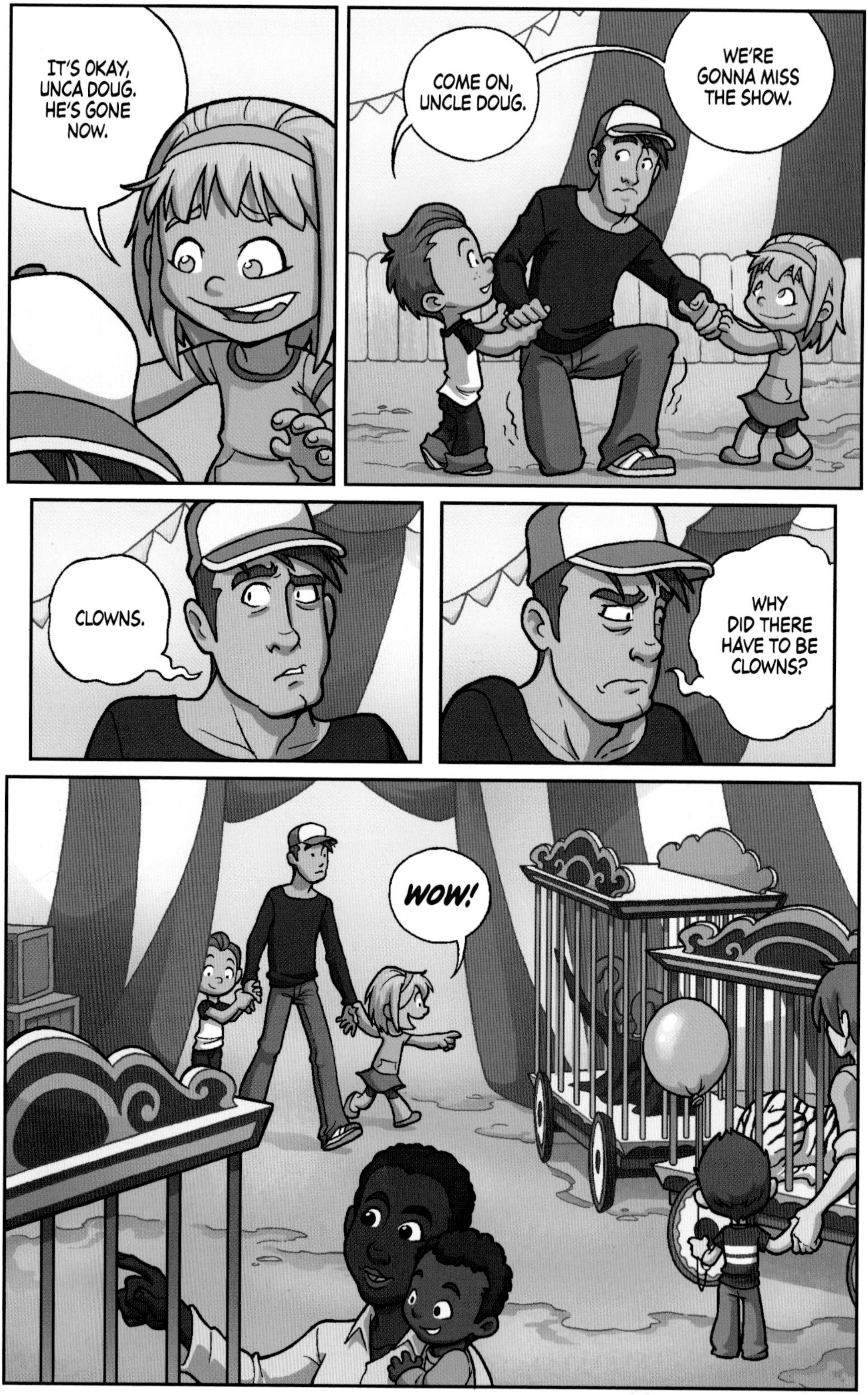
IT'S OKAY, UNCA DOUG. HE'S GONE NOW.
COME ON, UNCLE DOUG.
WE'RE GONNA MISS THE SHOW.
CLOWNS.
WHY DID THERE HAVE TO BE CLOWNS?
WOW!

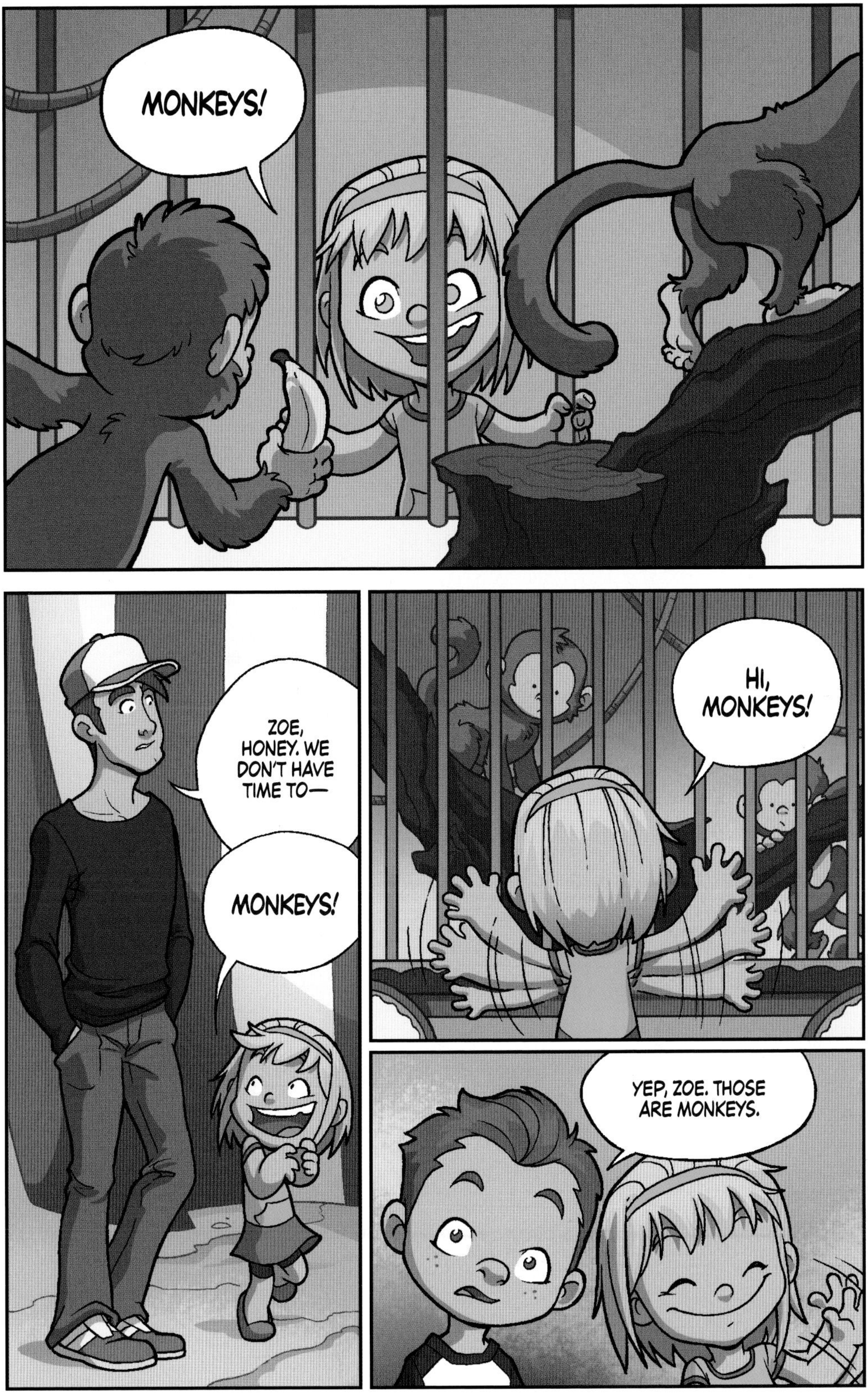
MONKEYS!
ZOE, HONEY. WE DON'T HAVE TIME TO—
MONKEYS!
HI, MONKEYS!
YEP, ZOE. THOSE ARE MONKEYS.

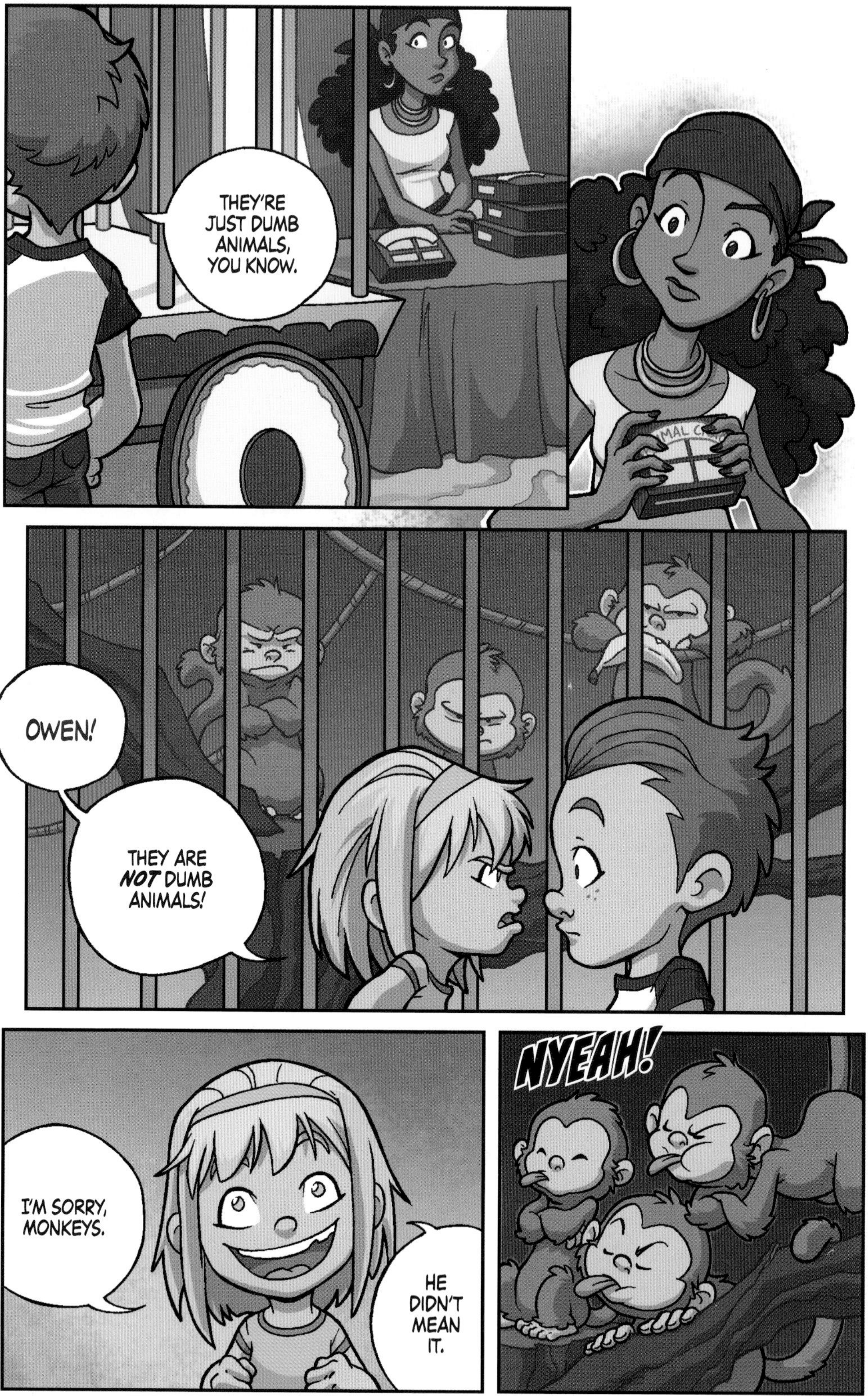
THEY'RE JUST DUMB ANIMALS, YOU KNOW.
OWEN!
THEY ARE *NOT* DUMB ANIMALS!
I'M SORRY, MONKEYS.
HE DIDN'T MEAN IT.
NYEAH!

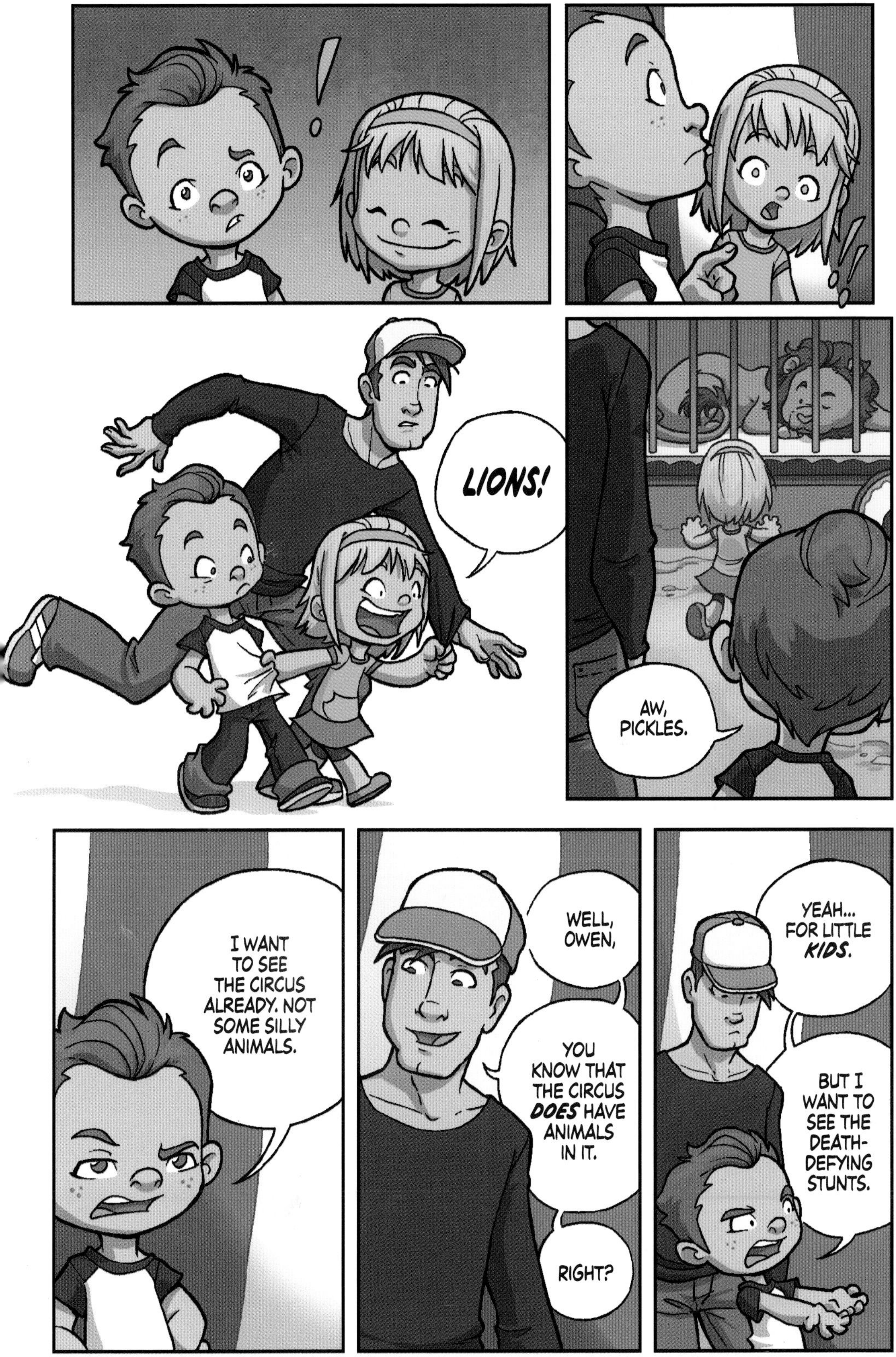
!
!!
LIONS!
AW, PICKLES.
I WANT TO SEE THE CIRCUS ALREADY. NOT SOME SILLY ANIMALS.
WELL, OWEN,
YOU KNOW THAT THE CIRCUS ***DOES*** HAVE ANIMALS IN IT.
RIGHT?
YEAH... FOR LITTLE ***KIDS***.
BUT I WANT TO SEE THE DEATH-DEFYING STUNTS.

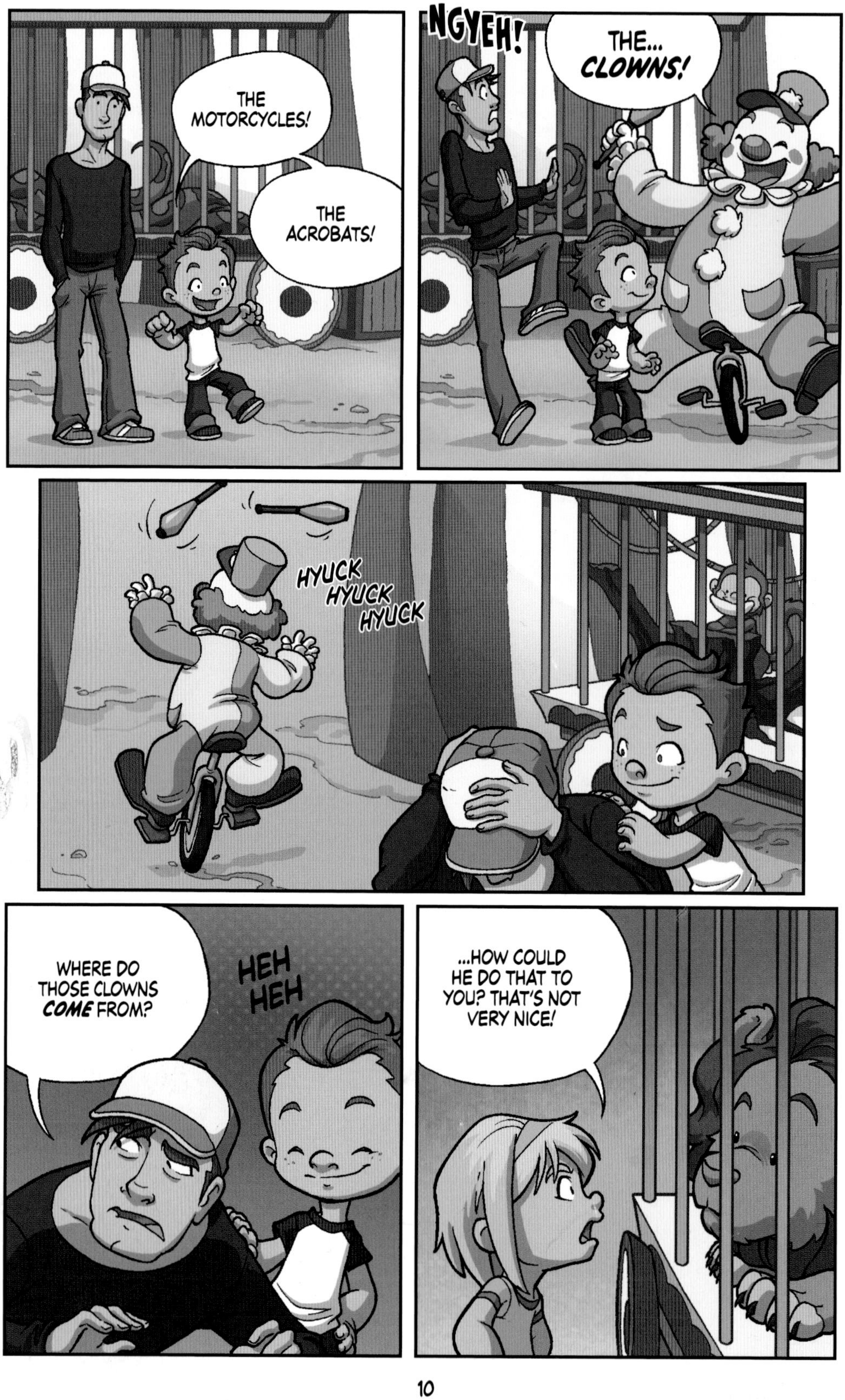

THE MOTORCYCLES!
THE ACROBATS!
NGYEH!
THE... CLOWNS!
HYUCK HYUCK HYUCK
WHERE DO THOSE CLOWNS COME FROM?
HEH HEH
...HOW COULD HE DO THAT TO YOU? THAT'S NOT VERY NICE!

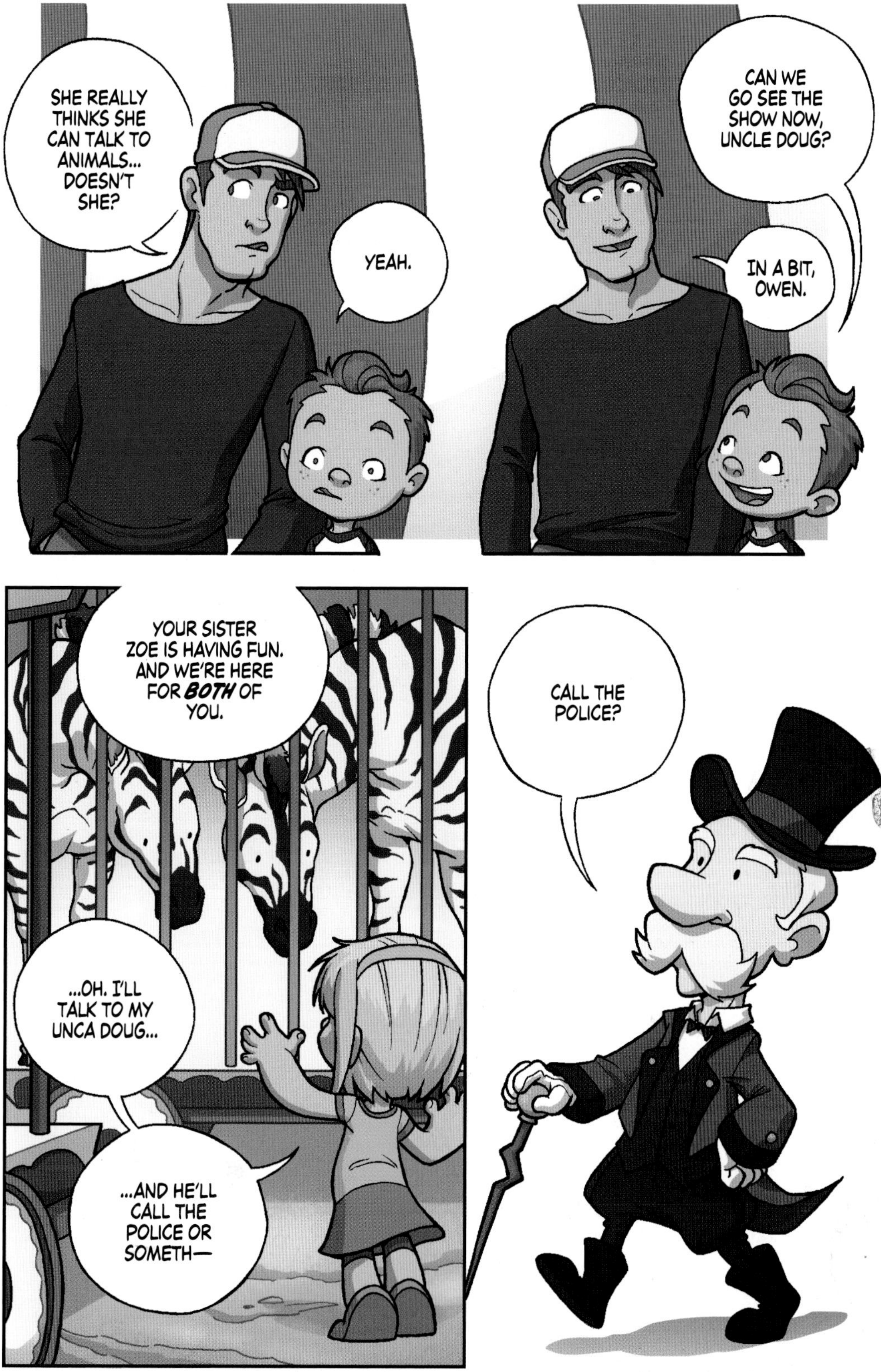
SHE REALLY THINKS SHE CAN TALK TO ANIMALS... DOESN'T SHE?
YEAH.
CAN WE GO SEE THE SHOW NOW, UNCLE DOUG?
IN A BIT, OWEN.
YOUR SISTER ZOE IS HAVING FUN. AND WE'RE HERE FOR *BOTH* OF YOU.
...OH. I'LL TALK TO MY UNCA DOUG...
...AND HE'LL CALL THE POLICE OR SOMETH—
CALL THE POLICE?

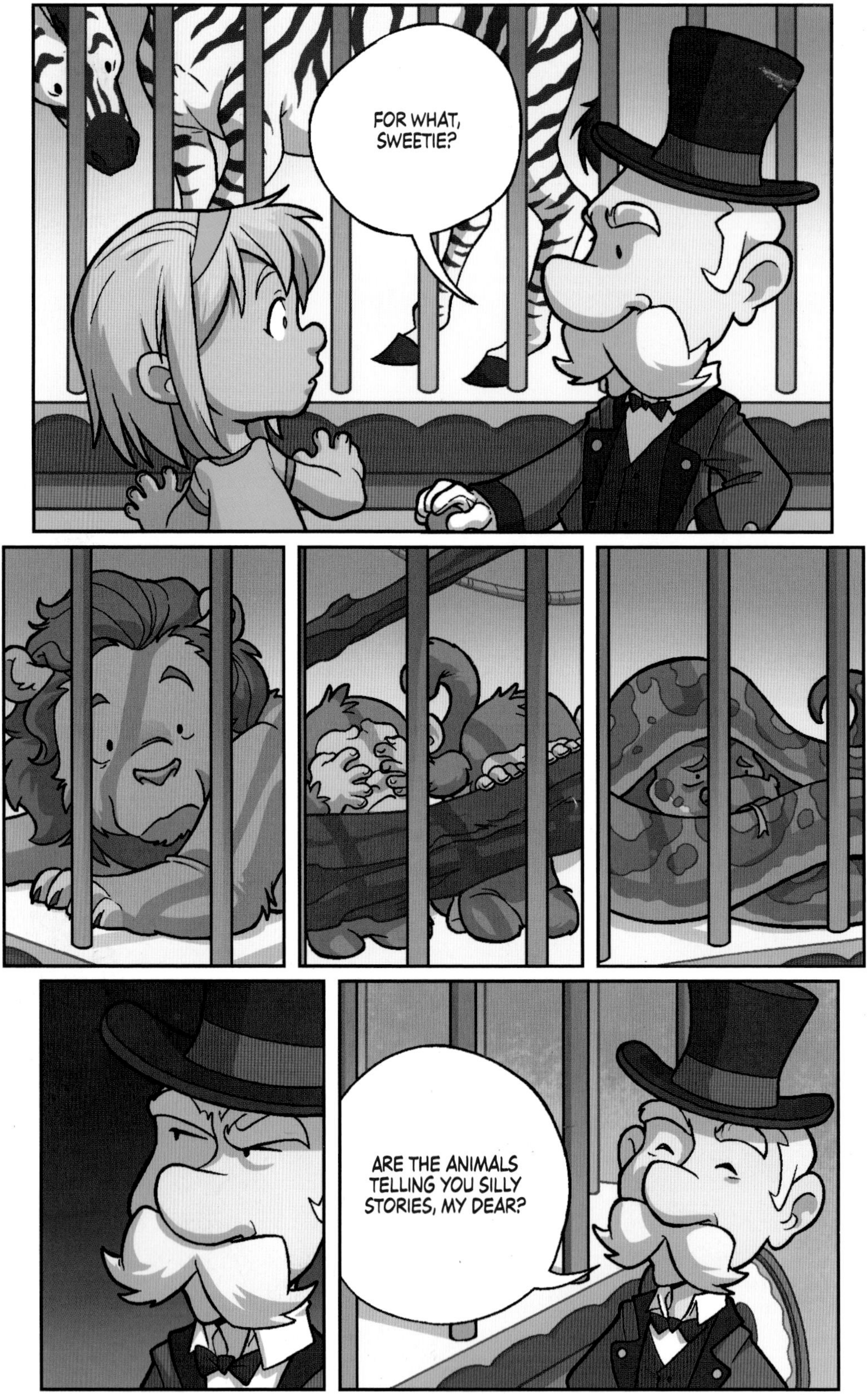
FOR WHAT, SWEETIE?
ARE THE ANIMALS TELLING YOU SILLY STORIES, MY DEAR?

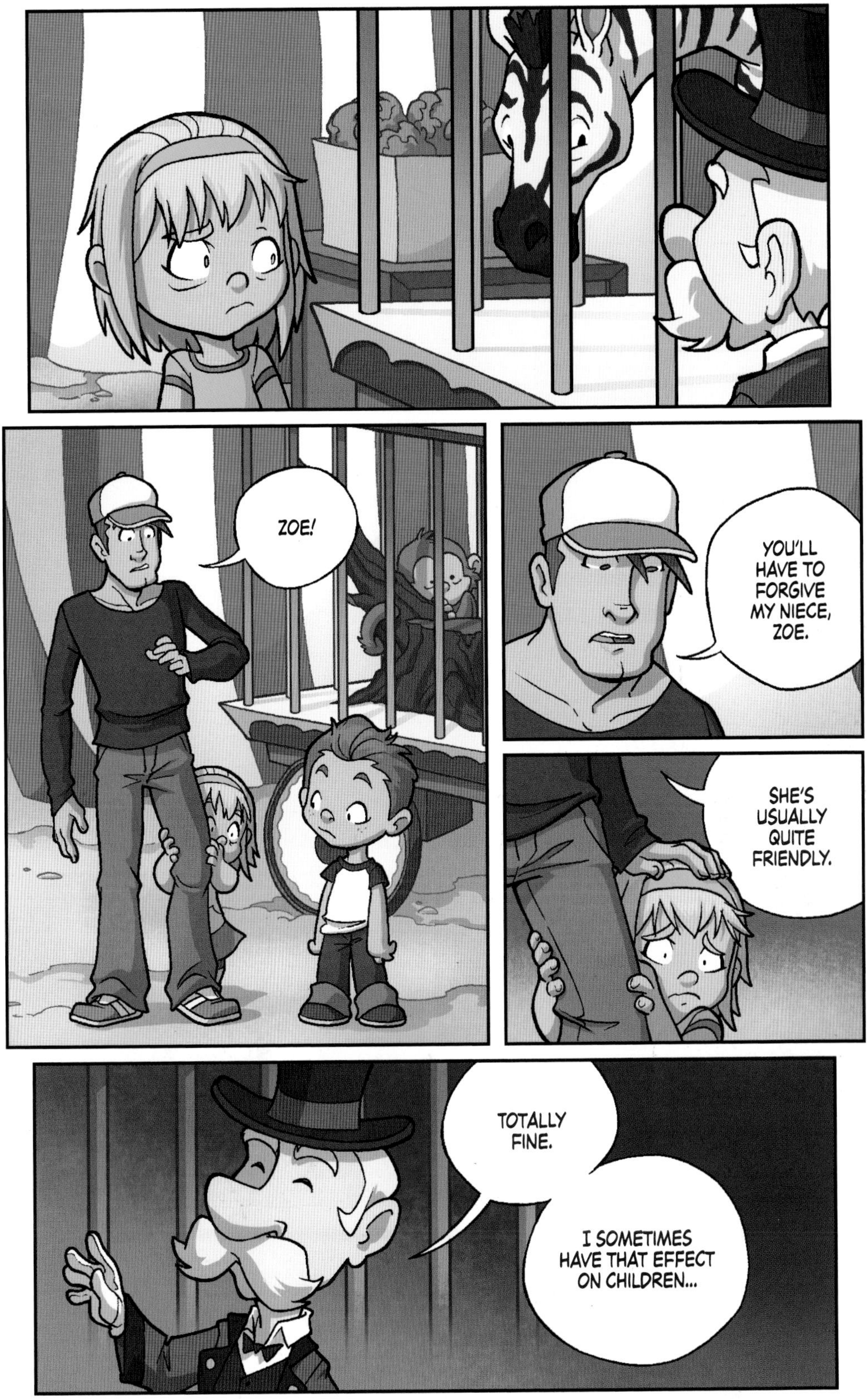
ZOE!
YOU'LL HAVE TO FORGIVE MY NIECE, ZOE.
SHE'S USUALLY QUITE FRIENDLY.
TOTALLY FINE.
I SOMETIMES HAVE THAT EFFECT ON CHILDREN...

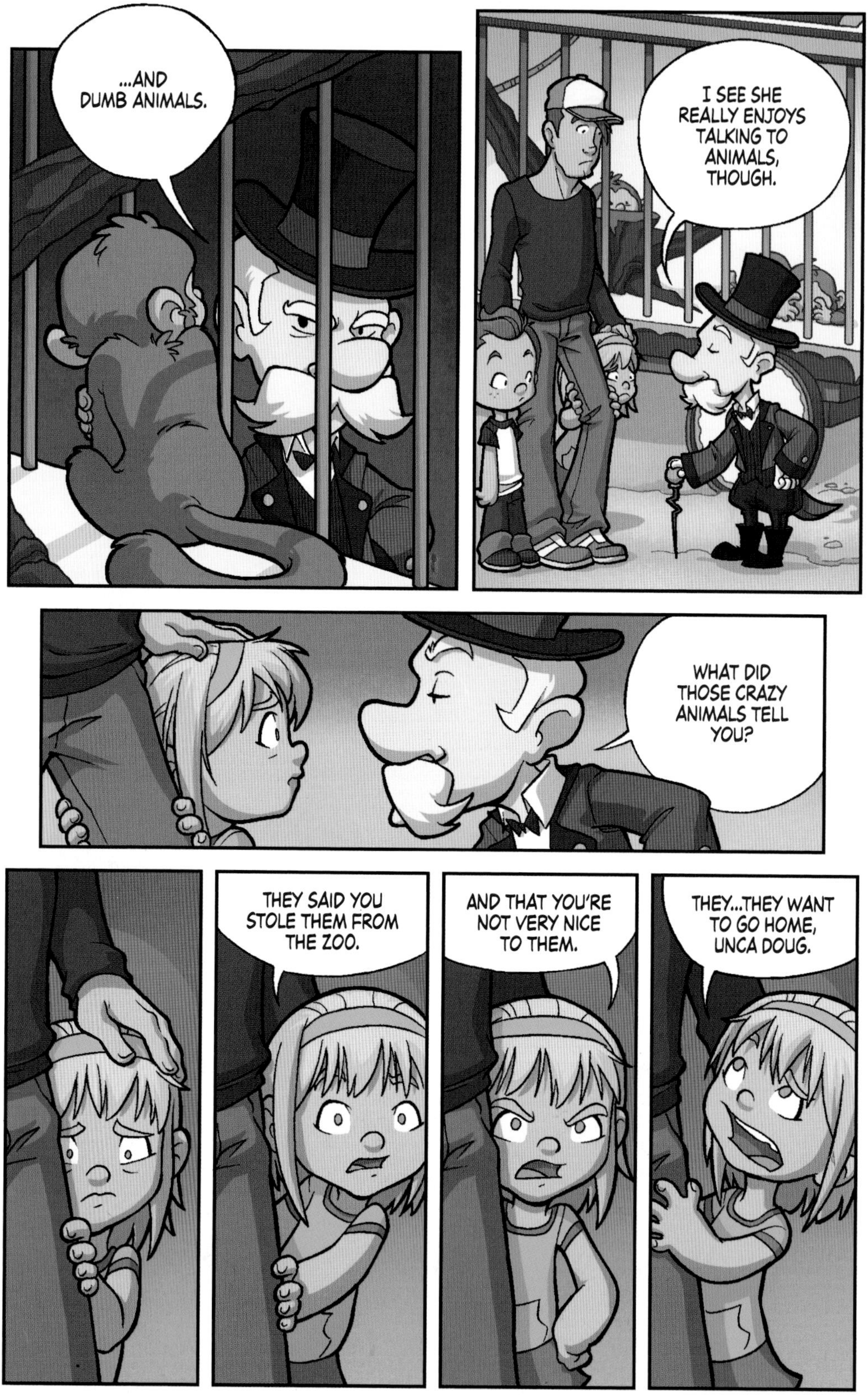
...AND DUMB ANIMALS.
I SEE SHE REALLY ENJOYS TALKING TO ANIMALS, THOUGH.
WHAT DID THOSE CRAZY ANIMALS TELL YOU?
THEY SAID YOU STOLE THEM FROM THE ZOO.
AND THAT YOU'RE NOT VERY NICE TO THEM.
THEY...THEY WANT TO GO HOME, UNCA DOUG.

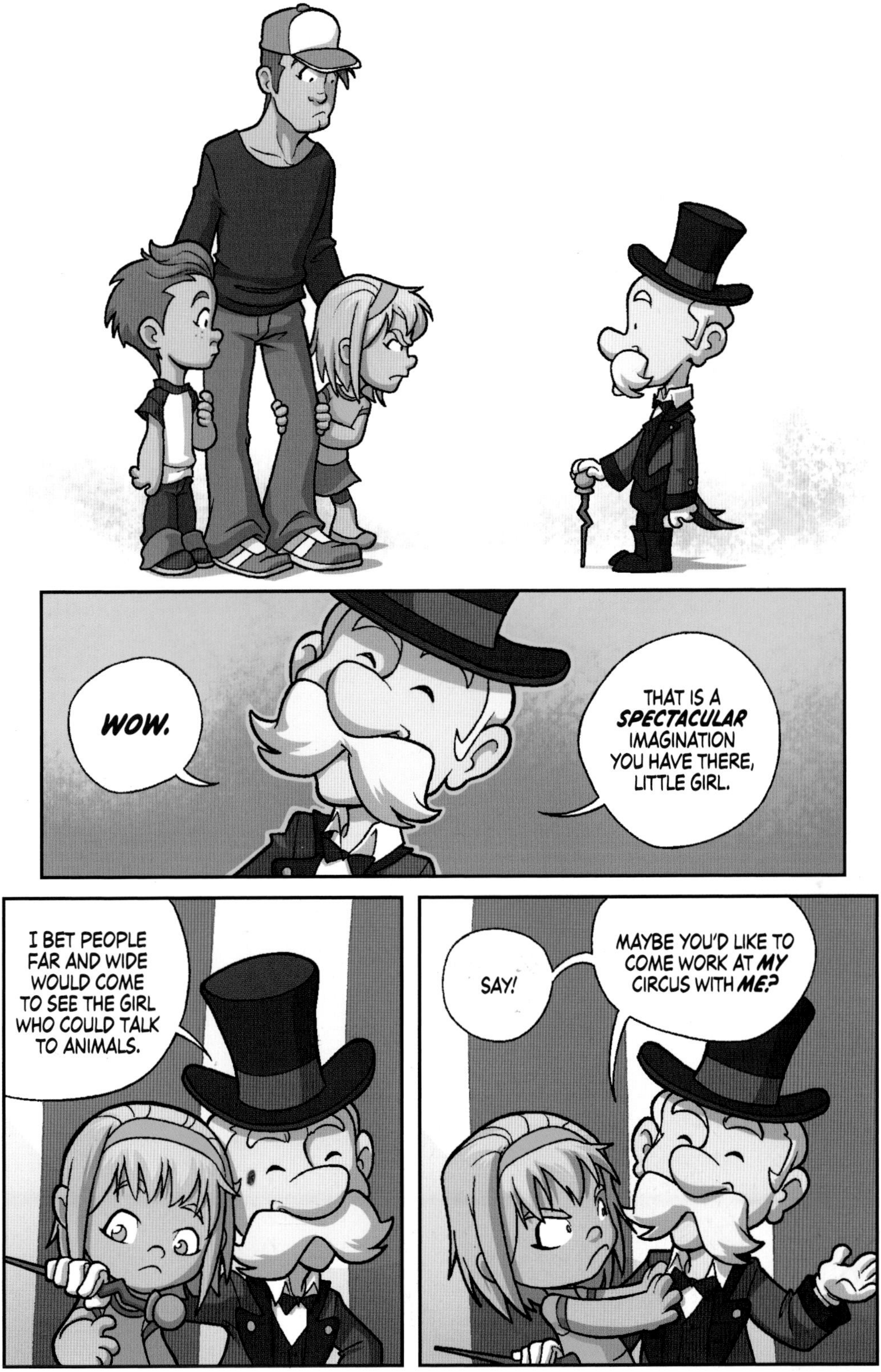

WOW.
THAT IS A SPECTACULAR IMAGINATION YOU HAVE THERE, LITTLE GIRL.
I BET PEOPLE FAR AND WIDE WOULD COME TO SEE THE GIRL WHO COULD TALK TO ANIMALS.
SAY!
MAYBE YOU'D LIKE TO COME WORK AT MY CIRCUS WITH ME?

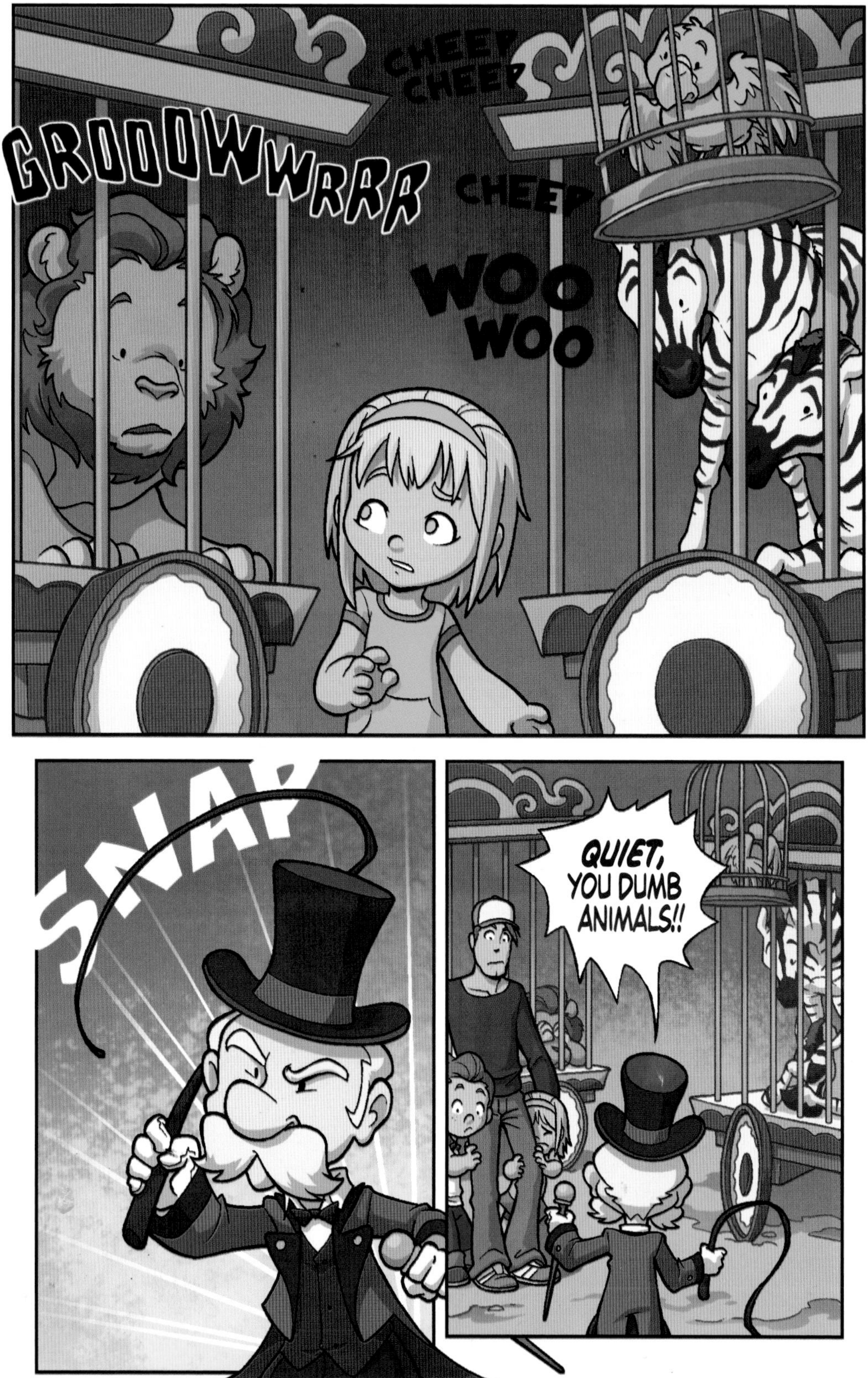
GROOOWWRRR
CHEEP CHEEP
CHEEP
WOO WOO
SNAP
QUIET, YOU DUMB ANIMALS!!

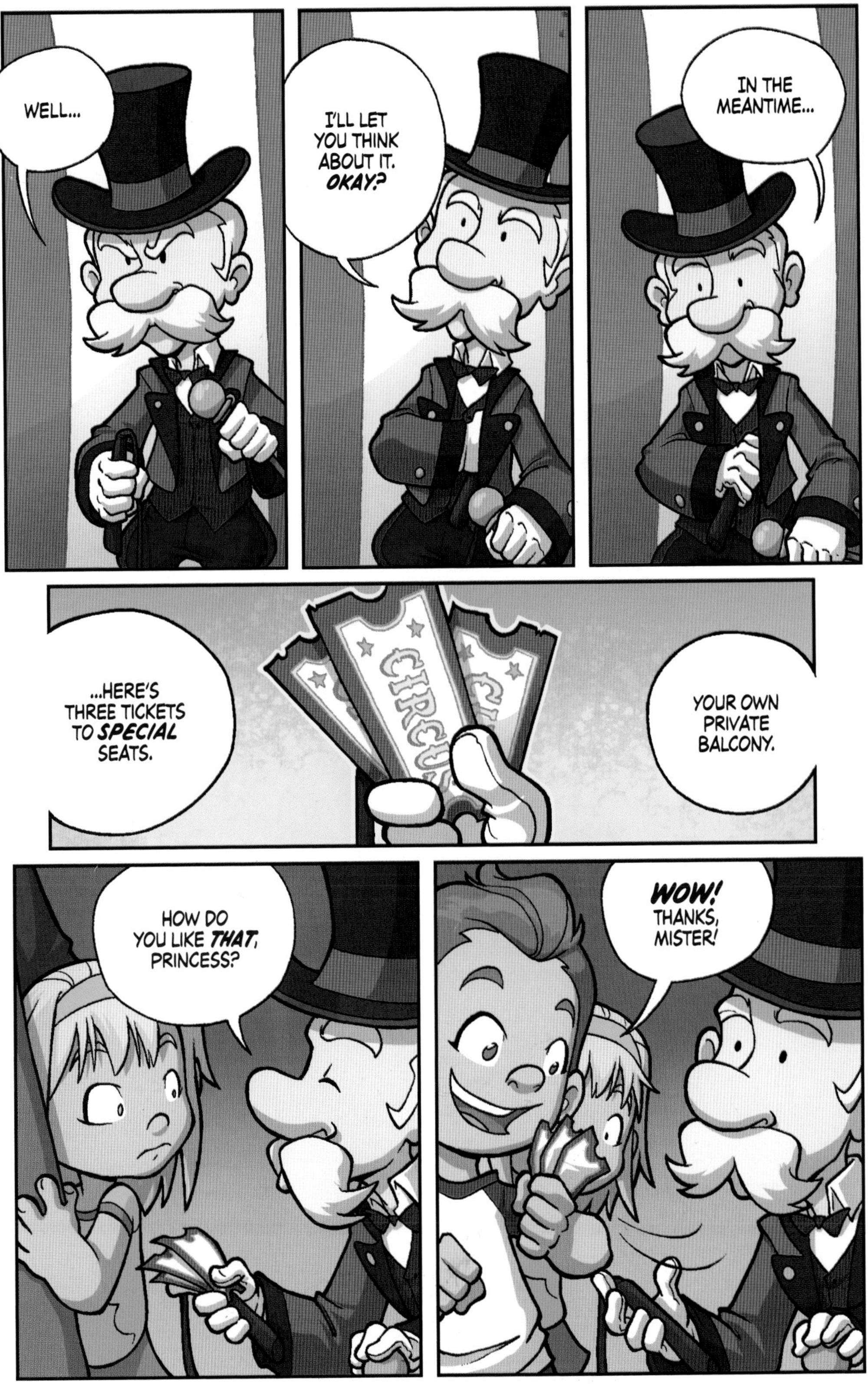
WELL...
I'LL LET YOU THINK ABOUT IT. *OKAY?*
IN THE MEANTIME...
...HERE'S THREE TICKETS TO *SPECIAL* SEATS.
CIRCUS
YOUR OWN PRIVATE BALCONY.
HOW DO YOU LIKE *THAT*, PRINCESS?
WOW! THANKS, MISTER!

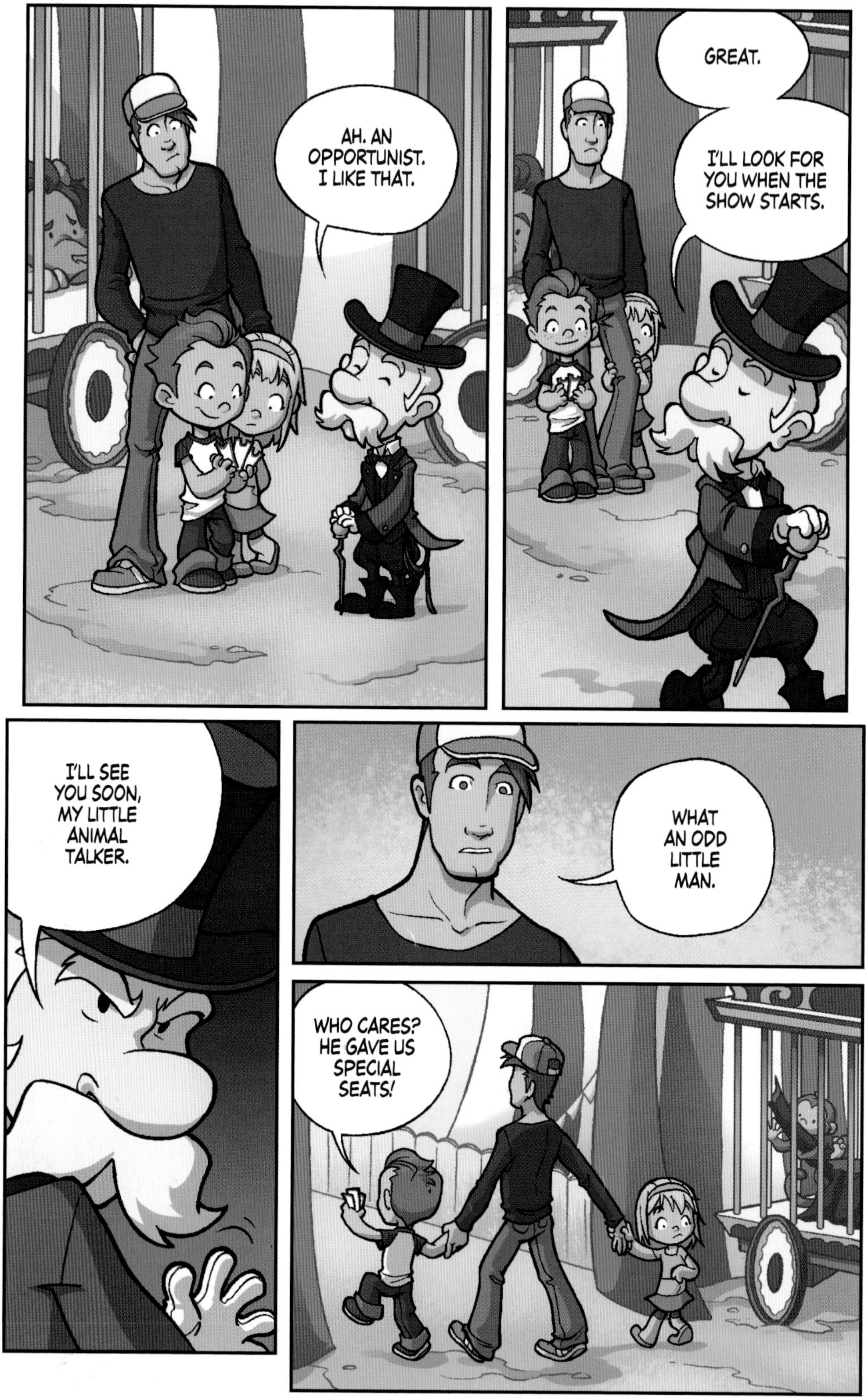
AH. AN OPPORTUNIST. I LIKE THAT.
GREAT.
I'LL LOOK FOR YOU WHEN THE SHOW STARTS.
I'LL SEE YOU SOON, MY LITTLE ANIMAL TALKER.
WHAT AN ODD LITTLE MAN.
WHO CARES? HE GAVE US SPECIAL SEATS!

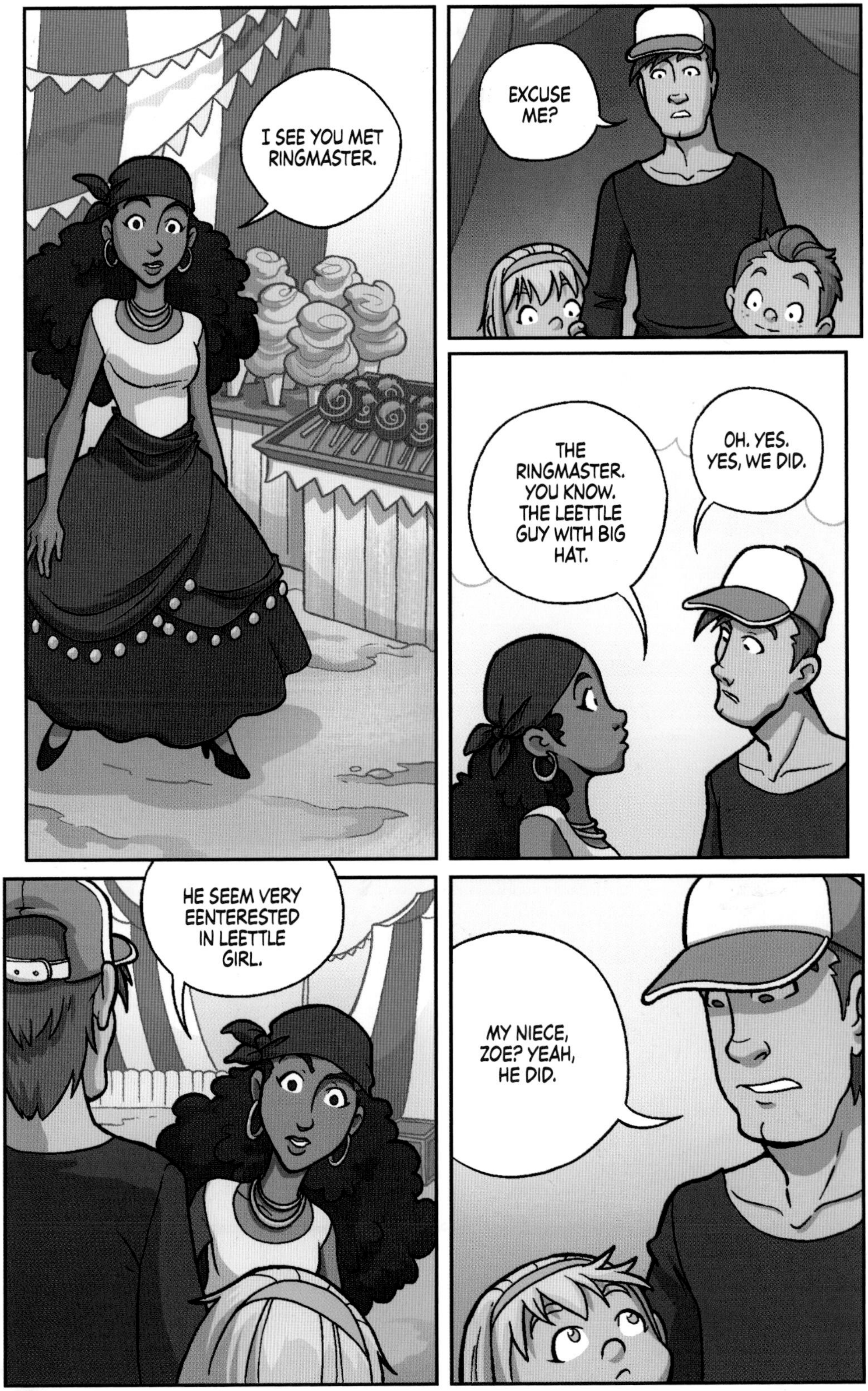
I SEE YOU MET RINGMASTER.
EXCUSE ME?
THE RINGMASTER. YOU KNOW. THE LEETTLE GUY WITH BIG HAT.
OH. YES. YES, WE DID.
HE SEEM VERY EENTERESTED IN LEETTLE GIRL.
MY NIECE, ZOE? YEAH, HE DID.

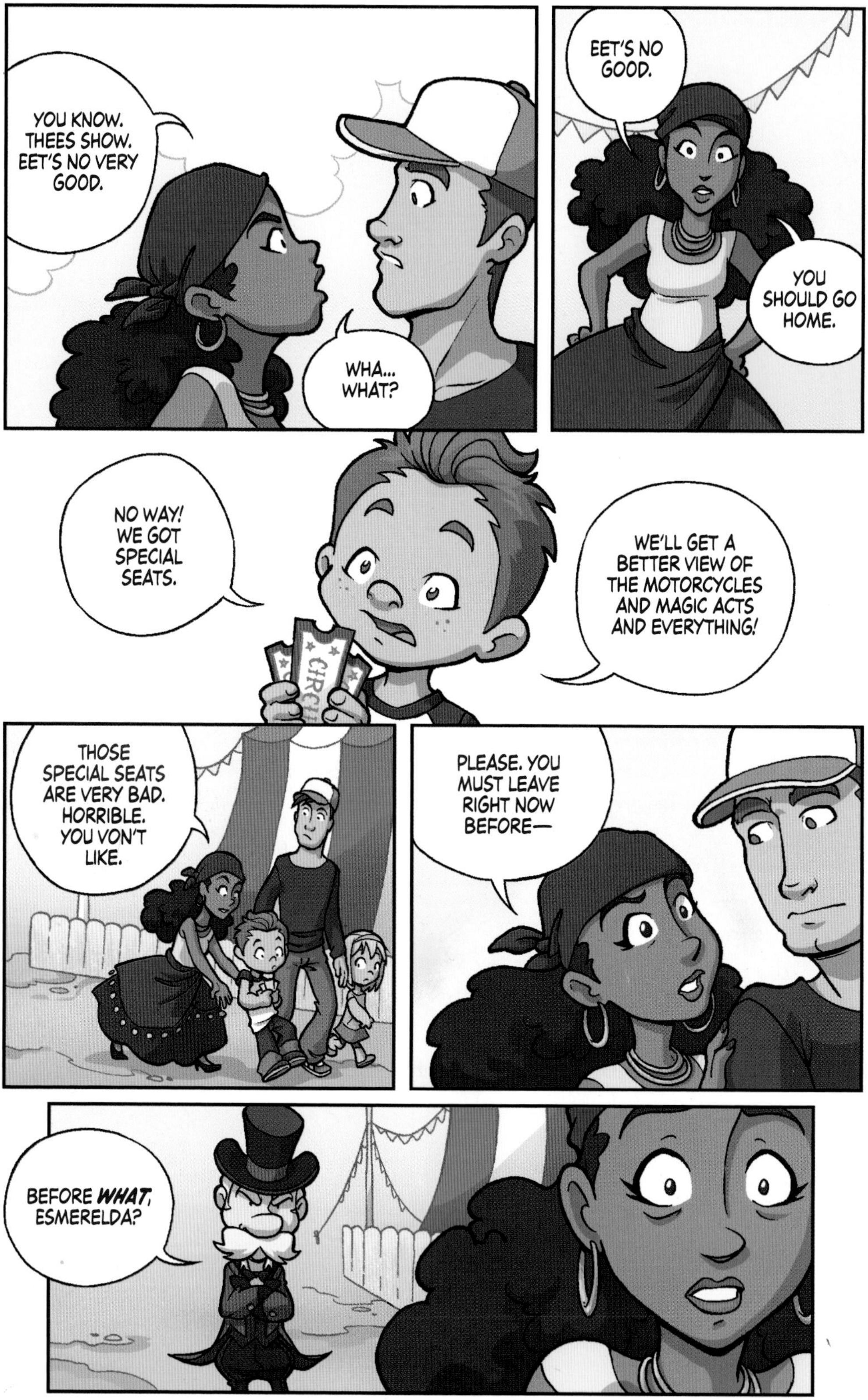

YOU KNOW. THEES SHOW. EET'S NO VERY GOOD.
WHA... WHAT?
EET'S NO GOOD.
YOU SHOULD GO HOME.
NO WAY! WE GOT SPECIAL SEATS.
WE'LL GET A BETTER VIEW OF THE MOTORCYCLES AND MAGIC ACTS AND EVERYTHING!
THOSE SPECIAL SEATS ARE VERY BAD. HORRIBLE. YOU VON'T LIKE.
PLEASE. YOU MUST LEAVE RIGHT NOW BEFORE—
BEFORE *WHAT*, ESMERELDA?

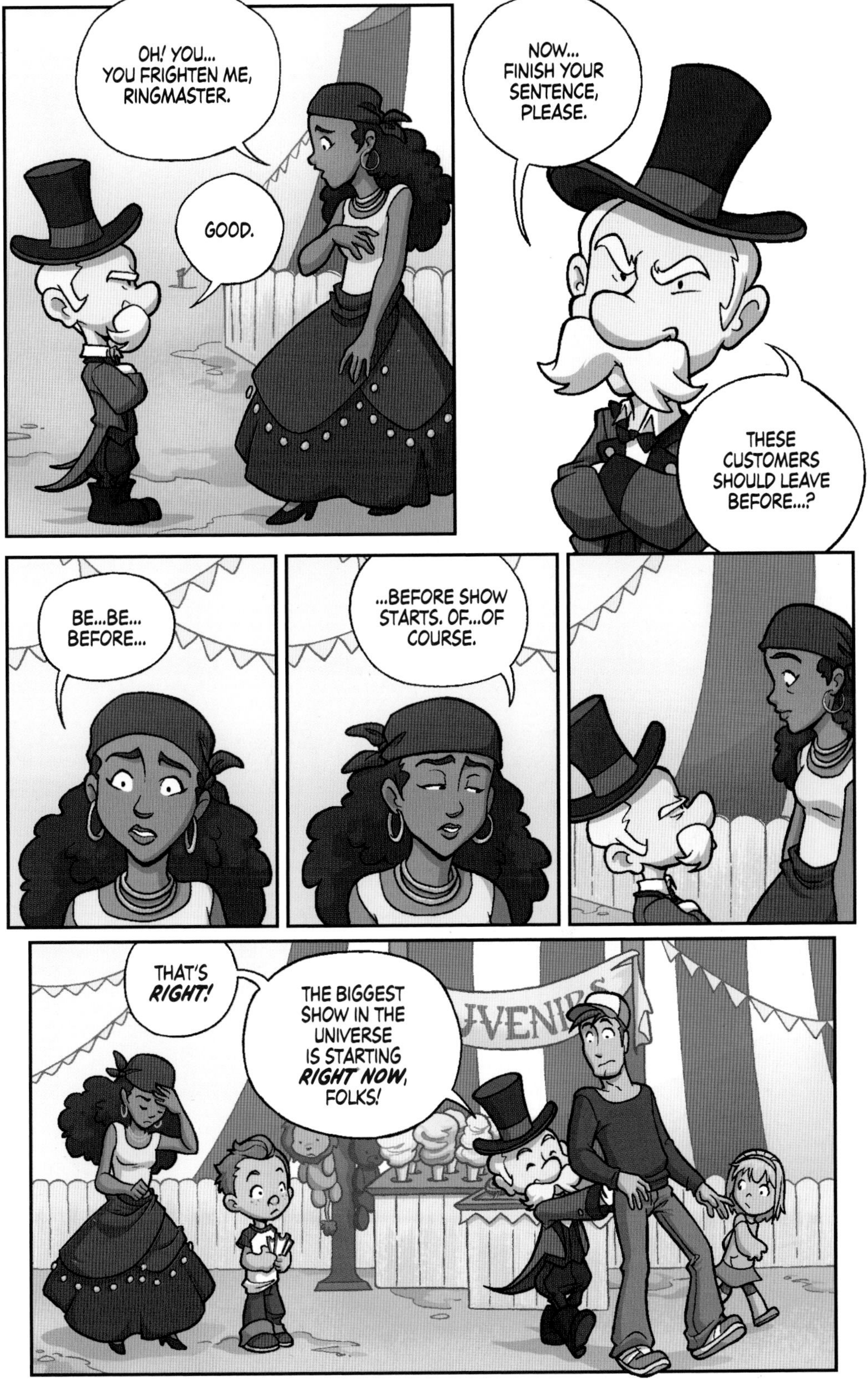
OH! YOU...
YOU FRIGHTEN ME, RINGMASTER.
GOOD.
NOW... FINISH YOUR SENTENCE, PLEASE.
THESE CUSTOMERS SHOULD LEAVE BEFORE...?
BE...BE... BEFORE...
...BEFORE SHOW STARTS. OF...OF COURSE.
THAT'S *RIGHT!*
THE BIGGEST SHOW IN THE UNIVERSE IS STARTING *RIGHT NOW*, FOLKS!

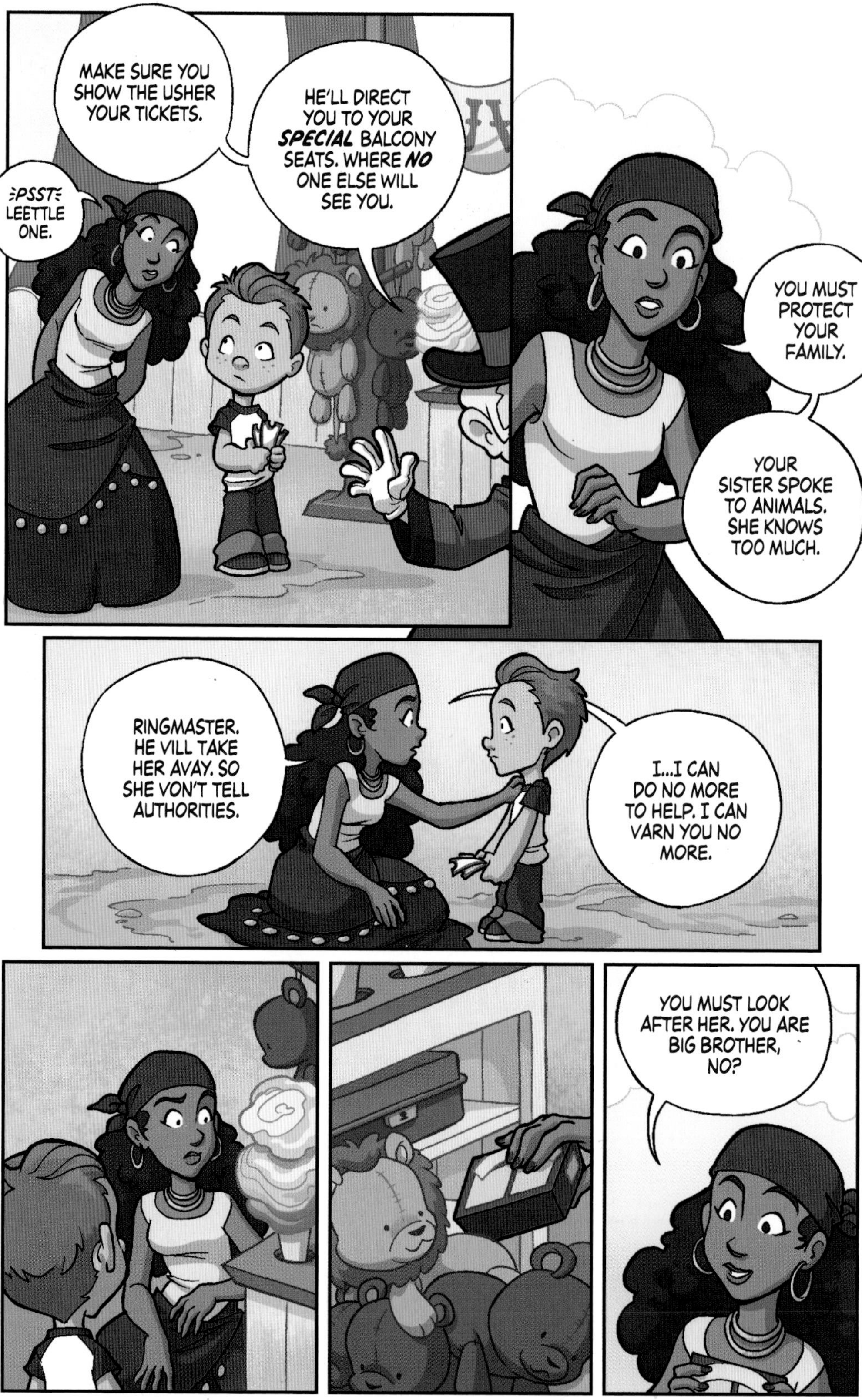
MAKE SURE YOU SHOW THE USHER YOUR TICKETS.
HE'LL DIRECT YOU TO YOUR *SPECIAL* BALCONY SEATS. WHERE *NO* ONE ELSE WILL SEE YOU.
PSST LEETTLE ONE.
YOU MUST PROTECT YOUR FAMILY.
YOUR SISTER SPOKE TO ANIMALS. SHE KNOWS TOO MUCH.
RINGMASTER. HE VILL TAKE HER AVAY. SO SHE VON'T TELL AUTHORITIES.
I...I CAN DO NO MORE TO HELP. I CAN VARN YOU NO MORE.
YOU MUST LOOK AFTER HER. YOU ARE BIG BROTHER, NO?

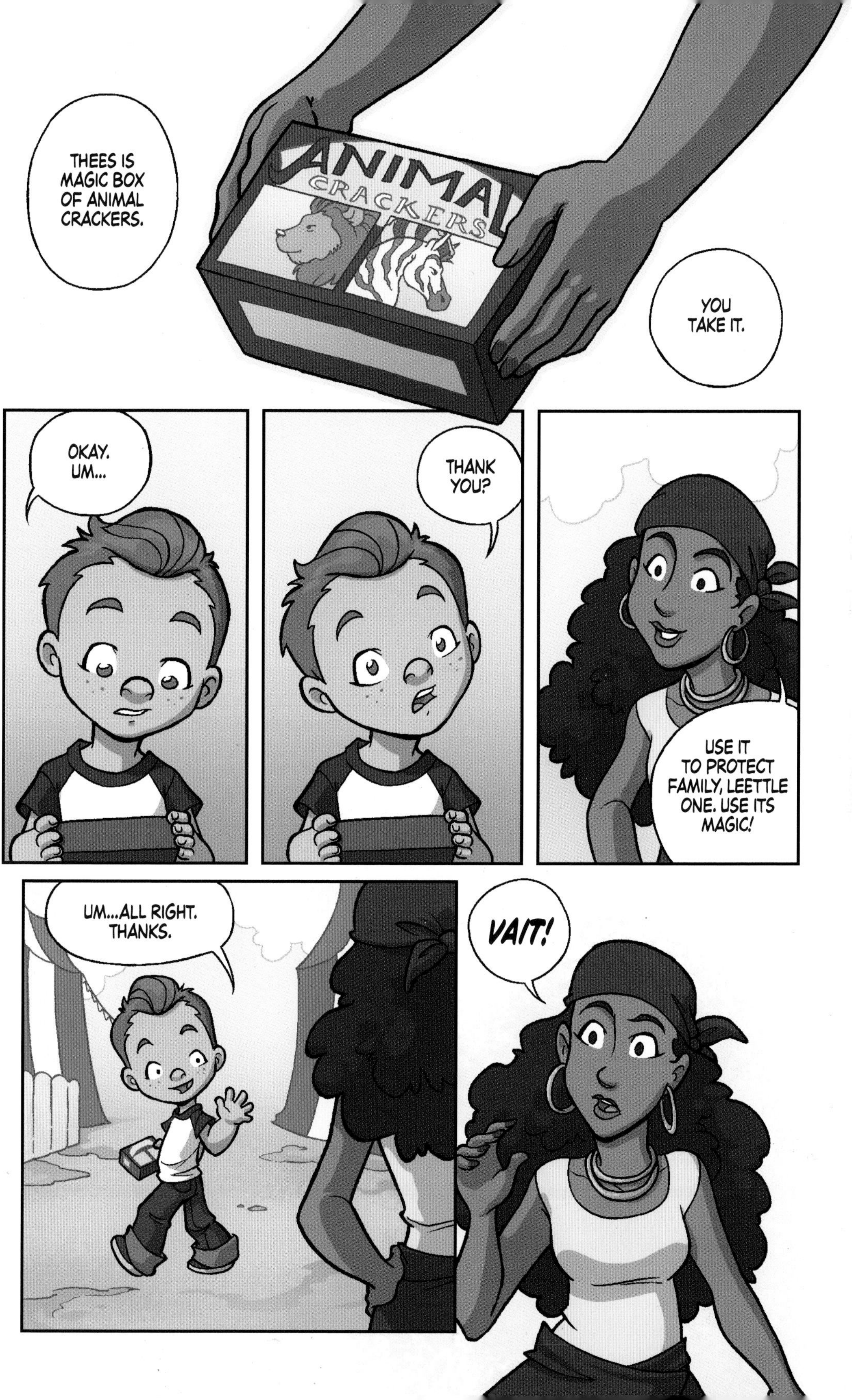
ANIMAL CRACKERS
THEES IS MAGIC BOX OF ANIMAL CRACKERS.
YOU TAKE IT.
OKAY. UM...
THANK YOU?
USE IT TO PROTECT FAMILY, LEETTLE ONE. USE ITS MAGIC!
UM...ALL RIGHT. THANKS.
VAIT!

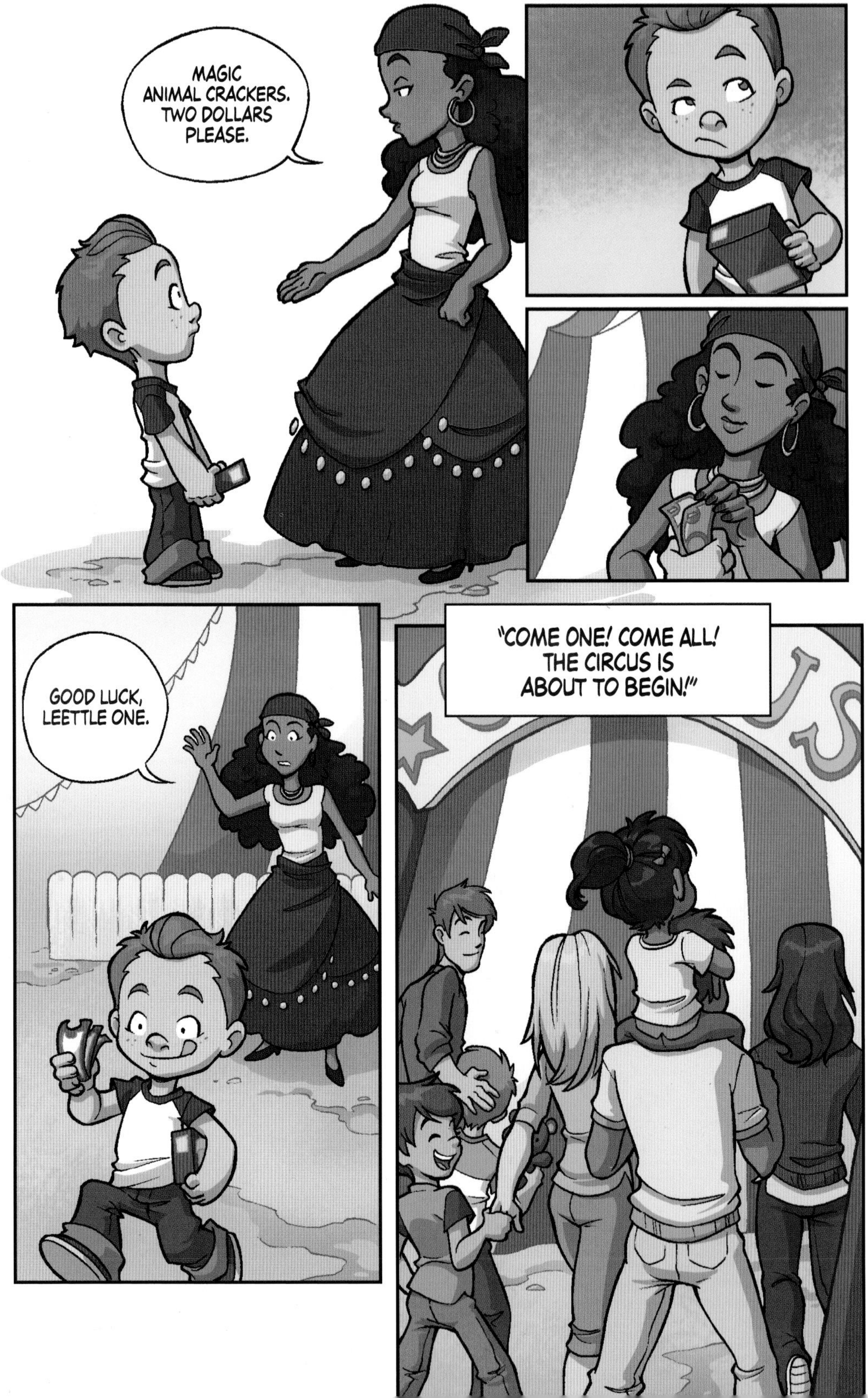
MAGIC ANIMAL CRACKERS. TWO DOLLARS PLEASE.
GOOD LUCK, LEETTLE ONE.
"COME ONE! COME ALL! THE CIRCUS IS ABOUT TO BEGIN!"

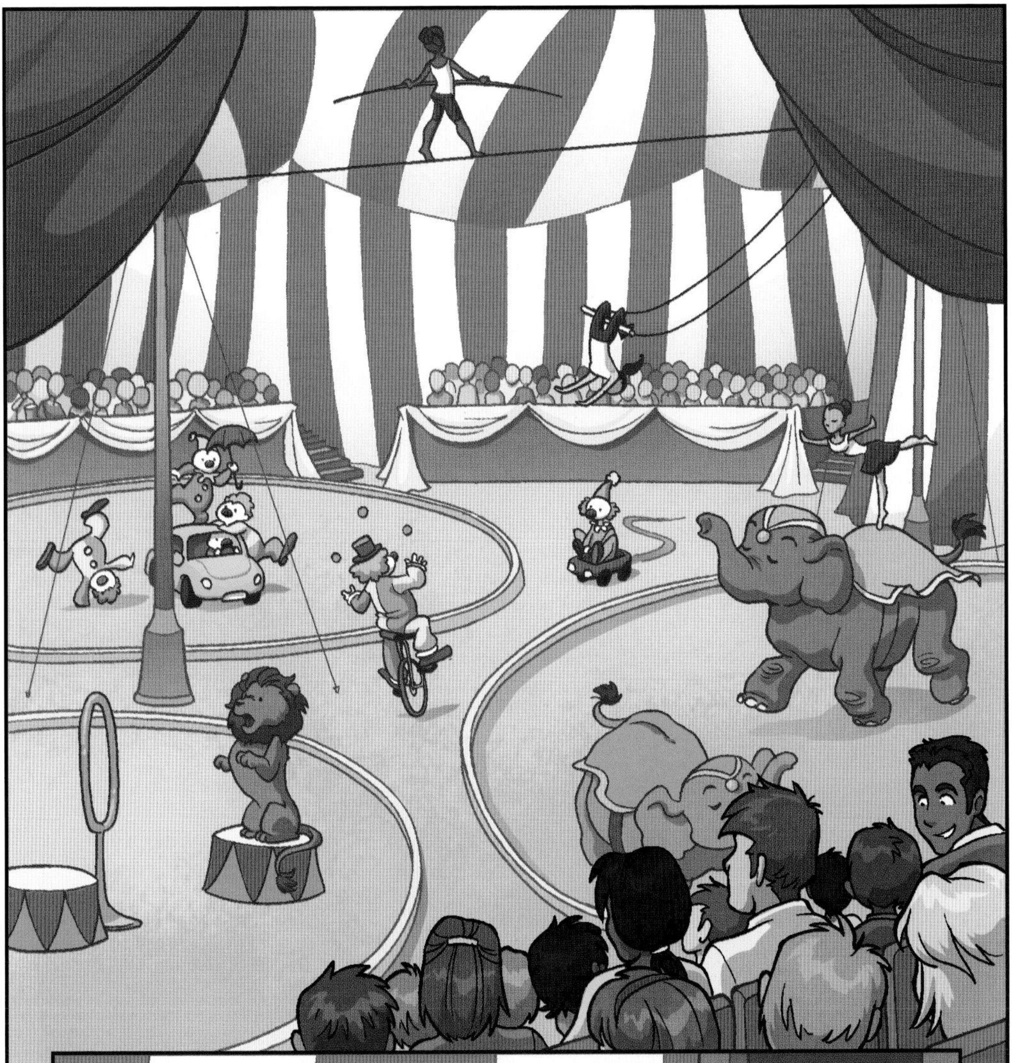

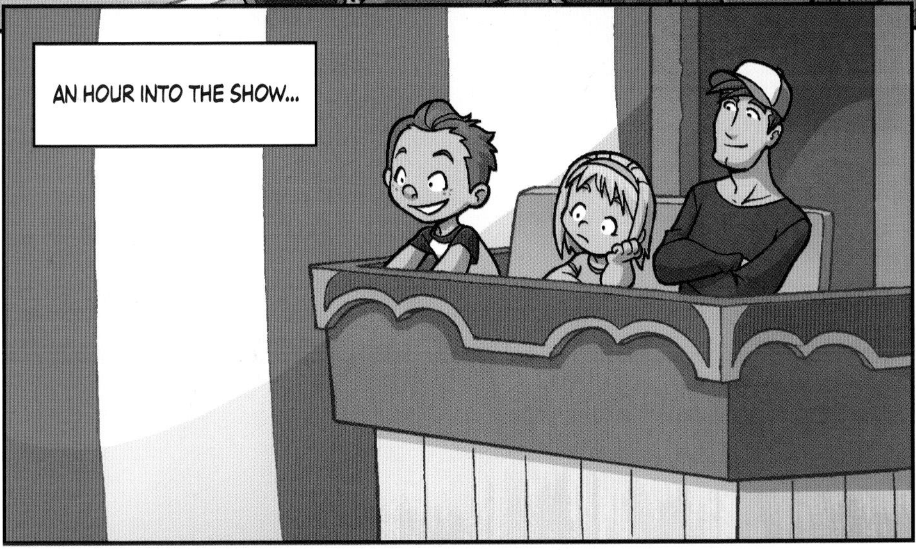
AN HOUR INTO THE SHOW...

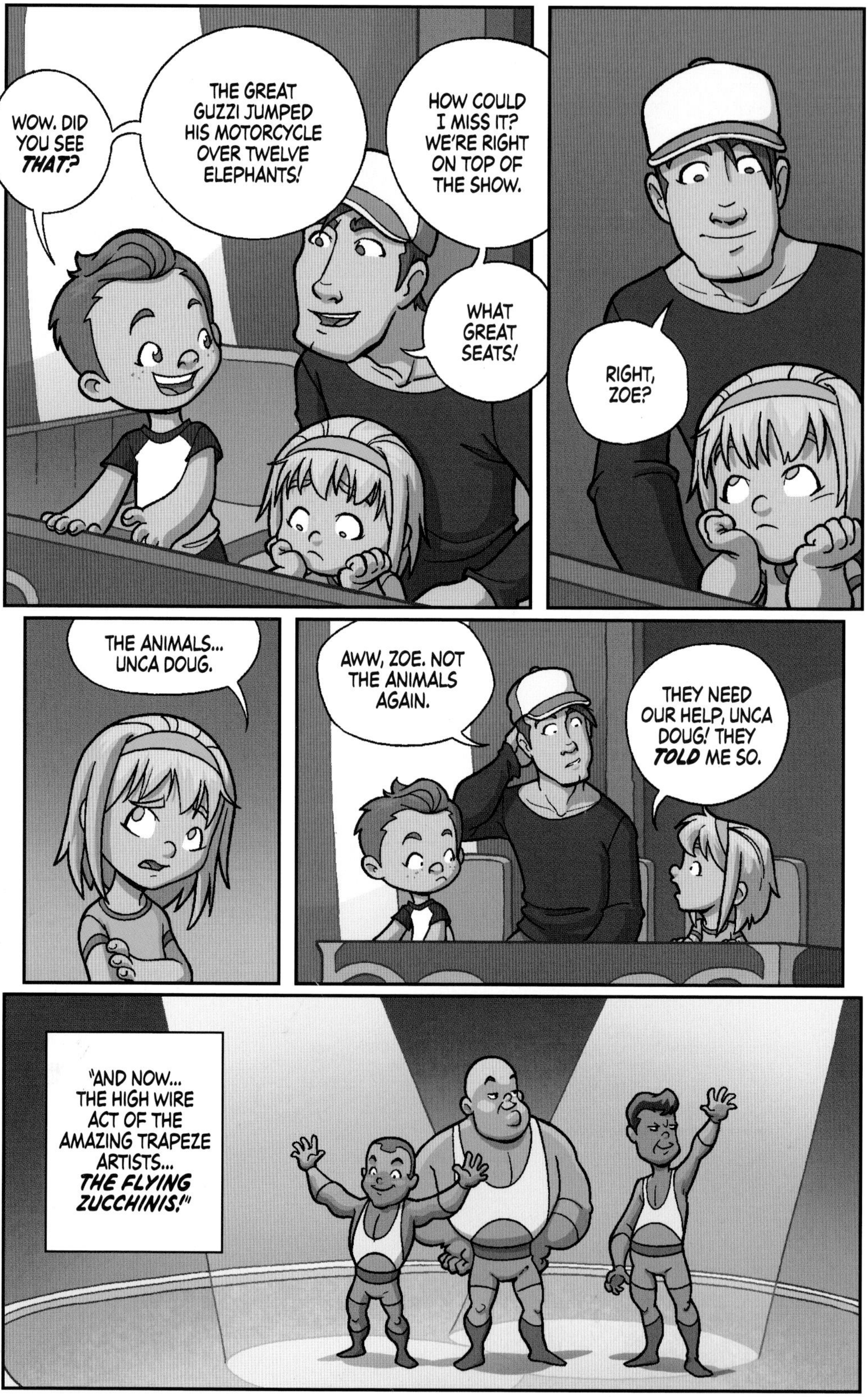
WOW. DID YOU SEE *THAT?*
THE GREAT GUZZI JUMPED HIS MOTORCYCLE OVER TWELVE ELEPHANTS!
HOW COULD I MISS IT? WE'RE RIGHT ON TOP OF THE SHOW.
WHAT GREAT SEATS!
RIGHT, ZOE?
THE ANIMALS... UNCA DOUG.
AWW, ZOE. NOT THE ANIMALS AGAIN.
THEY NEED OUR HELP, UNCA DOUG! THEY *TOLD* ME SO.
"AND NOW... THE HIGH WIRE ACT OF THE AMAZING TRAPEZE ARTISTS... *THE FLYING ZUCCHINIS!*"

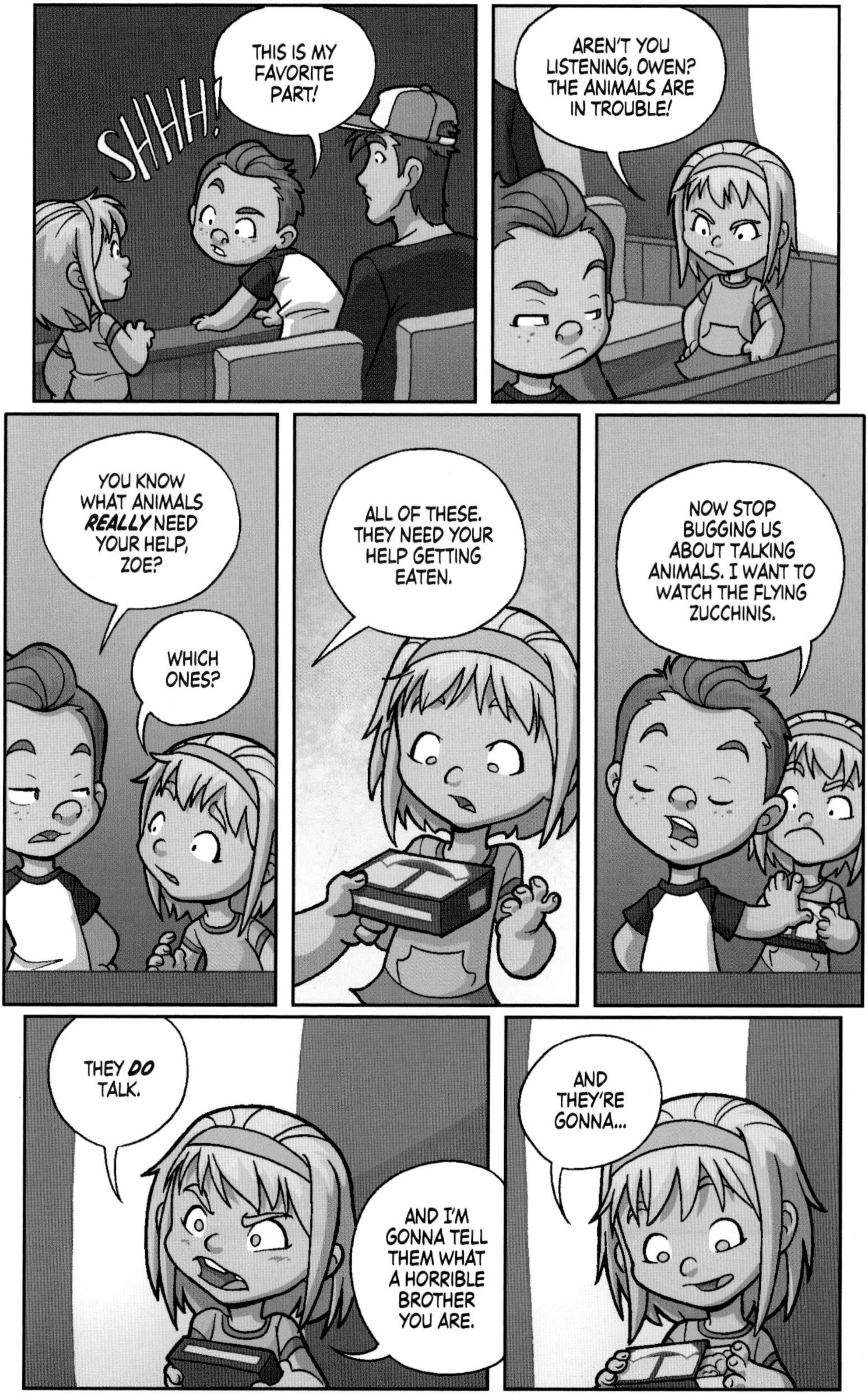
THIS IS MY FAVORITE PART!
SHHH!
AREN'T YOU LISTENING, OWEN? THE ANIMALS ARE IN TROUBLE!
YOU KNOW WHAT ANIMALS REALLY NEED YOUR HELP, ZOE?
WHICH ONES?
ALL OF THESE. THEY NEED YOUR HELP GETTING EATEN.
NOW STOP BUGGING US ABOUT TALKING ANIMALS. I WANT TO WATCH THE FLYING ZUCCHINIS.
THEY DO TALK.
AND I'M GONNA TELL THEM WHAT A HORRIBLE BROTHER YOU ARE.
AND THEY'RE GONNA...

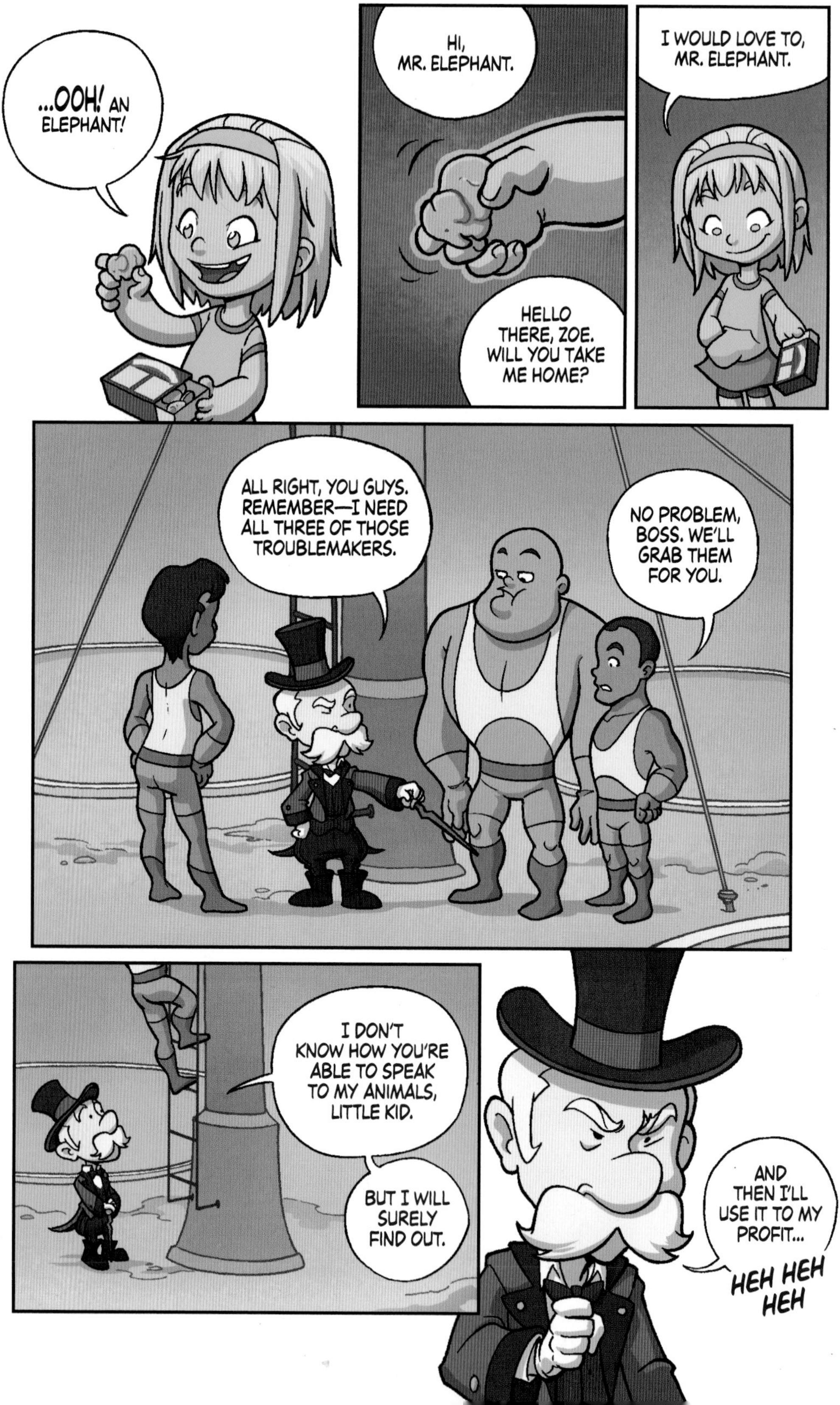
...OOH! AN ELEPHANT!
HI, MR. ELEPHANT.
HELLO THERE, ZOE. WILL YOU TAKE ME HOME?
I WOULD LOVE TO, MR. ELEPHANT.
ALL RIGHT, YOU GUYS. REMEMBER—I NEED ALL THREE OF THOSE TROUBLEMAKERS.
NO PROBLEM, BOSS. WE'LL GRAB THEM FOR YOU.
I DON'T KNOW HOW YOU'RE ABLE TO SPEAK TO MY ANIMALS, LITTLE KID.
BUT I WILL SURELY FIND OUT.
AND THEN I'LL USE IT TO MY PROFIT...
HEH HEH HEH

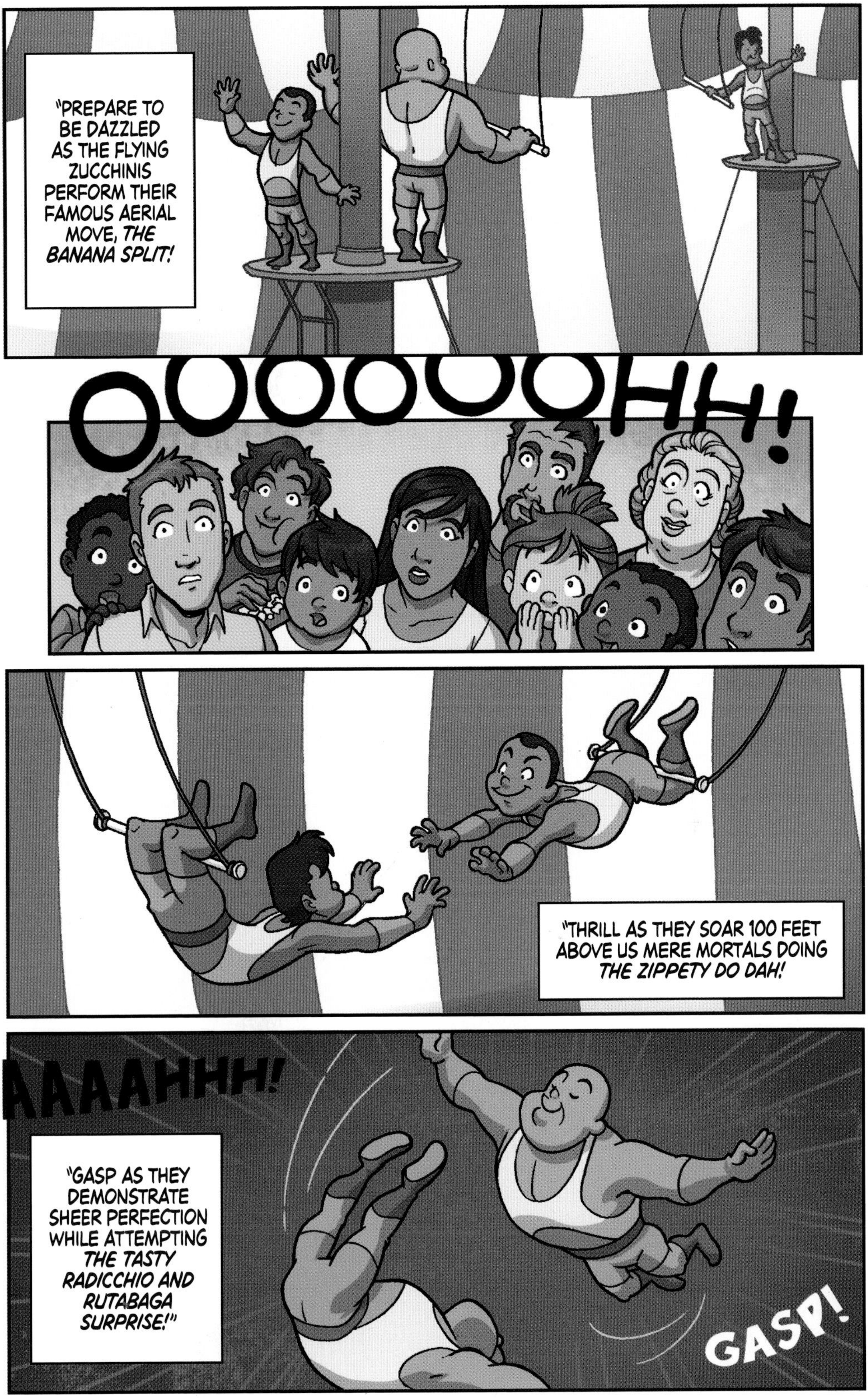
"PREPARE TO BE DAZZLED AS THE FLYING ZUCCHINIS PERFORM THEIR FAMOUS AERIAL MOVE, *THE BANANA SPLIT!*
OOOOOOHH!
"THRILL AS THEY SOAR 100 FEET ABOVE US MERE MORTALS DOING *THE ZIPPETY DO DAH!*
AAAAHHH!
"GASP AS THEY DEMONSTRATE SHEER PERFECTION WHILE ATTEMPTING *THE TASTY RADICCHIO AND RUTABAGA SURPRISE!*"
GASP!

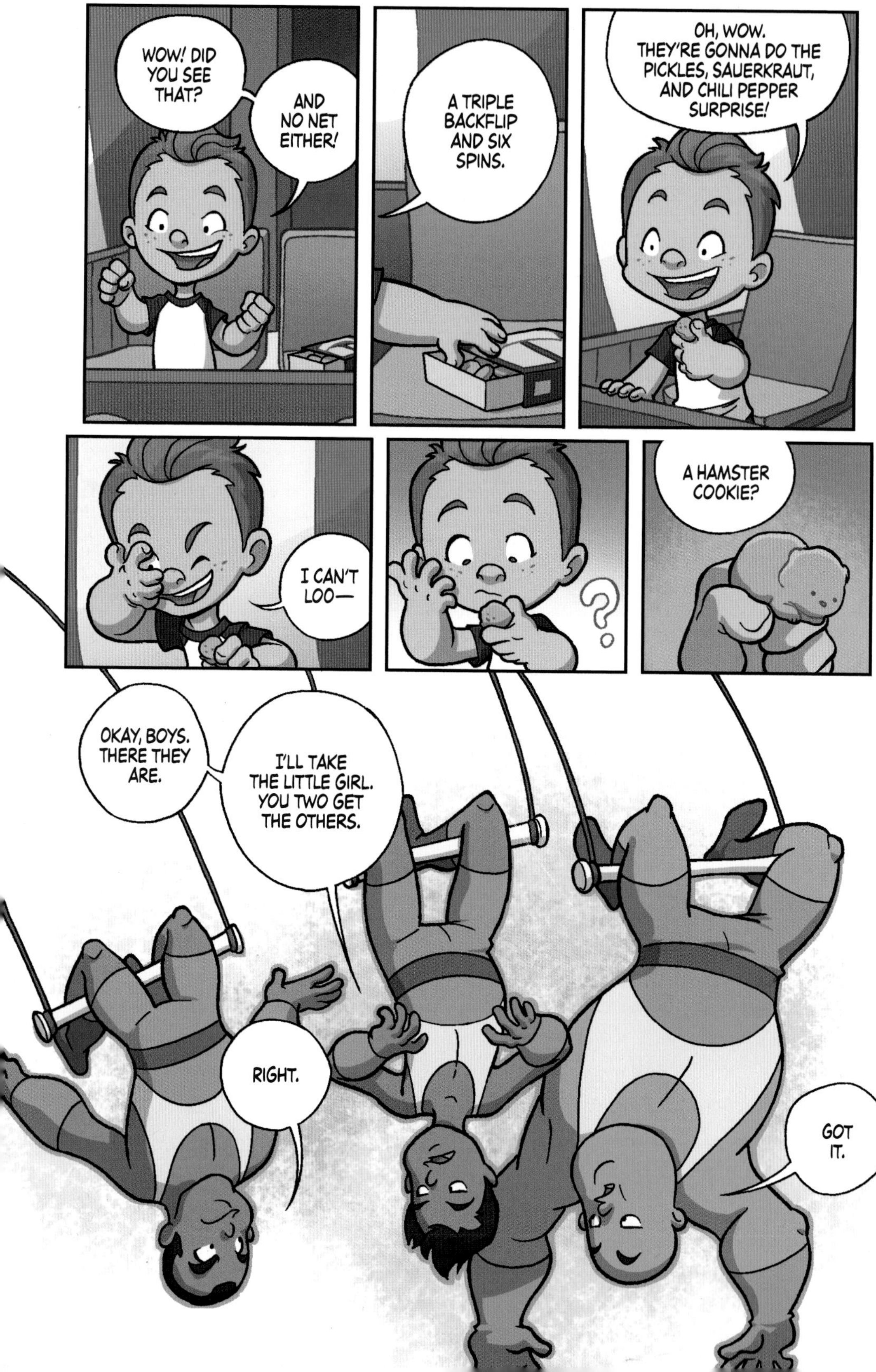
WOW! DID YOU SEE THAT?
AND NO NET EITHER!
A TRIPLE BACKFLIP AND SIX SPINS.
OH, WOW. THEY'RE GONNA DO THE PICKLES, SAUERKRAUT, AND CHILI PEPPER SURPRISE!
I CAN'T LOO—
A HAMSTER COOKIE?
OKAY, BOYS. THERE THEY ARE.
I'LL TAKE THE LITTLE GIRL. YOU TWO GET THE OTHERS.
RIGHT.
GOT IT.

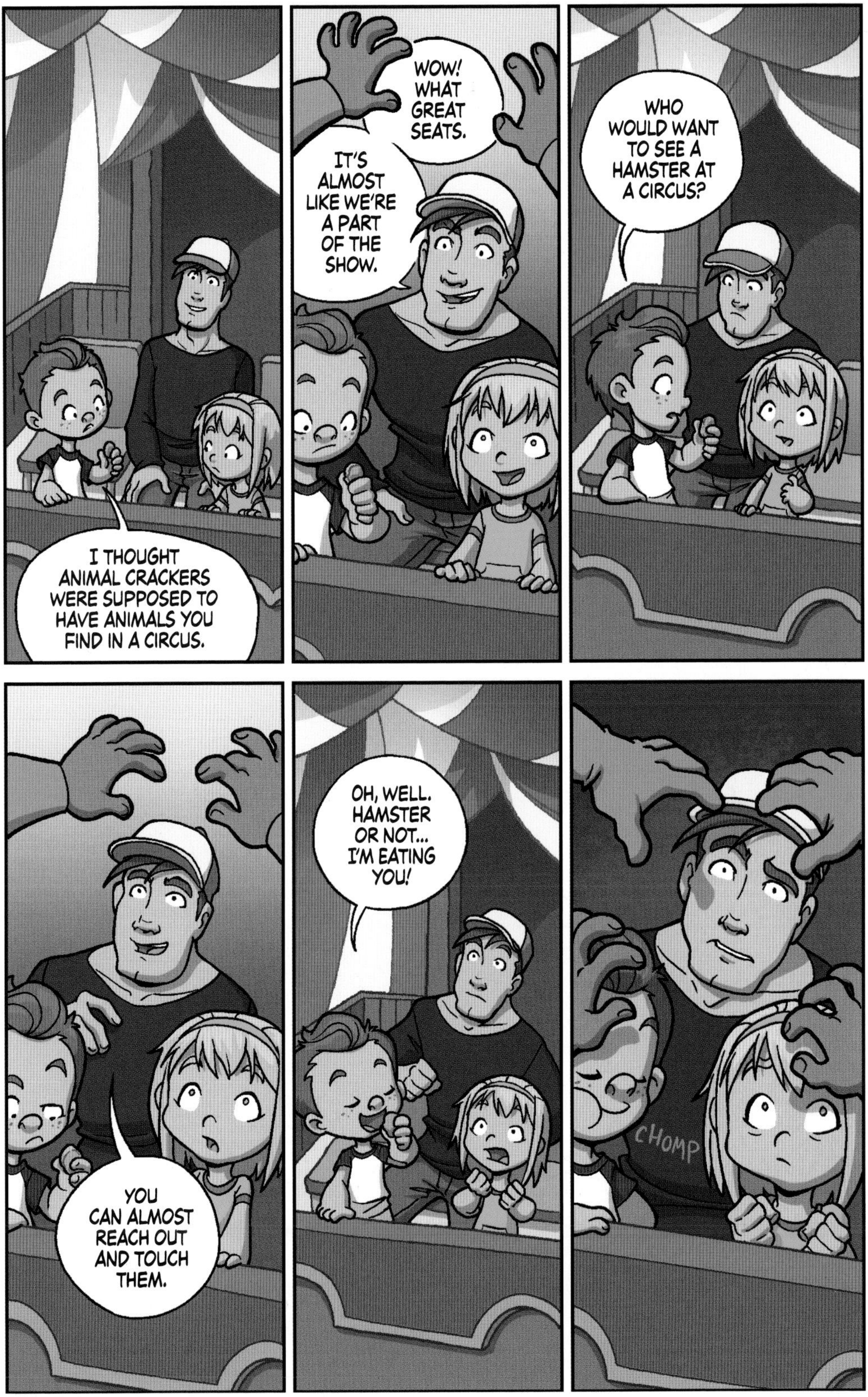
I THOUGHT ANIMAL CRACKERS WERE SUPPOSED TO HAVE ANIMALS YOU FIND IN A CIRCUS.
WOW! WHAT GREAT SEATS.
IT'S ALMOST LIKE WE'RE A PART OF THE SHOW.
WHO WOULD WANT TO SEE A HAMSTER AT A CIRCUS?
YOU CAN ALMOST REACH OUT AND TOUCH THEM.
OH, WELL. HAMSTER OR NOT... I'M EATING YOU!
CHOMP

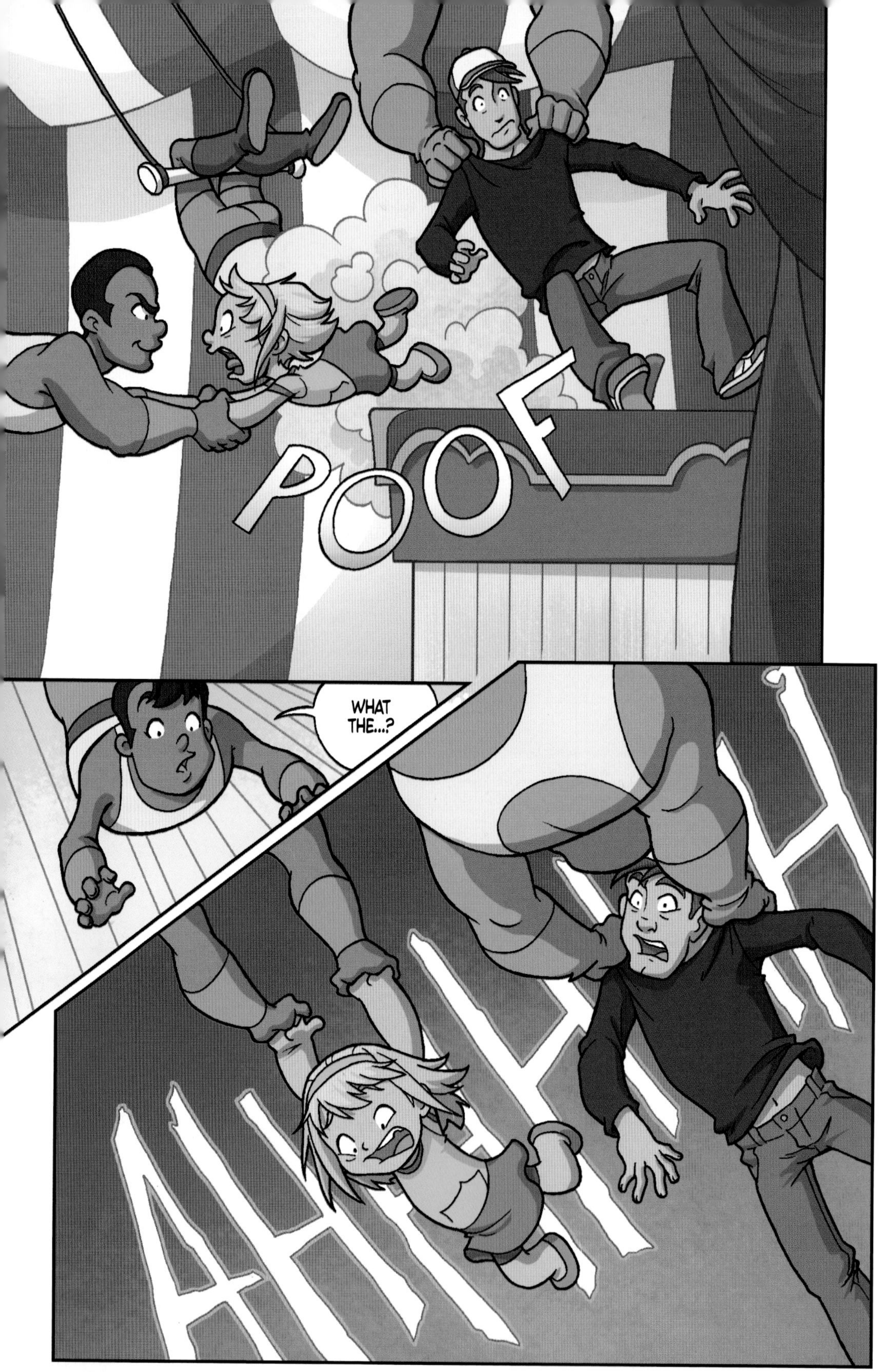
POOF
WHAT THE...?
AHHHH

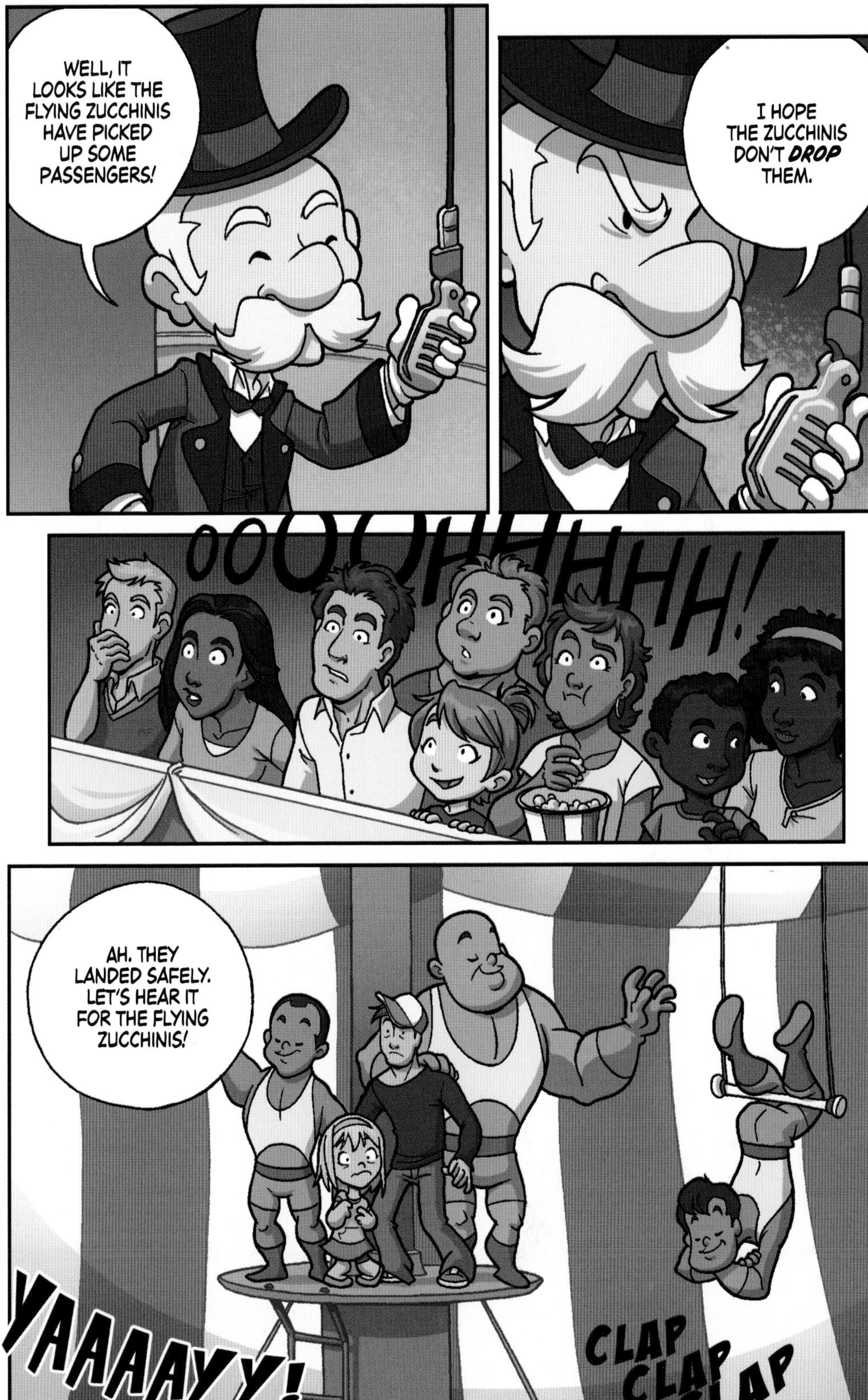
WELL, IT LOOKS LIKE THE FLYING ZUCCHINIS HAVE PICKED UP SOME PASSENGERS!
I HOPE THE ZUCCHINIS DON'T DROP THEM.
OOOOOHHHHH!
AH. THEY LANDED SAFELY. LET'S HEAR IT FOR THE FLYING ZUCCHINIS!
YAAAAYY!
CLAP CLAP CLAP

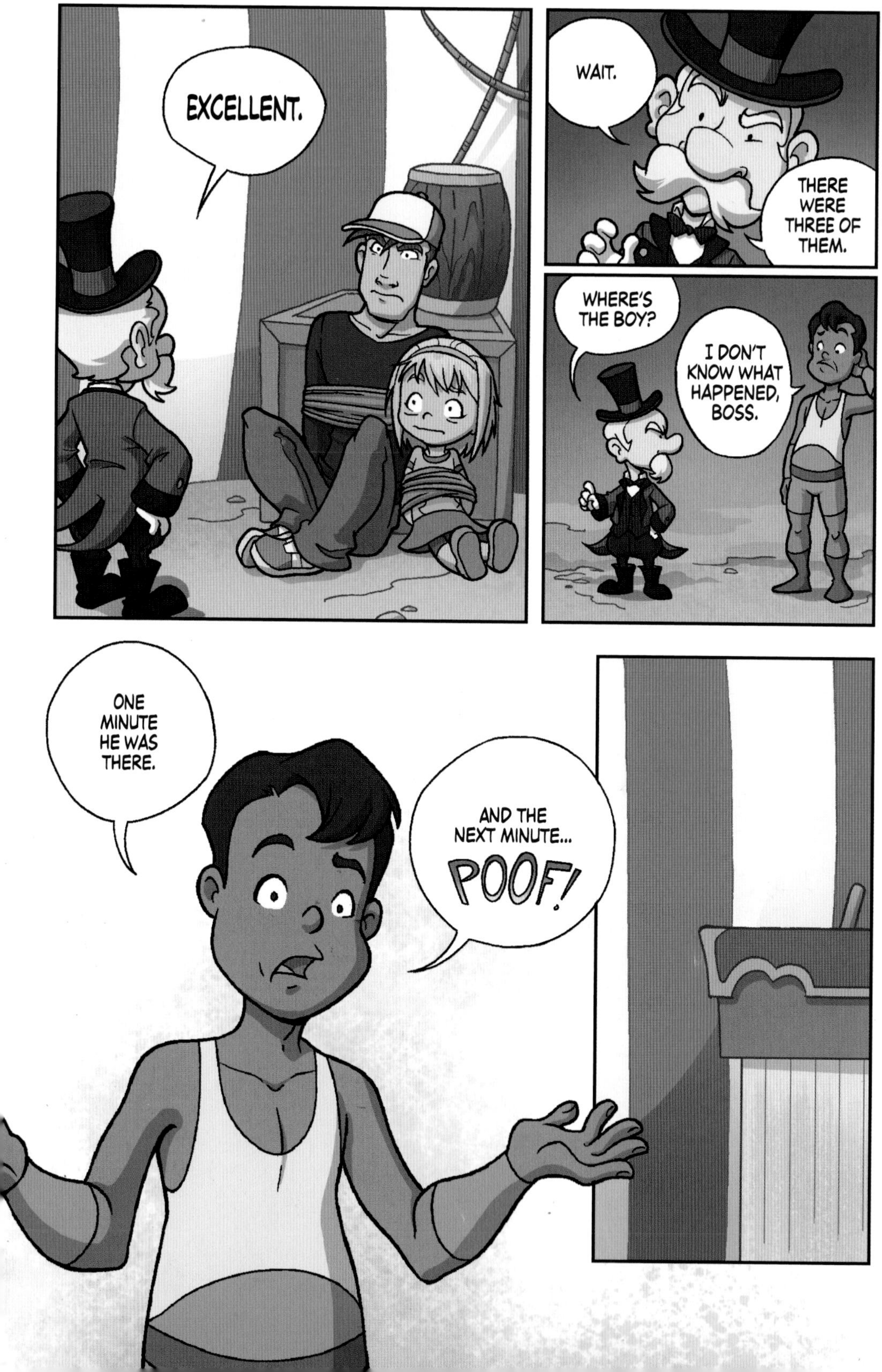
EXCELLENT.
WAIT.
THERE WERE THREE OF THEM.
WHERE'S THE BOY?
I DON'T KNOW WHAT HAPPENED, BOSS.
ONE MINUTE HE WAS THERE.
AND THE NEXT MINUTE...
POOF!

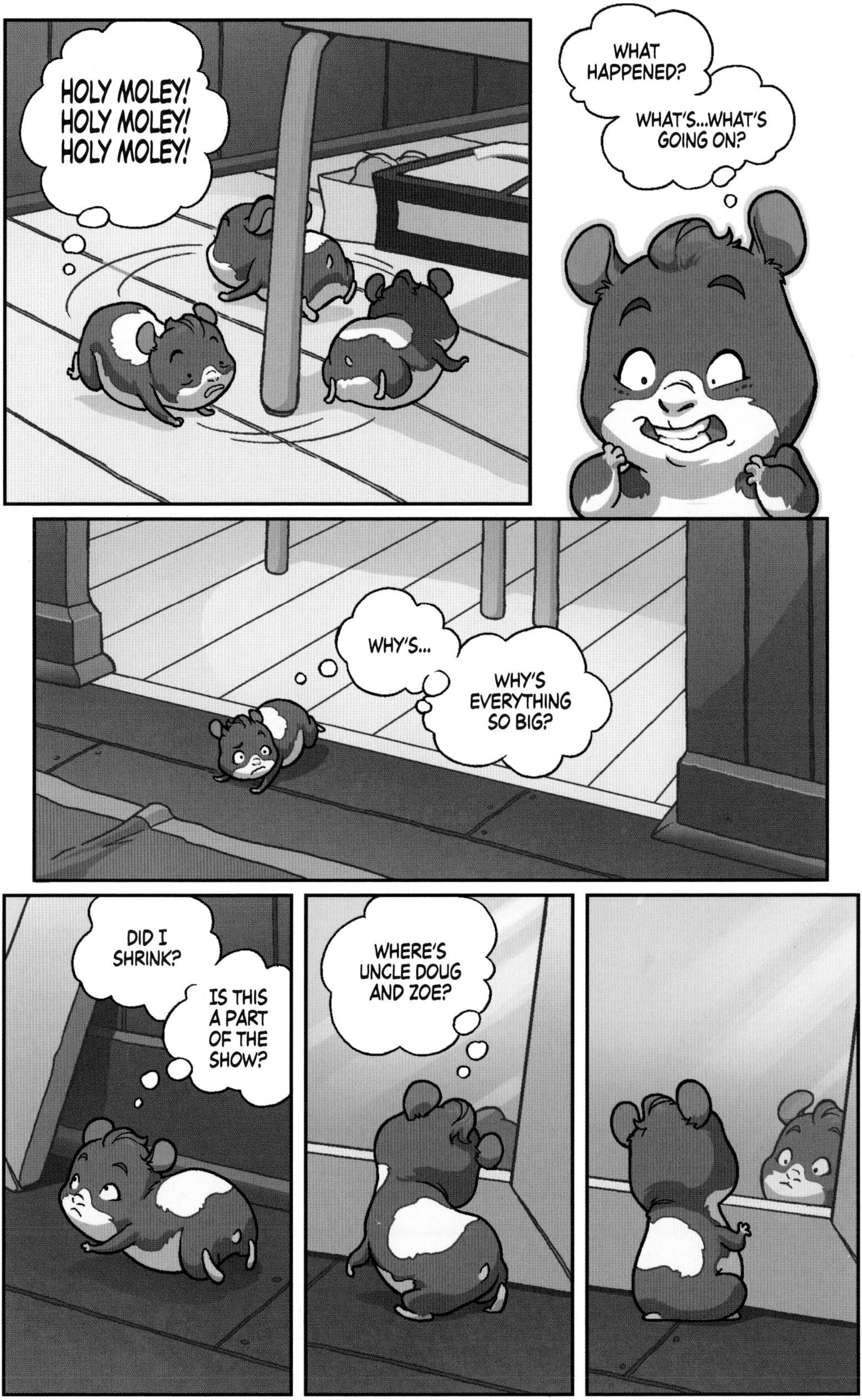
HOLY MOLEY!
HOLY MOLEY!
HOLY MOLEY!
WHAT HAPPENED?
WHAT'S...WHAT'S GOING ON?
WHY'S...
WHY'S EVERYTHING SO BIG?
DID I SHRINK?
IS THIS A PART OF THE SHOW?
WHERE'S UNCLE DOUG AND ZOE?

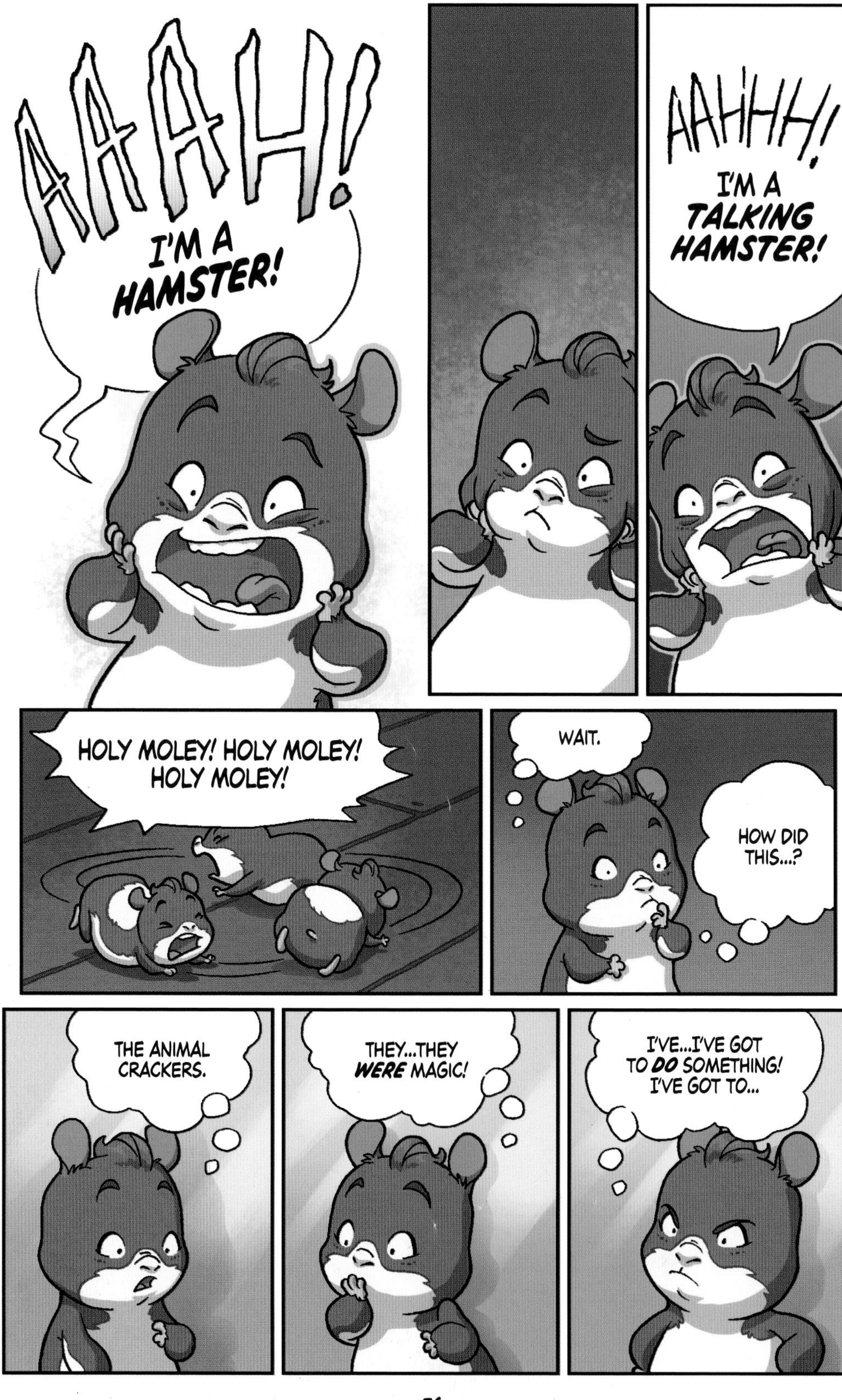
AAAH!
I'M A HAMSTER!
AAHHH!
I'M A TALKING HAMSTER!
HOLY MOLEY! HOLY MOLEY! HOLY MOLEY!
WAIT.
HOW DID THIS...?
THE ANIMAL CRACKERS.
THEY...THEY WERE MAGIC!
I'VE...I'VE GOT TO DO SOMETHING! I'VE GOT TO...

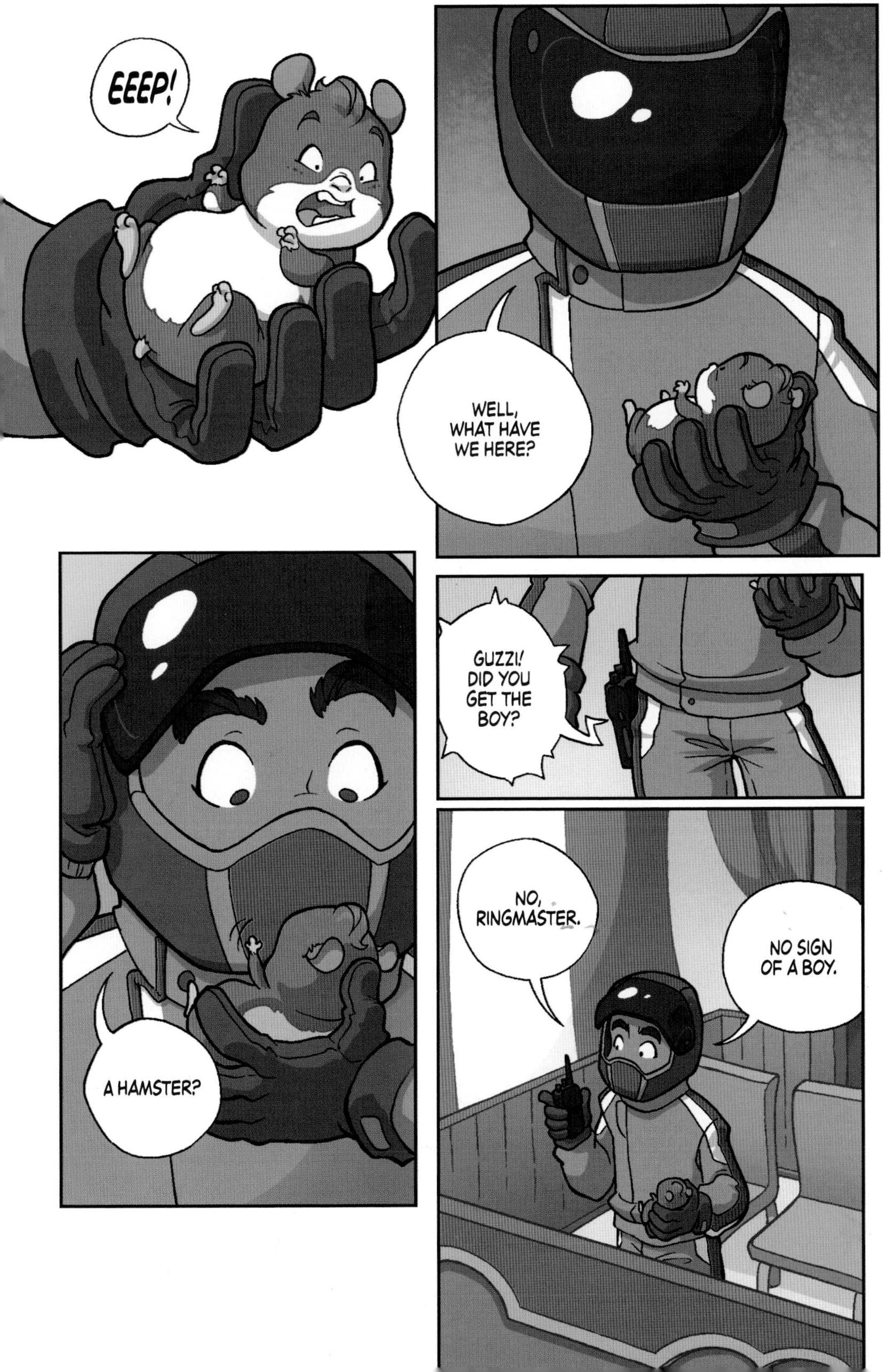
EEEP!
WELL, WHAT HAVE WE HERE?
A HAMSTER?
GUZZI! DID YOU GET THE BOY?
NO, RINGMASTER.
NO SIGN OF A BOY.

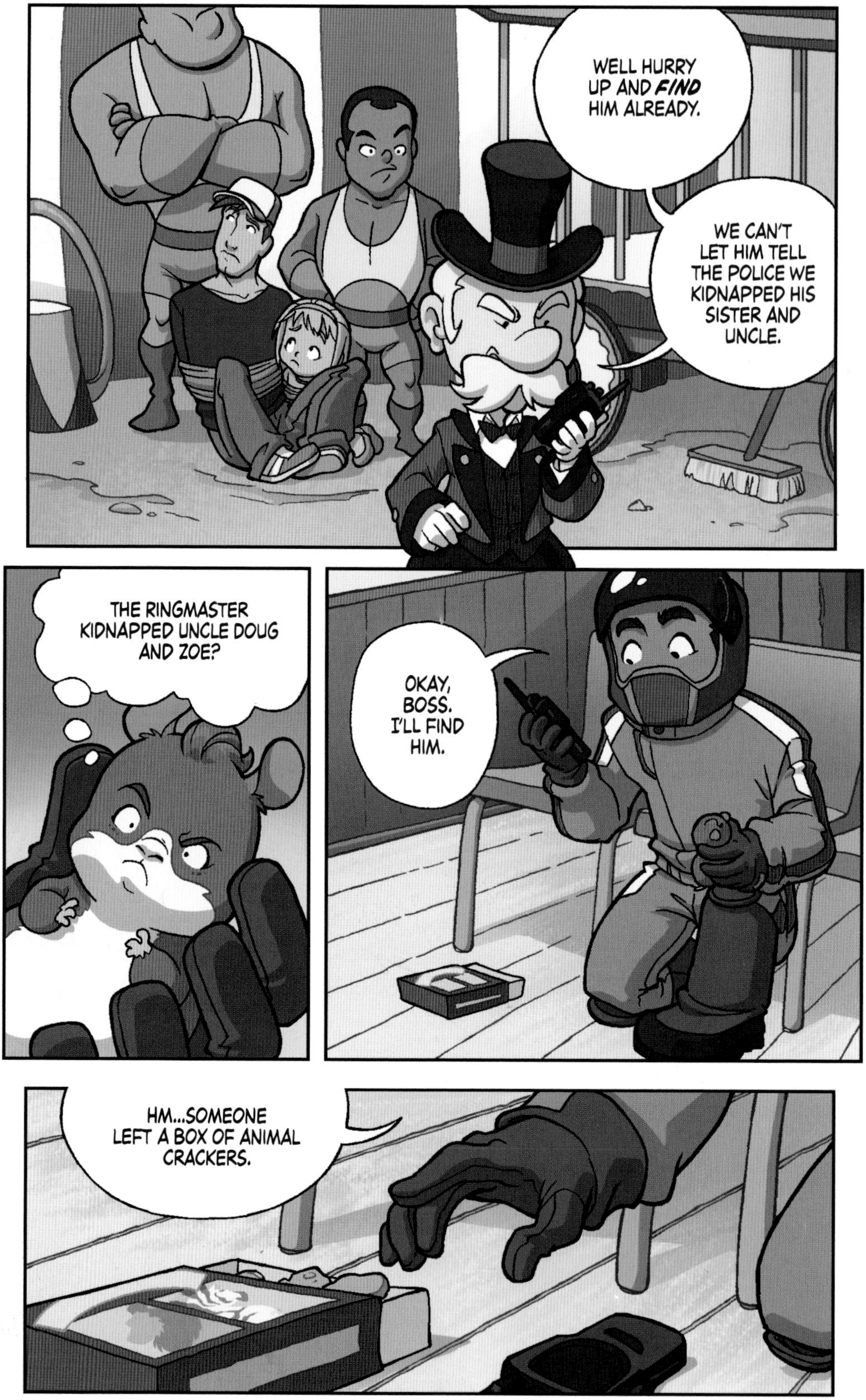
WELL HURRY UP AND FIND HIM ALREADY.
WE CAN'T LET HIM TELL THE POLICE WE KIDNAPPED HIS SISTER AND UNCLE.
THE RINGMASTER KIDNAPPED UNCLE DOUG AND ZOE?
OKAY, BOSS. I'LL FIND HIM.
HM...SOMEONE LEFT A BOX OF ANIMAL CRACKERS.

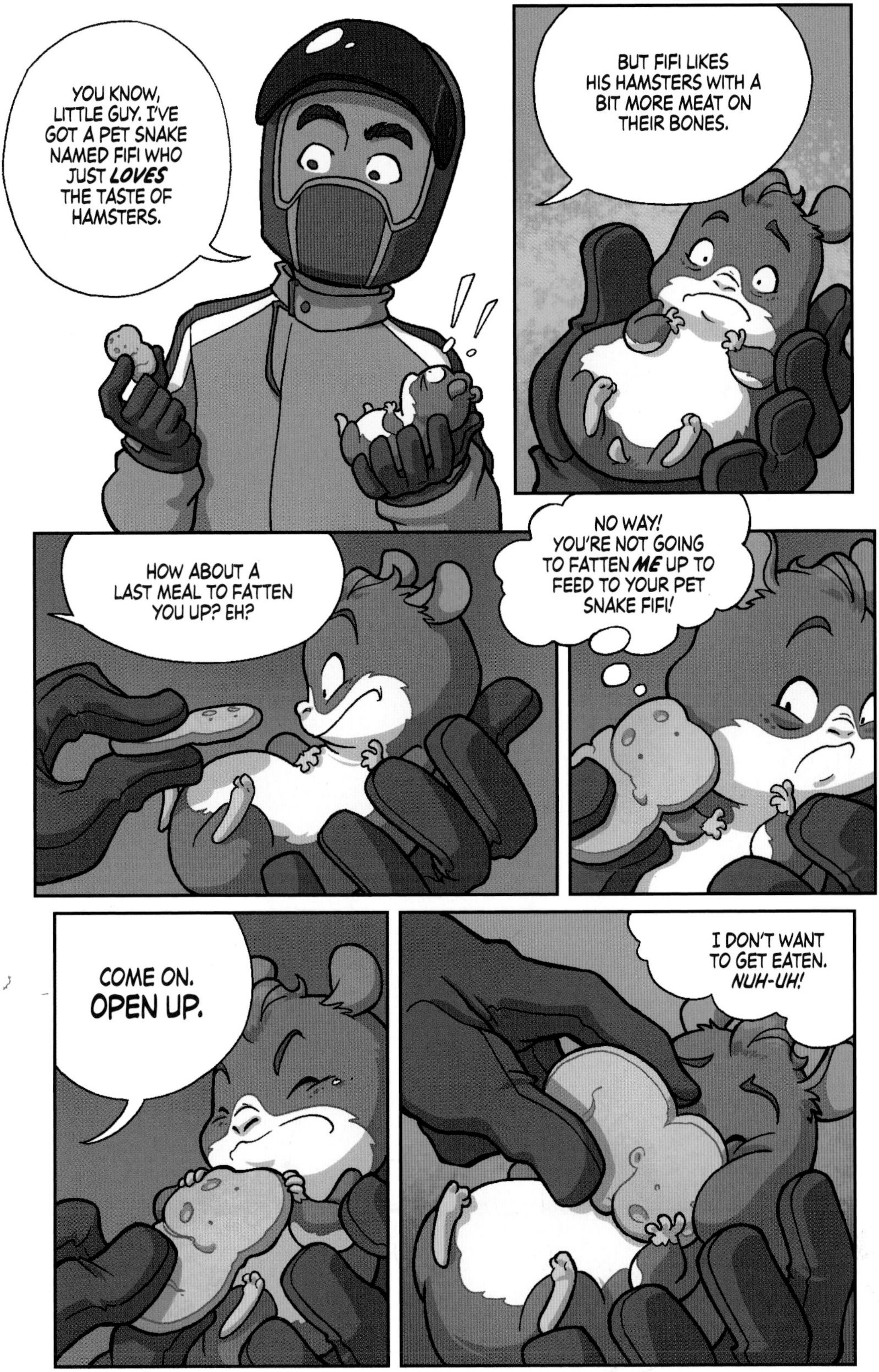
YOU KNOW, LITTLE GUY. I'VE GOT A PET SNAKE NAMED FIFI WHO JUST *LOVES* THE TASTE OF HAMSTERS.
BUT FIFI LIKES HIS HAMSTERS WITH A BIT MORE MEAT ON THEIR BONES.
HOW ABOUT A LAST MEAL TO FATTEN YOU UP? EH?
NO WAY! YOU'RE NOT GOING TO FATTEN *ME* UP TO FEED TO YOUR PET SNAKE FIFI!
COME ON. OPEN UP.
I DON'T WANT TO GET EATEN. *NUH-UH!*

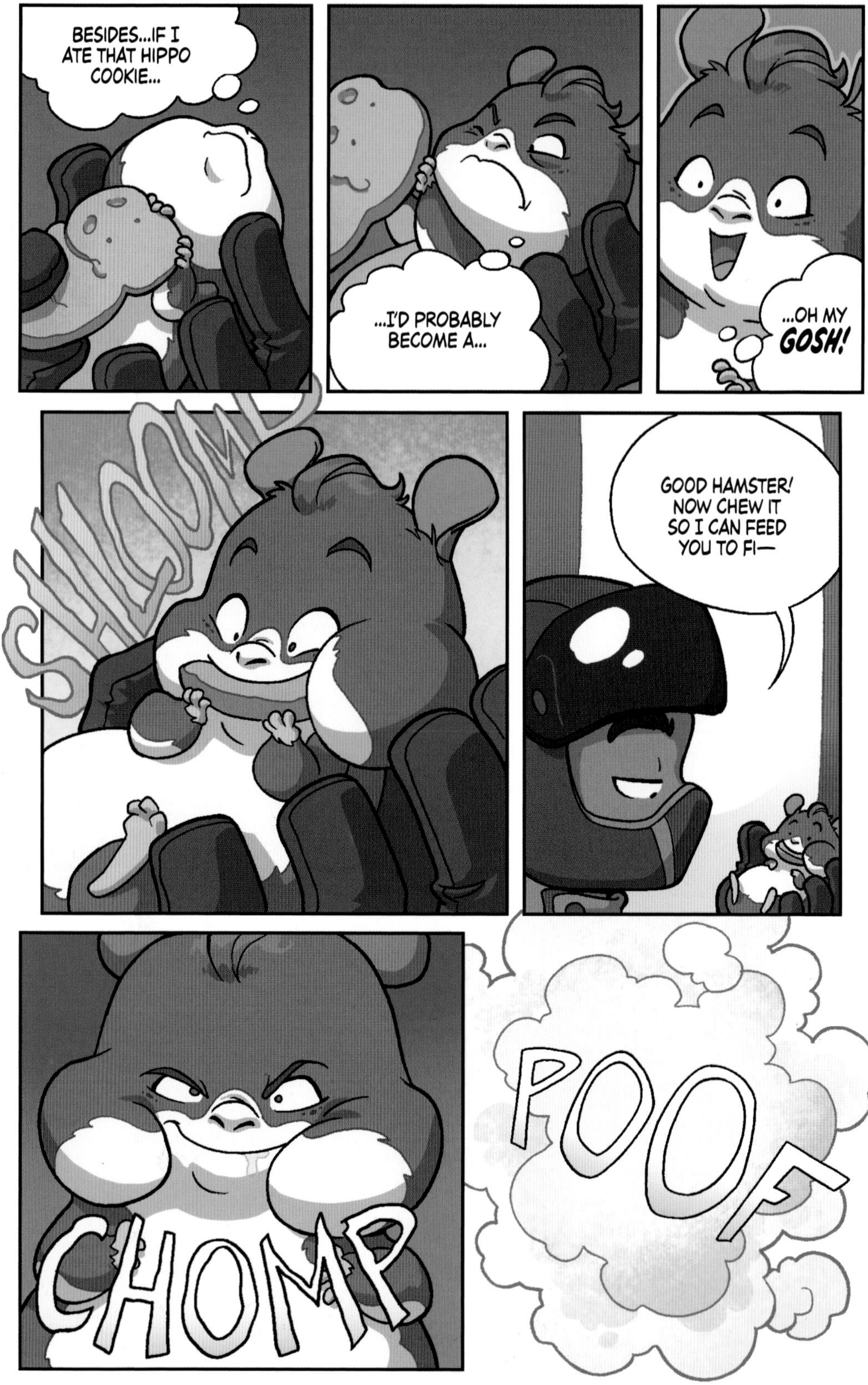
BESIDES...IF I ATE THAT HIPPO COOKIE...
...I'D PROBABLY BECOME A...
...OH MY **GOSH!**
SHLOOMP
GOOD HAMSTER! NOW CHEW IT SO I CAN FEED YOU TO FI—
CHOMP
POOF

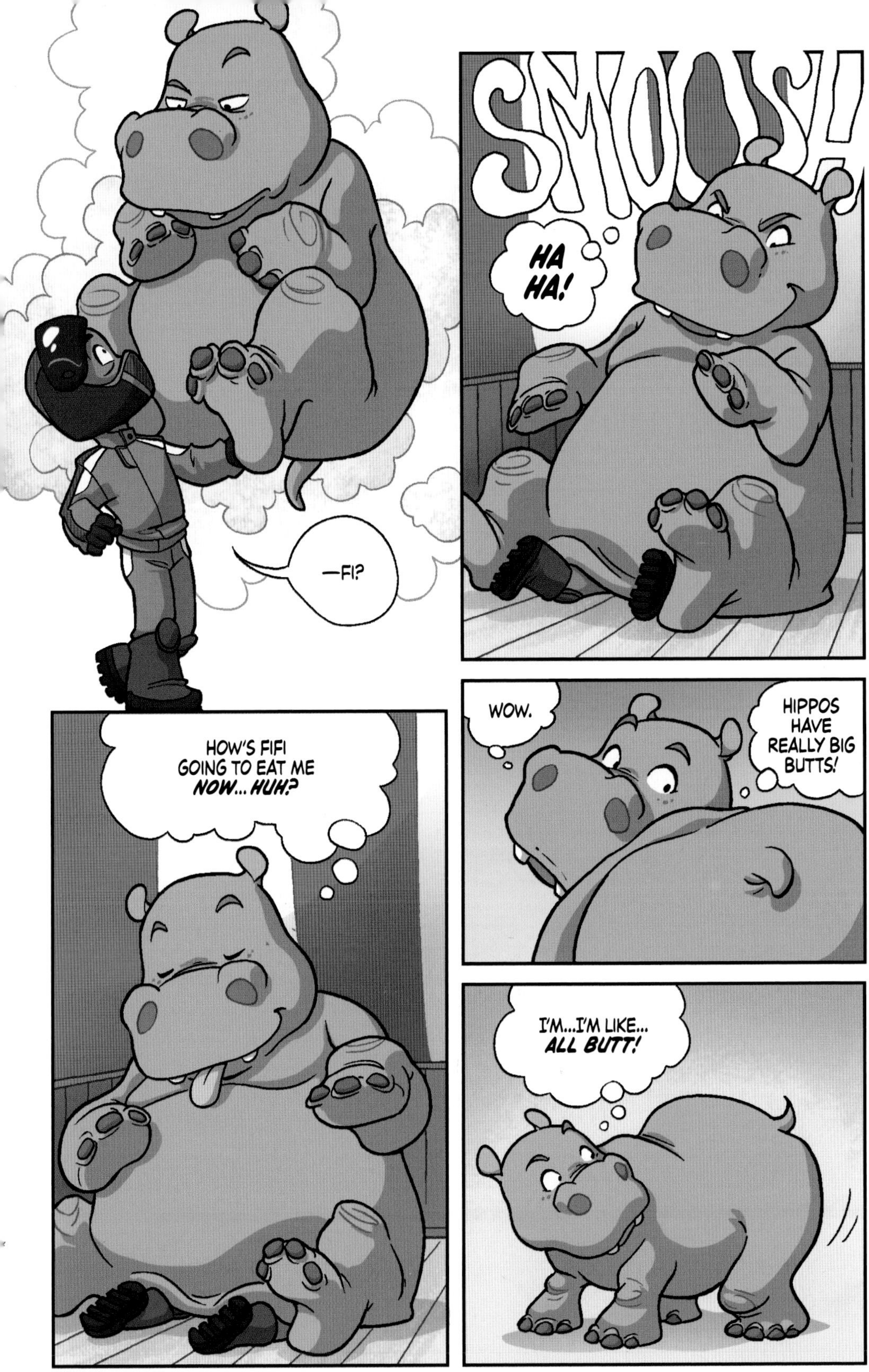
—FI?
SMOOSH!
HA HA!
HOW'S FIFI GOING TO EAT ME NOW... HUH?
WOW.
HIPPOS HAVE REALLY BIG BUTTS!
I'M...I'M LIKE... ALL BUTT!

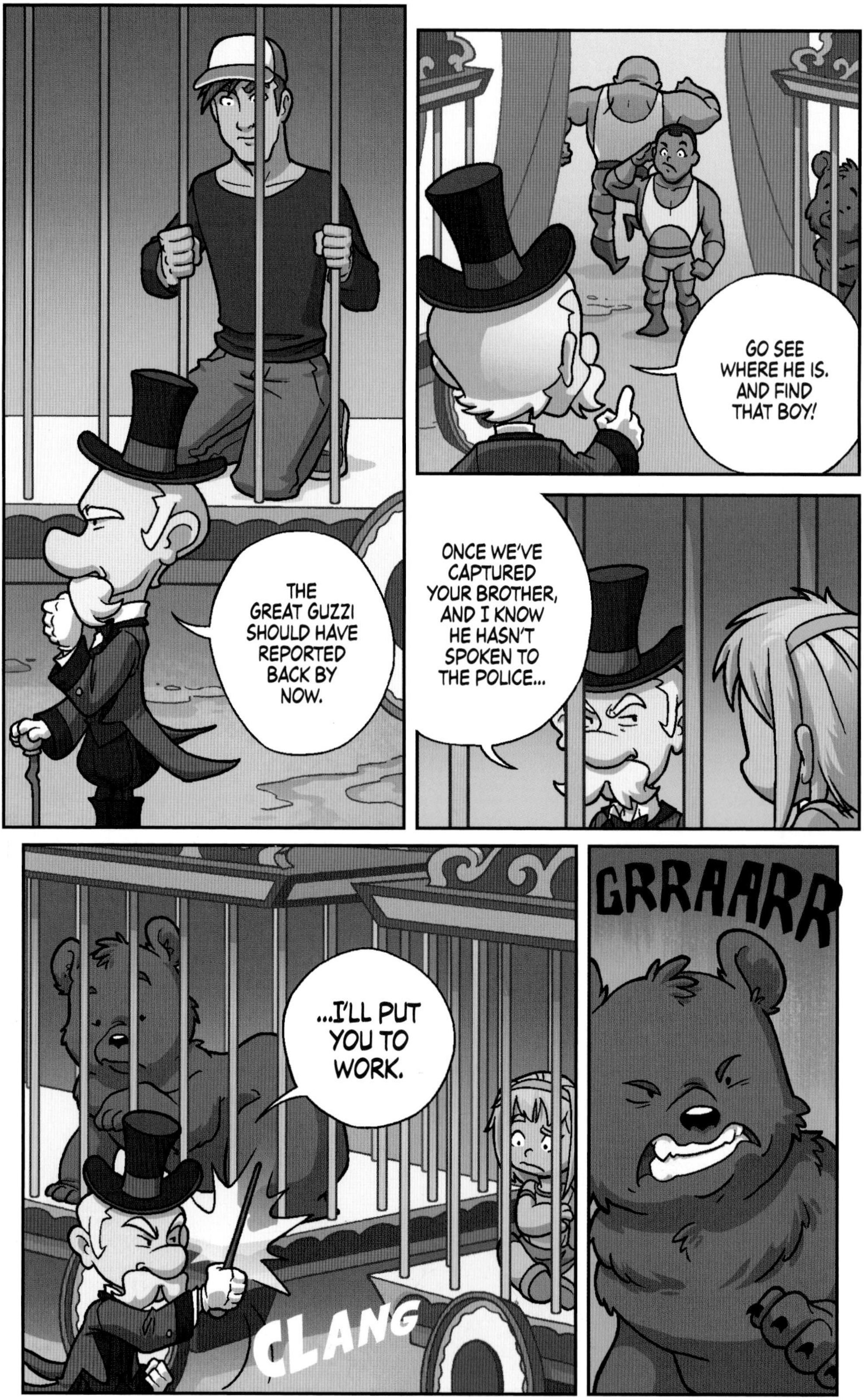
THE GREAT GUZZI SHOULD HAVE REPORTED BACK BY NOW.
GO SEE WHERE HE IS. AND FIND THAT BOY!
ONCE WE'VE CAPTURED YOUR BROTHER, AND I KNOW HE HASN'T SPOKEN TO THE POLICE...
...I'LL PUT YOU TO WORK.
CLANG
GRRAARR

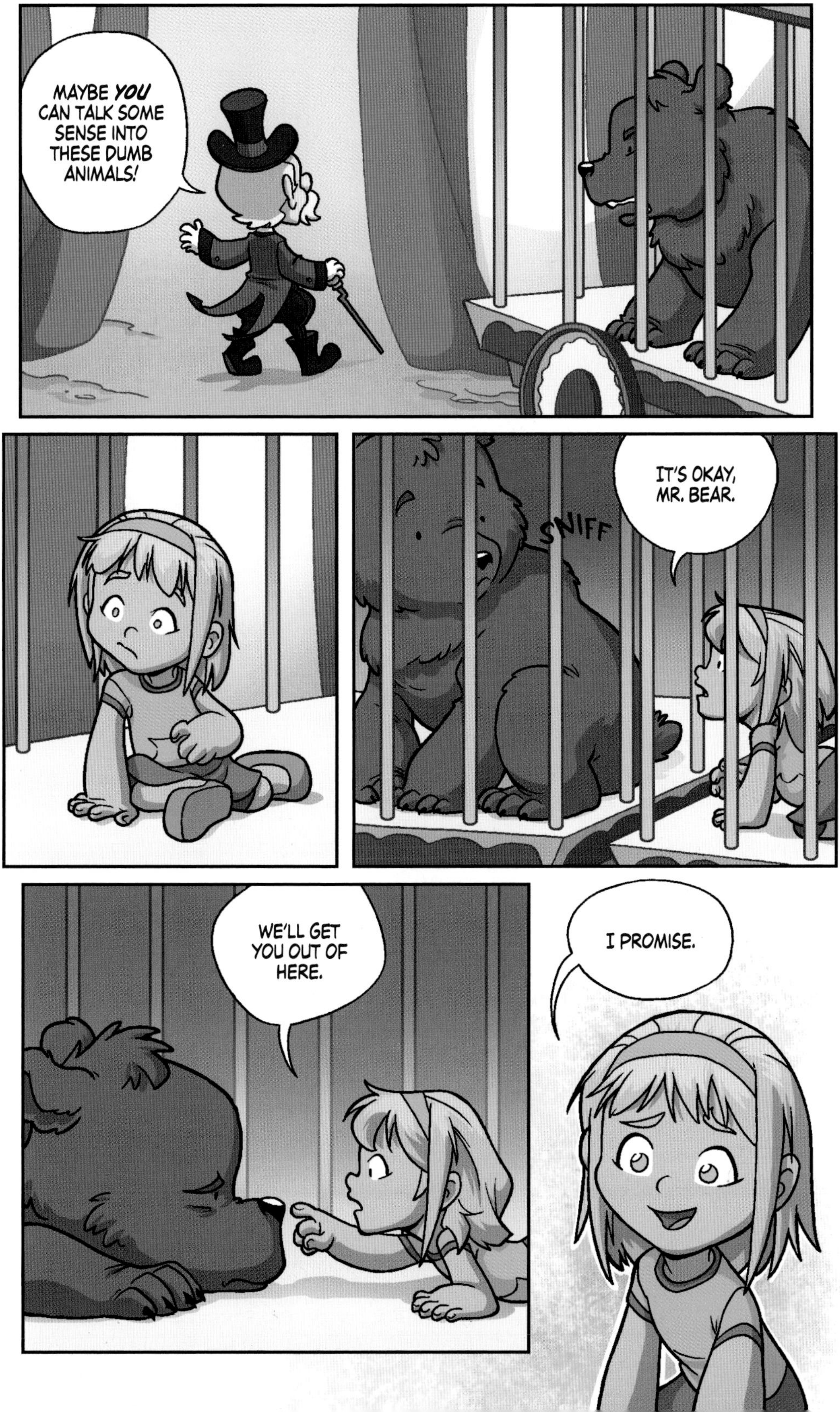
MAYBE *YOU* CAN TALK SOME SENSE INTO THESE DUMB ANIMALS!
SNIFF
IT'S OKAY, MR. BEAR.
WE'LL GET YOU OUT OF HERE.
I PROMISE.

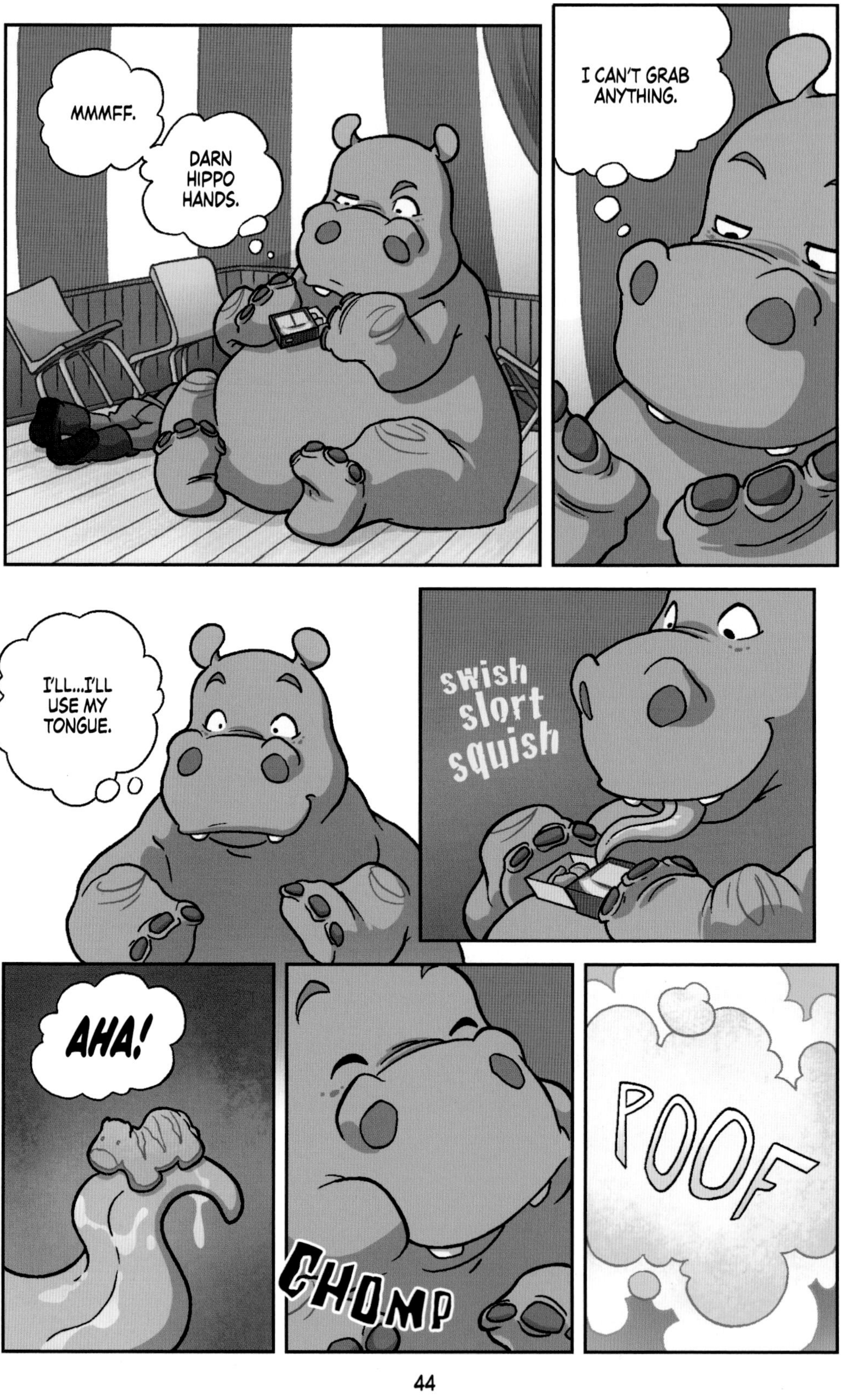
MMMFF.
DARN HIPPO HANDS.
I CAN'T GRAB ANYTHING.
I'LL...I'LL USE MY TONGUE.
swish slort squish
AHA!
CHOMP
POOF

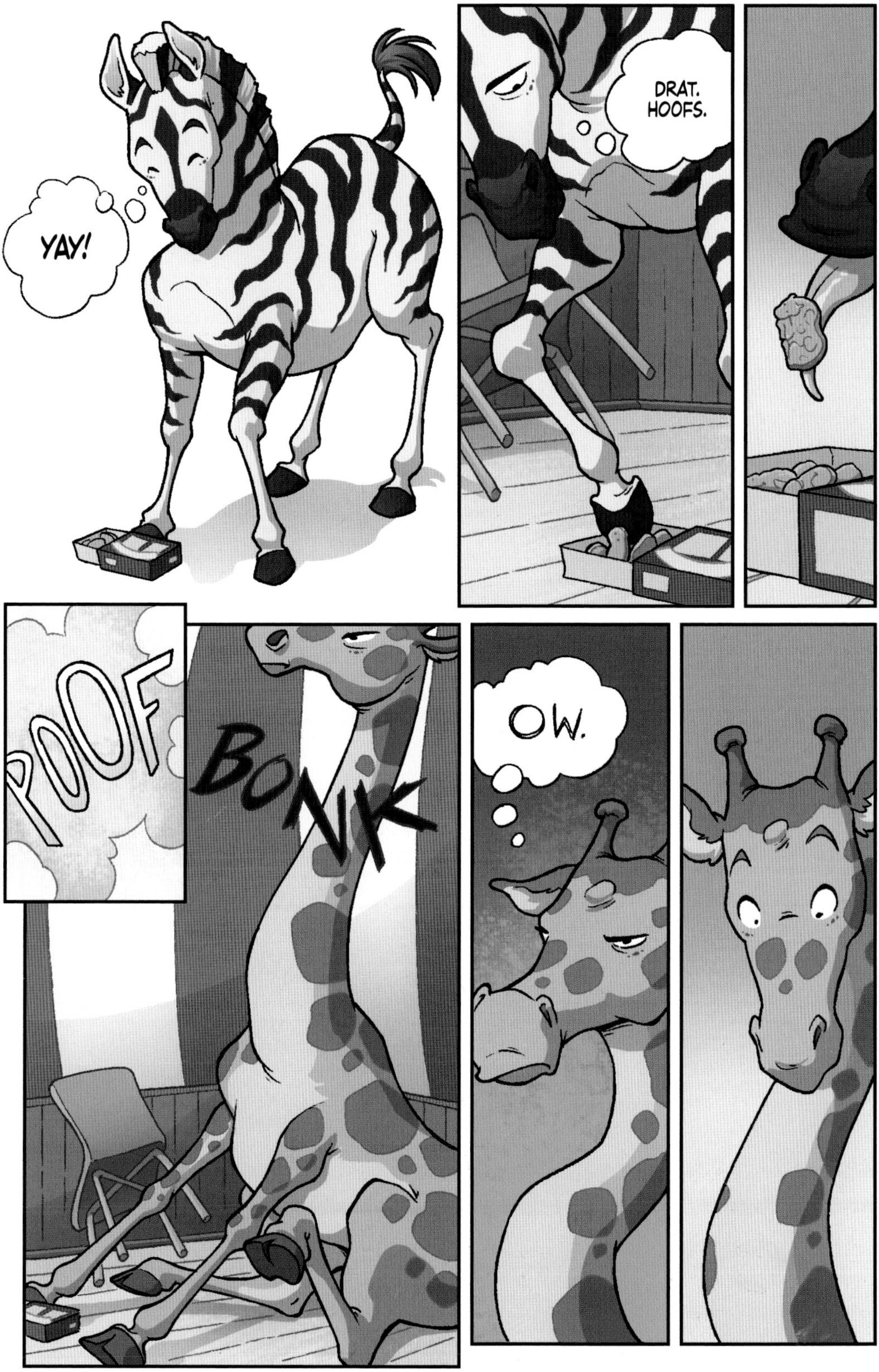
YAY!
DRAT. HOOFS.
POOF
BONK
OW.

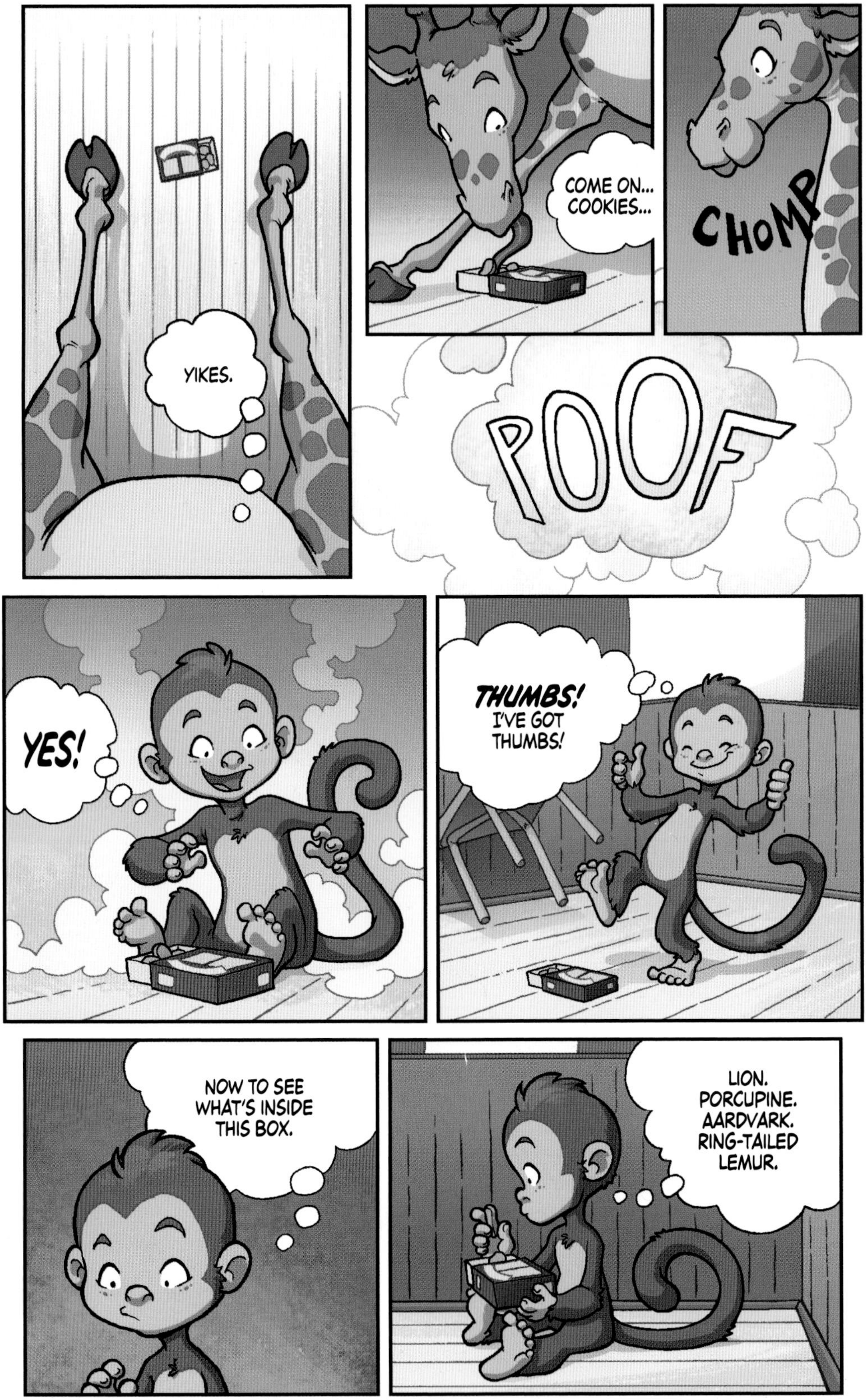
YIKES.
COME ON... COOKIES...
CHOMP
POOF
YES!
THUMBS! I'VE GOT THUMBS!
NOW TO SEE WHAT'S INSIDE THIS BOX.
LION. PORCUPINE. AARDVARK. RING-TAILED LEMUR.

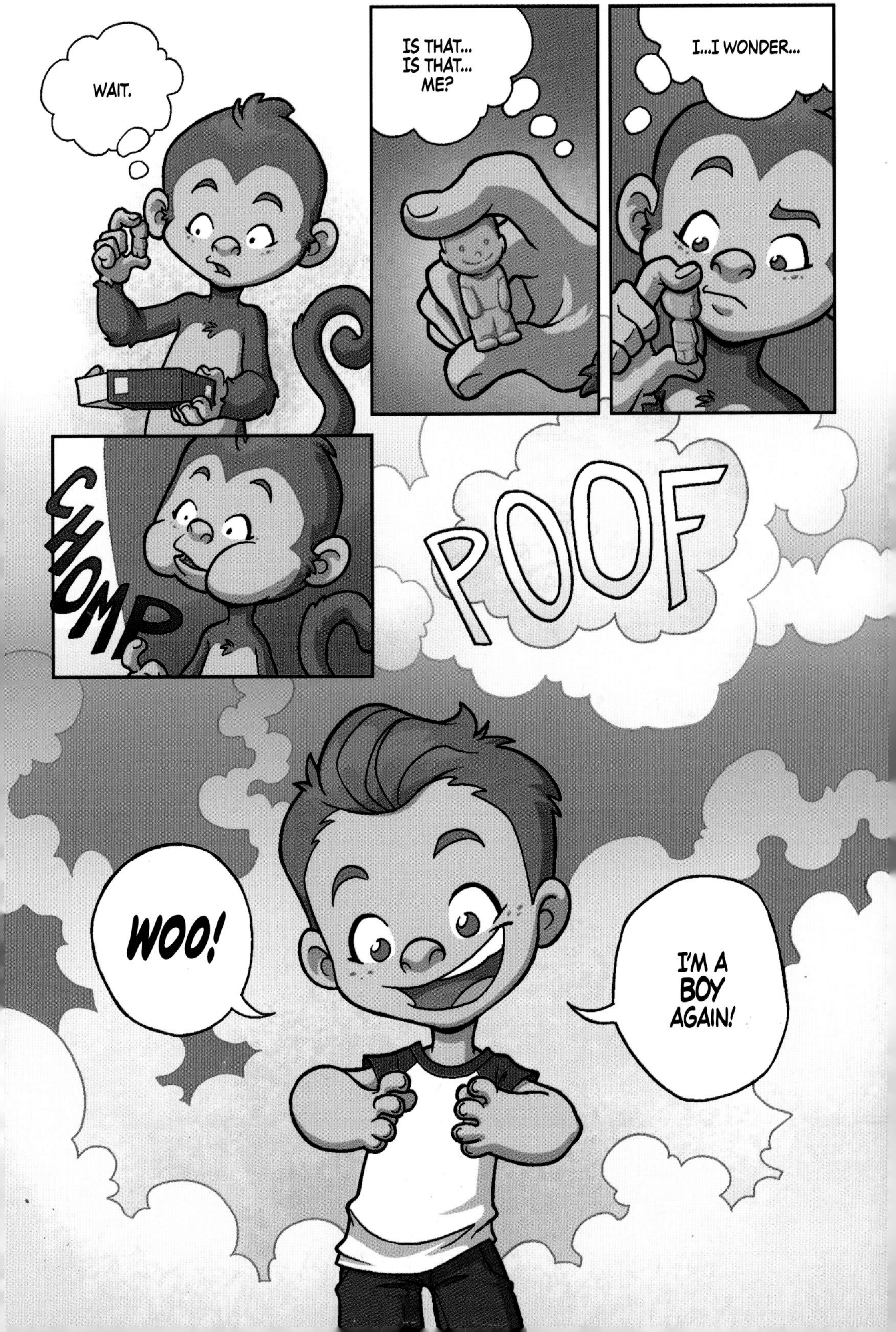
WAIT.
IS THAT... IS THAT... ME?
I...I WONDER...
CHOMP
POOF
WOO!
I'M A BOY AGAIN!

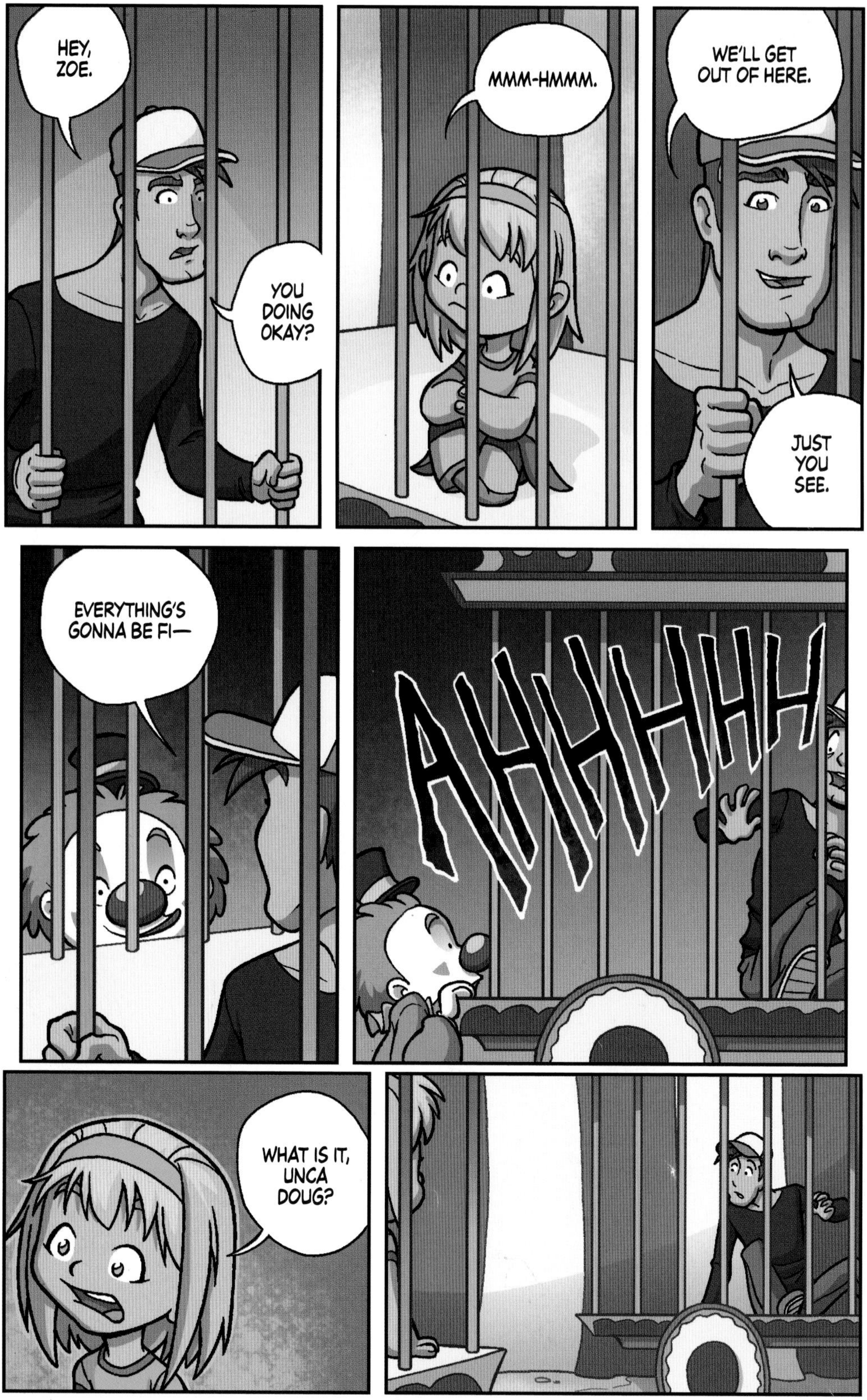
HEY, ZOE.
YOU DOING OKAY?
MMM-HMMM.
WE'LL GET OUT OF HERE.
JUST YOU SEE.
EVERYTHING'S GONNA BE FI—
AHHHHHH
WHAT IS IT, UNCA DOUG?

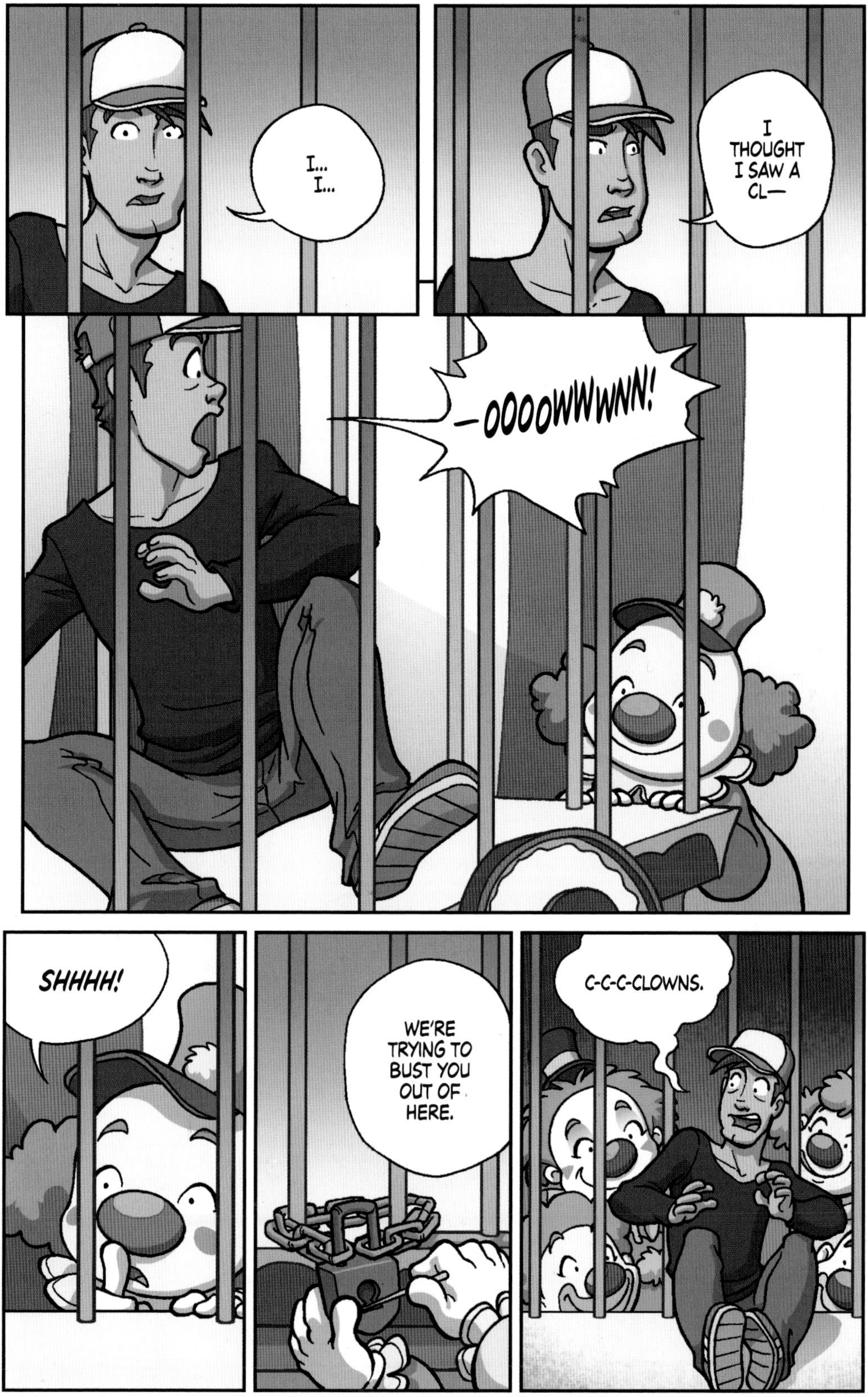
I... I...
I THOUGHT I SAW A CL—
—OOOOWWWNN!
SHHHH!
WE'RE TRYING TO BUST YOU OUT OF HERE.
C-C-C-CLOWNS.

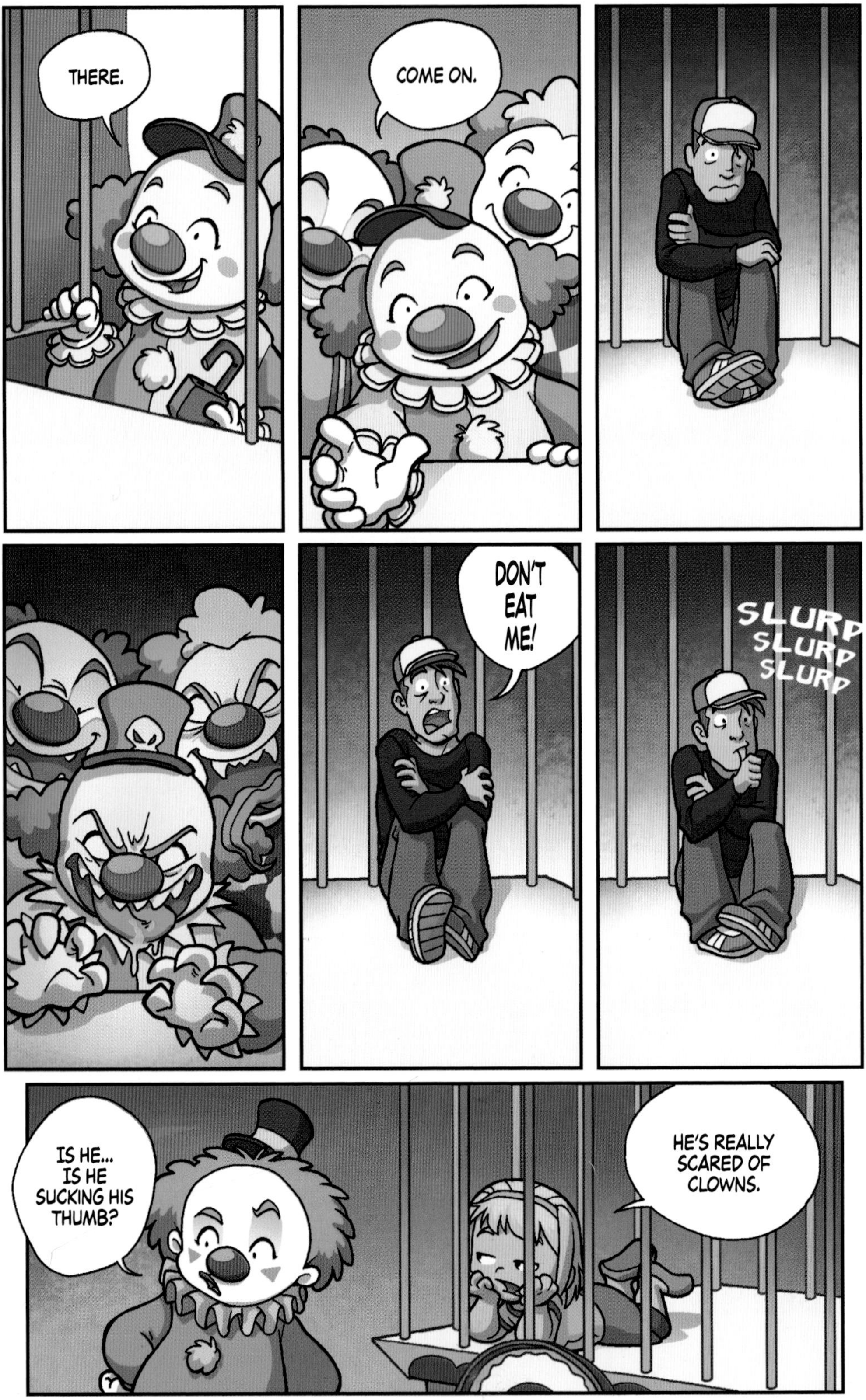
THERE.
COME ON.
DON'T EAT ME!
SLURP SLURP SLURP
IS HE... IS HE SUCKING HIS THUMB?
HE'S REALLY SCARED OF CLOWNS.

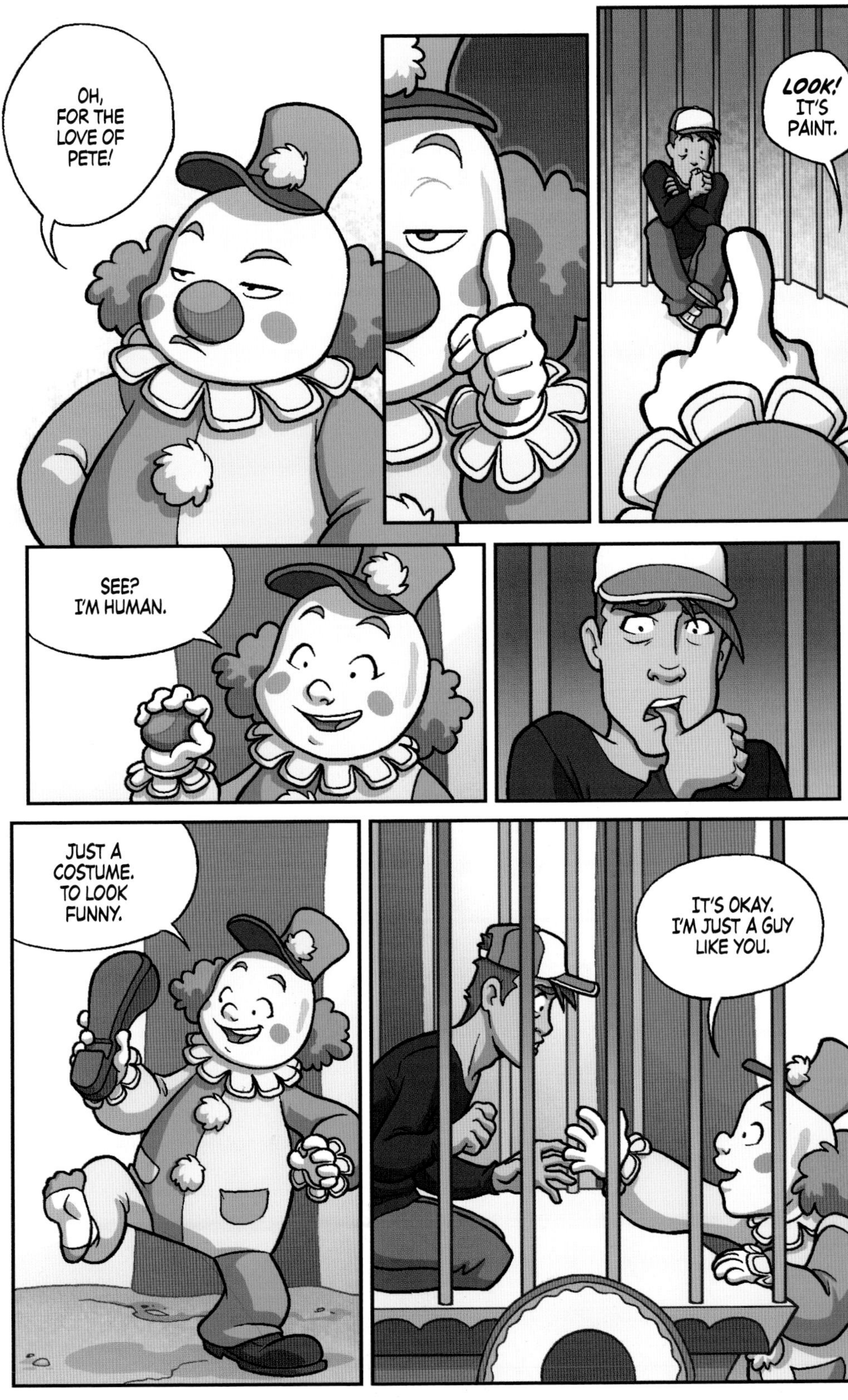
OH, FOR THE LOVE OF PETE!
LOOK! IT'S PAINT.
SEE? I'M HUMAN.
JUST A COSTUME. TO LOOK FUNNY.
IT'S OKAY. I'M JUST A GUY LIKE YOU.

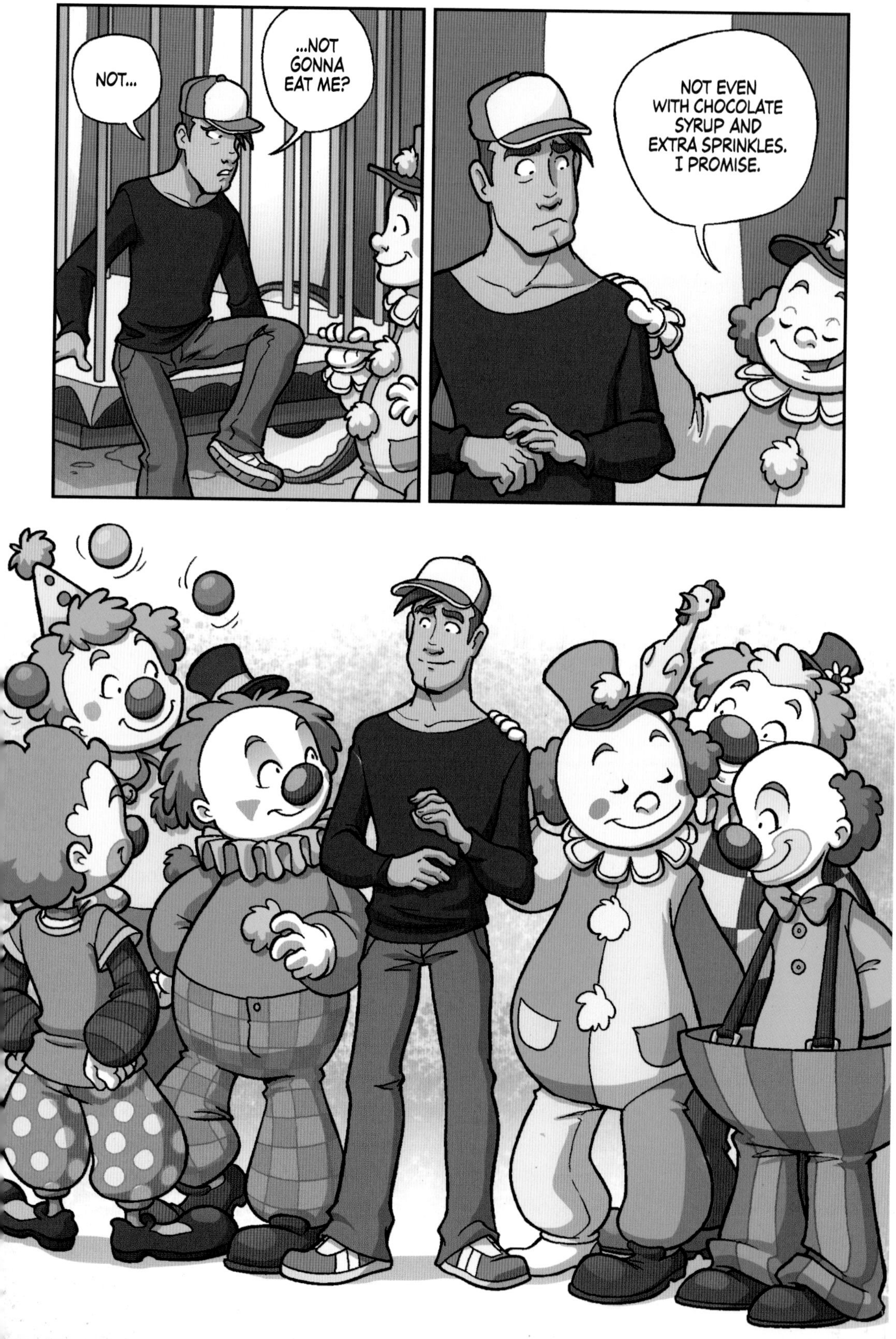
NOT...
...NOT GONNA EAT ME?
NOT EVEN WITH CHOCOLATE SYRUP AND EXTRA SPRINKLES. I PROMISE.

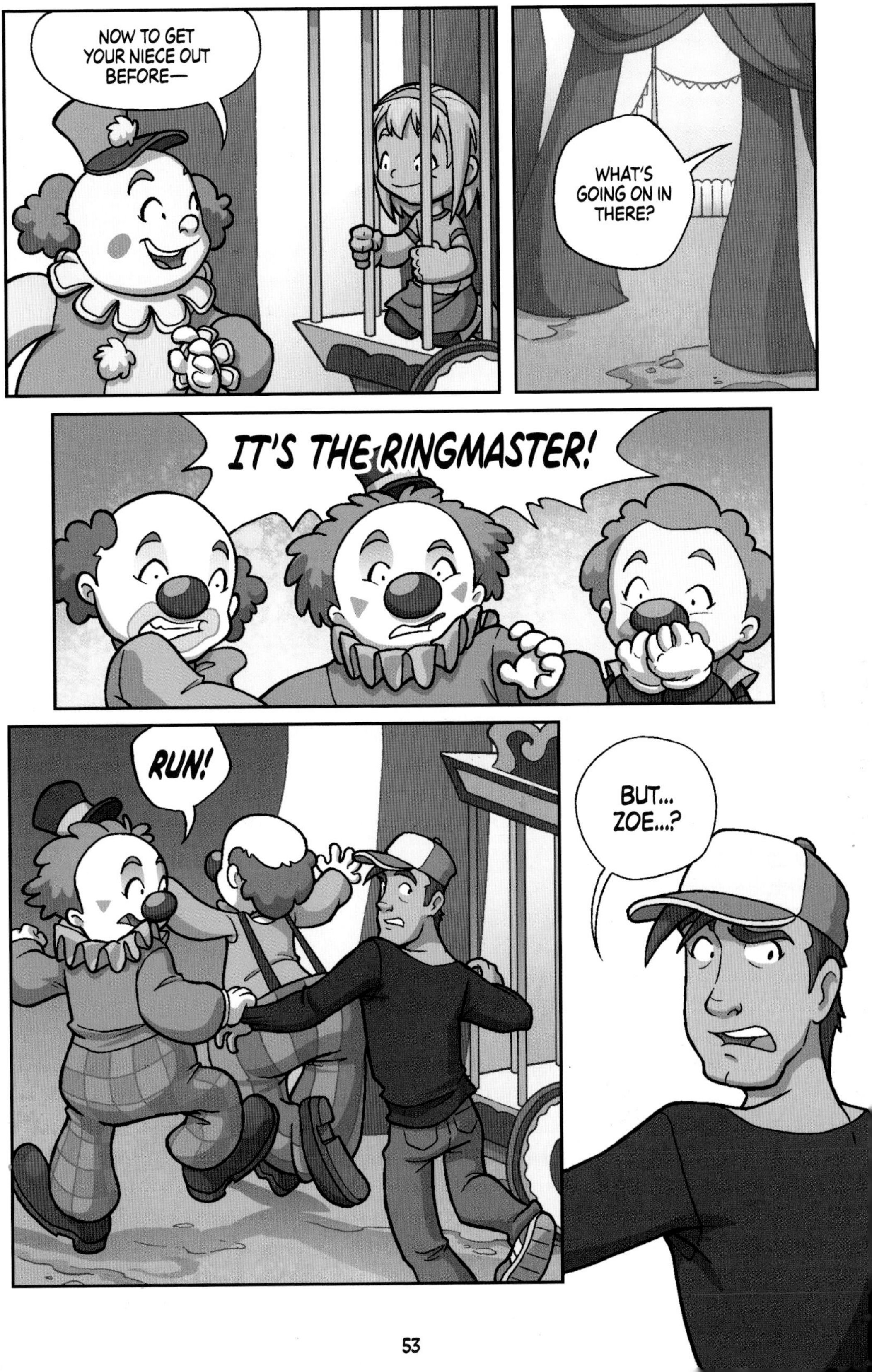
NOW TO GET YOUR NIECE OUT BEFORE—
WHAT'S GOING ON IN THERE?
IT'S THE RINGMASTER!
RUN!
BUT... ZOE...?

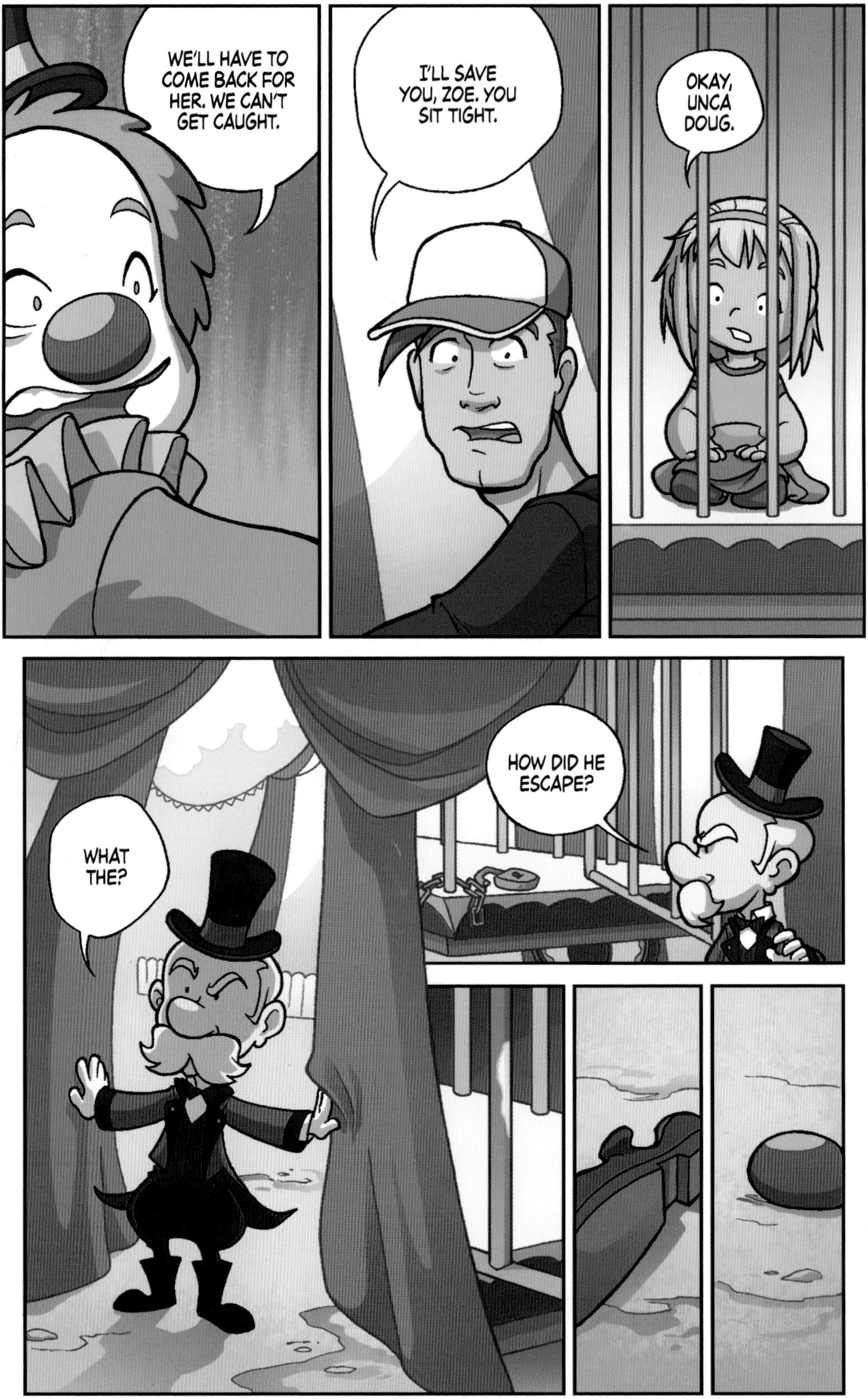
WE'LL HAVE TO COME BACK FOR HER. WE CAN'T GET CAUGHT.
I'LL SAVE YOU, ZOE. YOU SIT TIGHT.
OKAY, UNCA DOUG.
WHAT THE?
HOW DID HE ESCAPE?

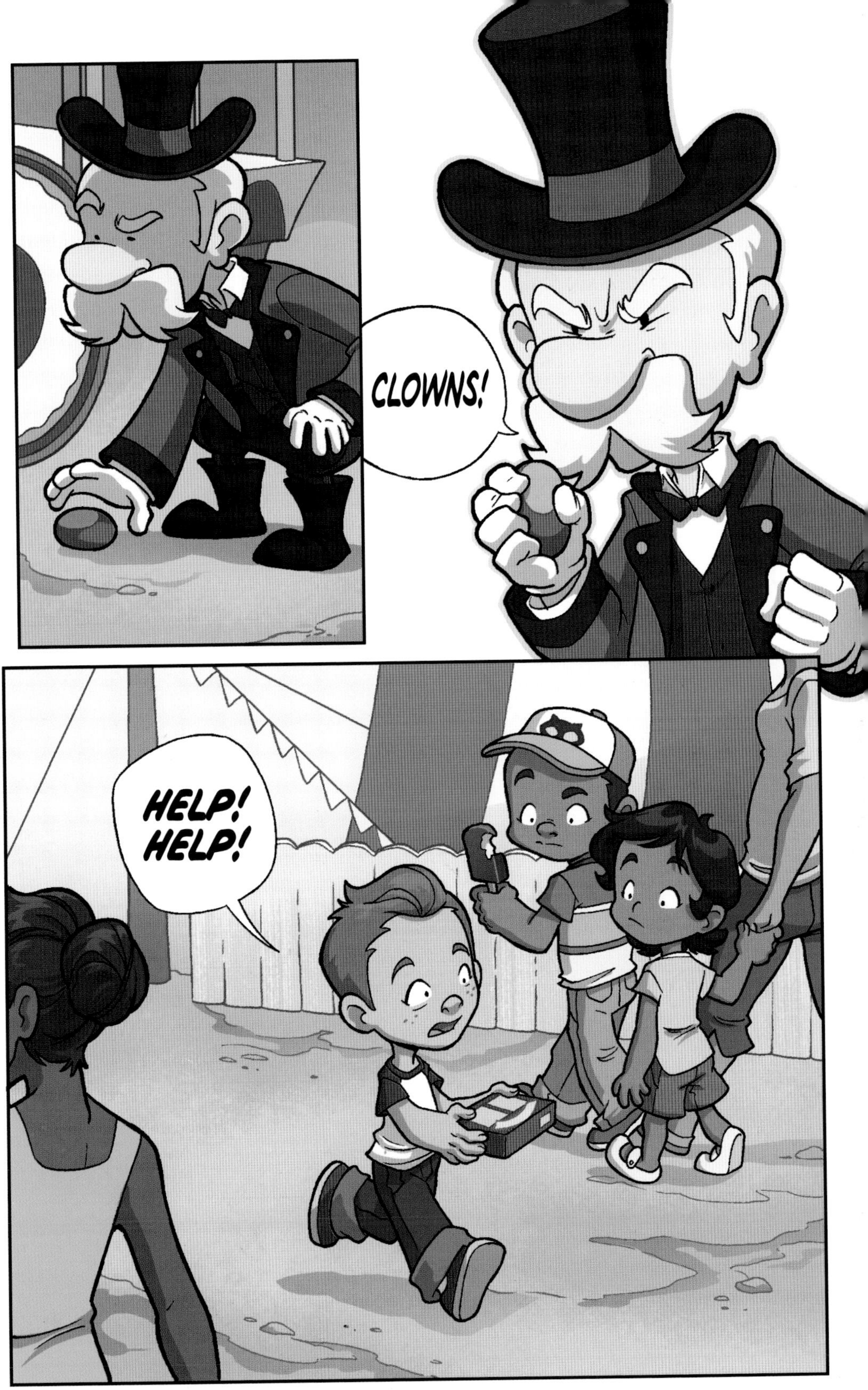
CLOWNS!
HELP! HELP!

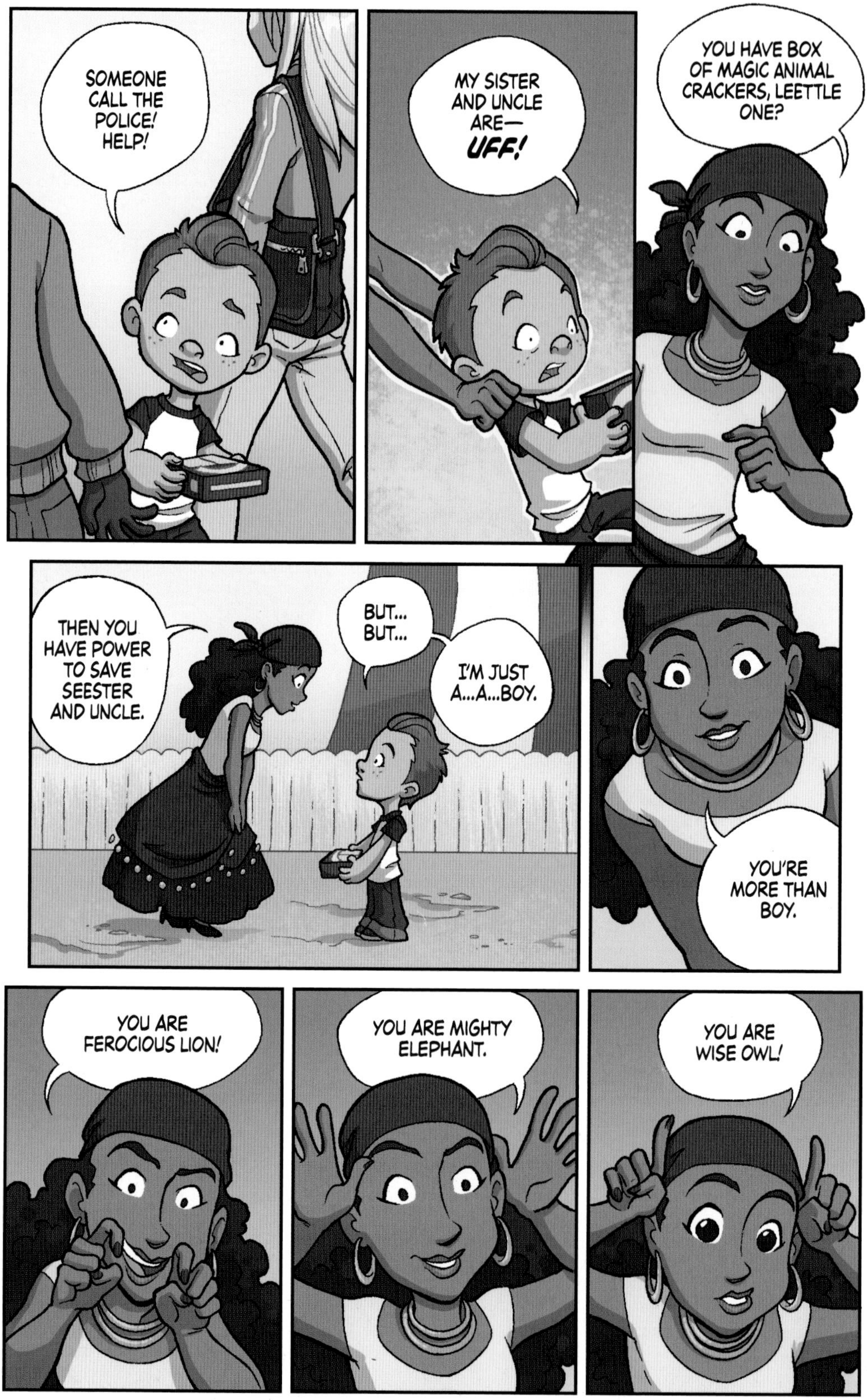
SOMEONE CALL THE POLICE! HELP!
MY SISTER AND UNCLE ARE— UFF!
YOU HAVE BOX OF MAGIC ANIMAL CRACKERS, LEETTLE ONE?
THEN YOU HAVE POWER TO SAVE SEESTER AND UNCLE.
BUT... BUT...
I'M JUST A...A...BOY.
YOU'RE MORE THAN BOY.
YOU ARE FEROCIOUS LION!
YOU ARE MIGHTY ELEPHANT.
YOU ARE WISE OWL!

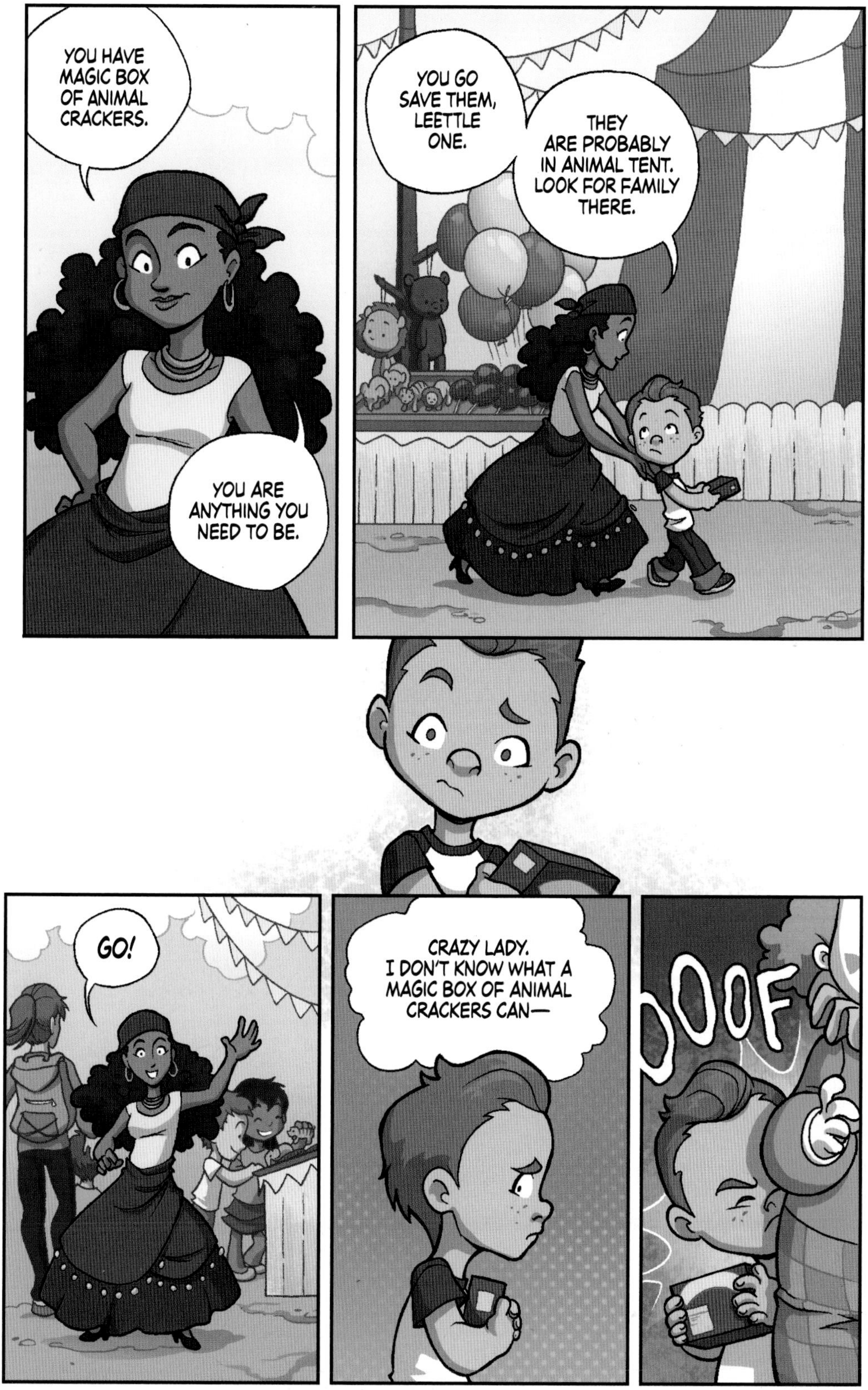
YOU HAVE MAGIC BOX OF ANIMAL CRACKERS.
YOU ARE ANYTHING YOU NEED TO BE.
YOU GO SAVE THEM, LEETTLE ONE.
THEY ARE PROBABLY IN ANIMAL TENT. LOOK FOR FAMILY THERE.
GO!
CRAZY LADY. I DON'T KNOW WHAT A MAGIC BOX OF ANIMAL CRACKERS CAN—
OOOF

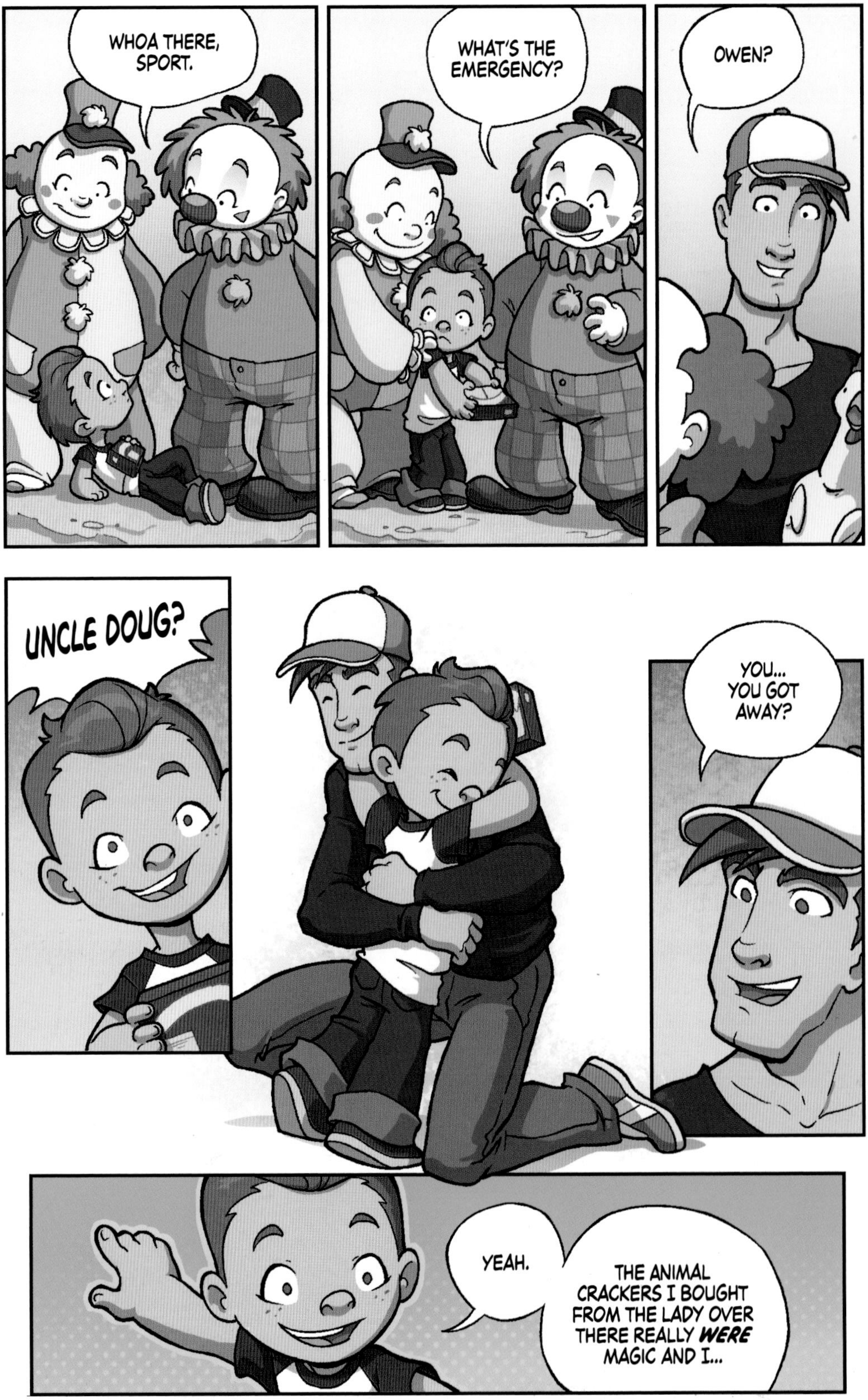
WHOA THERE, SPORT.
WHAT'S THE EMERGENCY?
OWEN?
UNCLE DOUG?
YOU... YOU GOT AWAY?
YEAH.
THE ANIMAL CRACKERS I BOUGHT FROM THE LADY OVER THERE REALLY WERE MAGIC AND I...

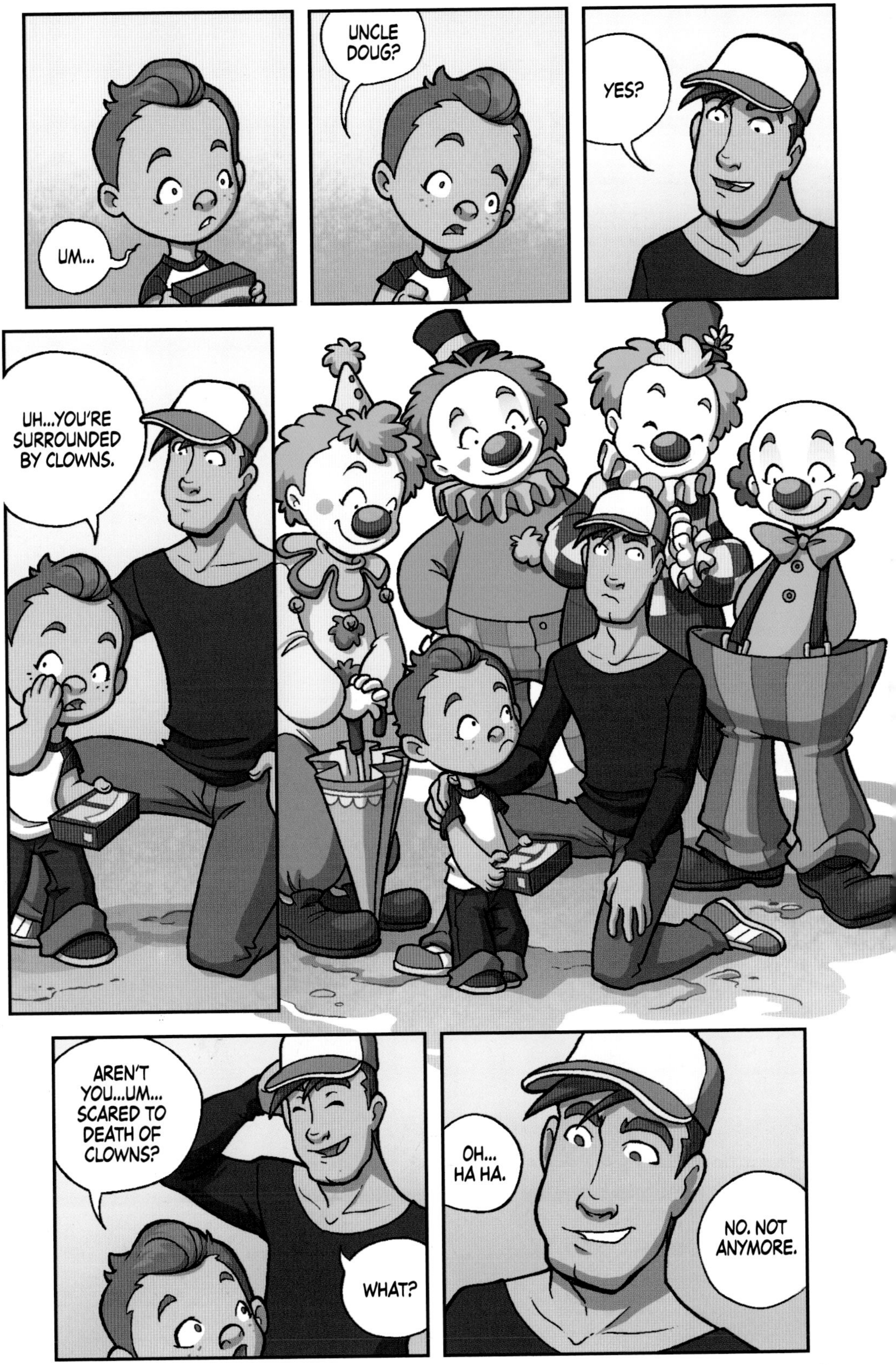
UM...
UNCLE DOUG?
YES?
UH...YOU'RE SURROUNDED BY CLOWNS.
AREN'T YOU...UM... SCARED TO DEATH OF CLOWNS?
WHAT?
OH... HA HA.
NO. NOT ANYMORE.

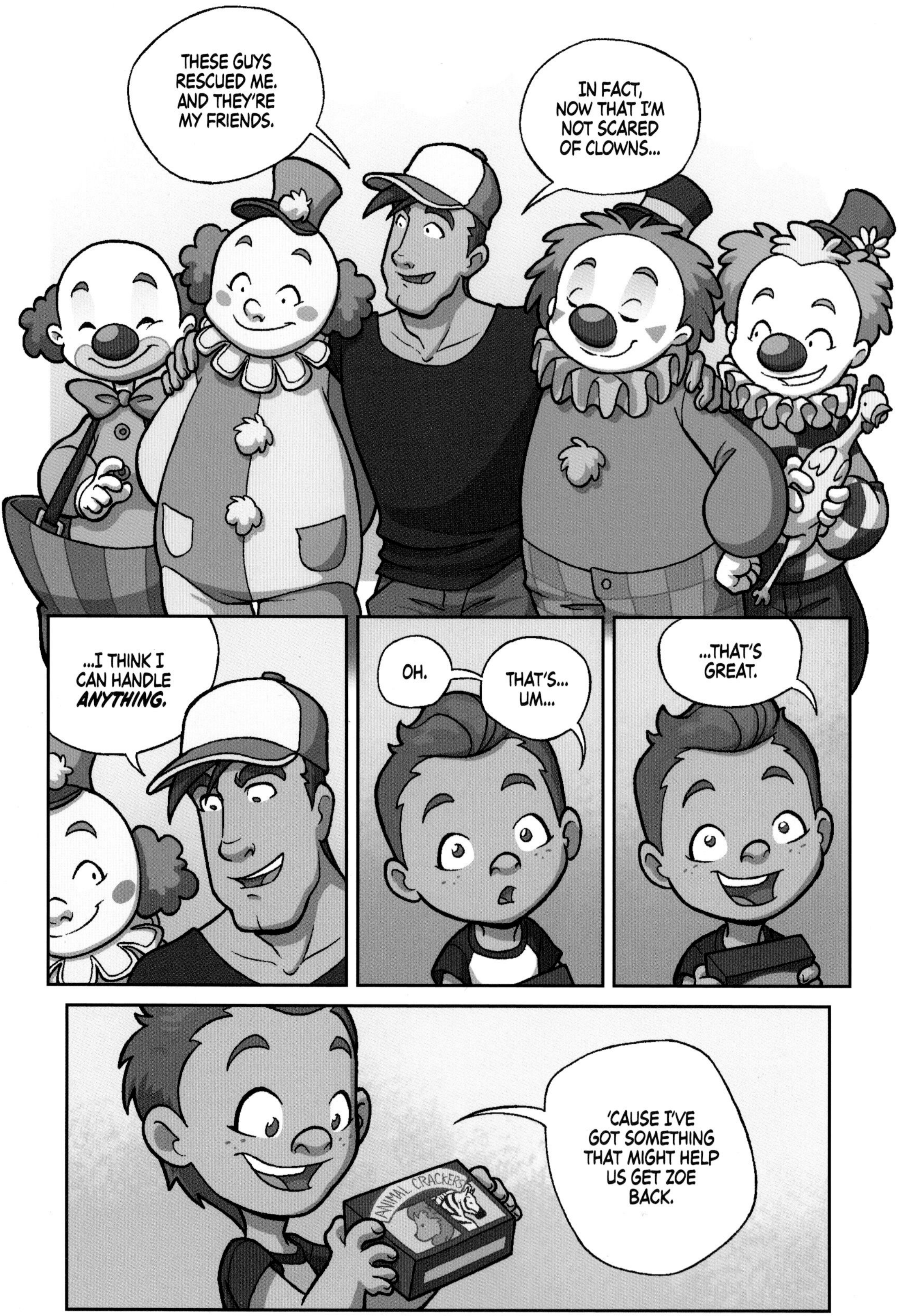
THESE GUYS RESCUED ME. AND THEY'RE MY FRIENDS.
IN FACT, NOW THAT I'M NOT SCARED OF CLOWNS...
...I THINK I CAN HANDLE *ANYTHING.*
OH.
THAT'S... UM...
...THAT'S GREAT.
'CAUSE I'VE GOT SOMETHING THAT MIGHT HELP US GET ZOE BACK.
ANIMAL CRACKERS

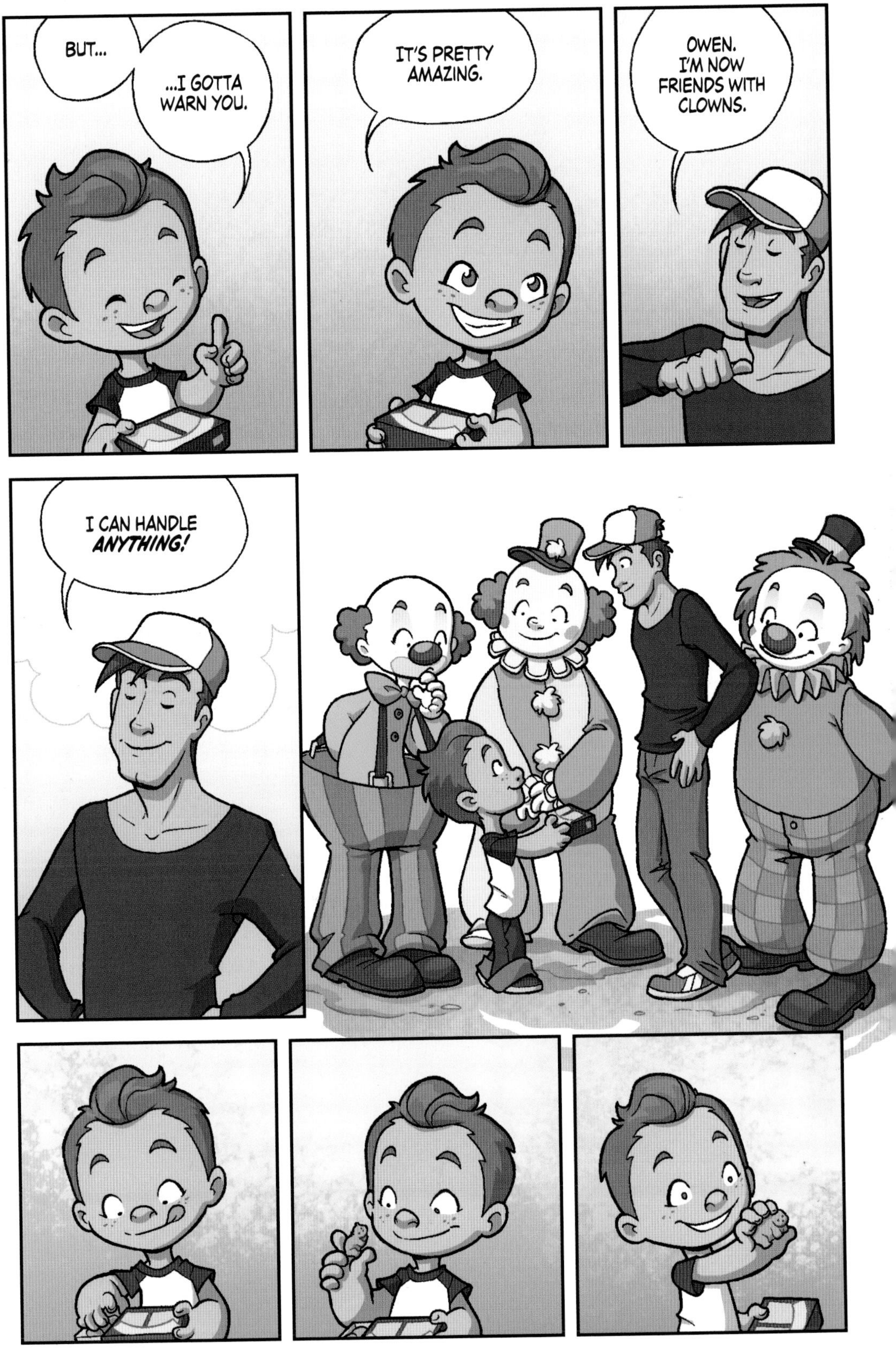
BUT...
...I GOTTA WARN YOU.
IT'S PRETTY AMAZING.
OWEN. I'M NOW FRIENDS WITH CLOWNS.
I CAN HANDLE ANYTHING!

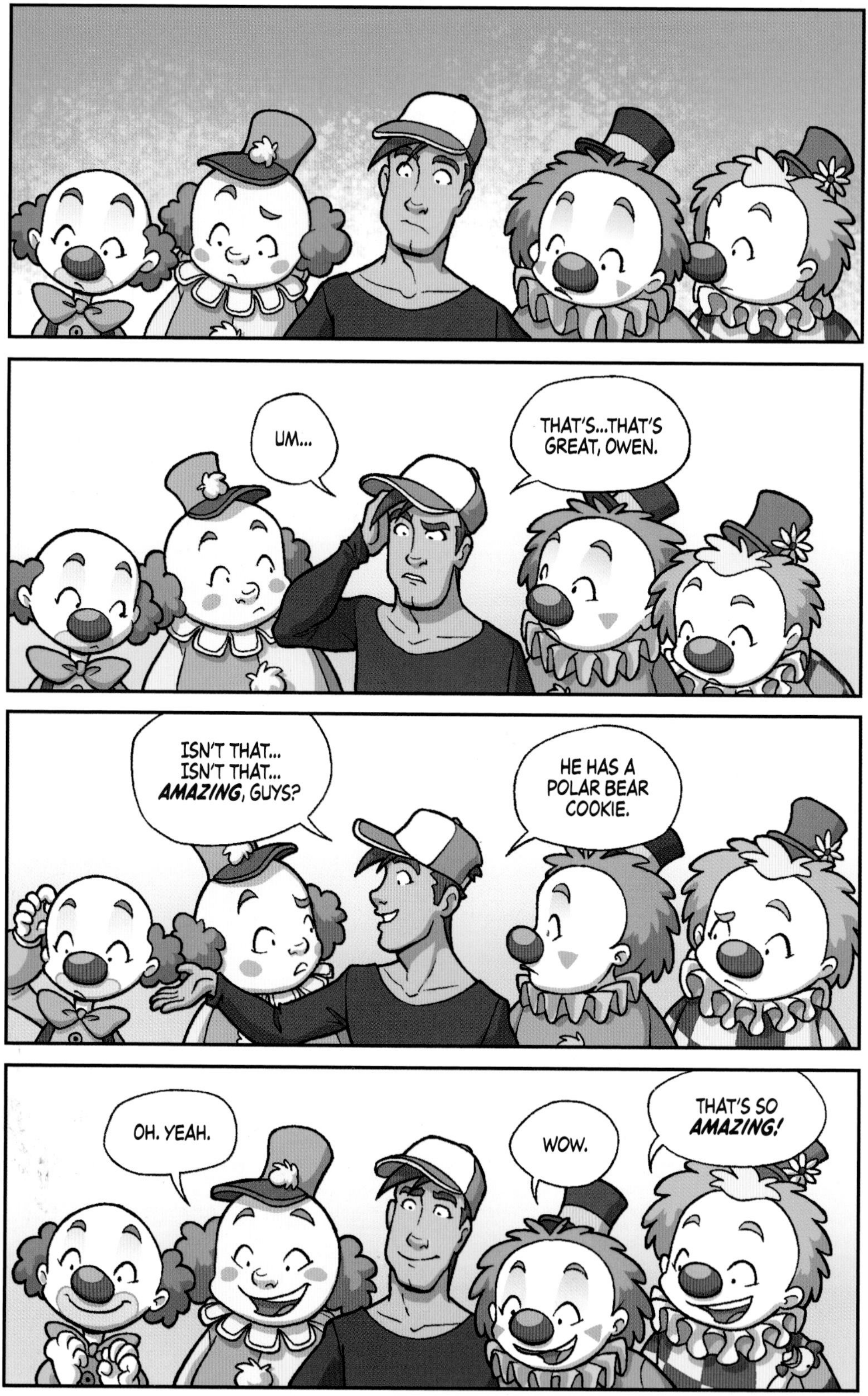
UM...
THAT'S...THAT'S GREAT, OWEN.
ISN'T THAT... ISN'T THAT... AMAZING, GUYS?
HE HAS A POLAR BEAR COOKIE.
OH. YEAH.
WOW.
THAT'S SO AMAZING!

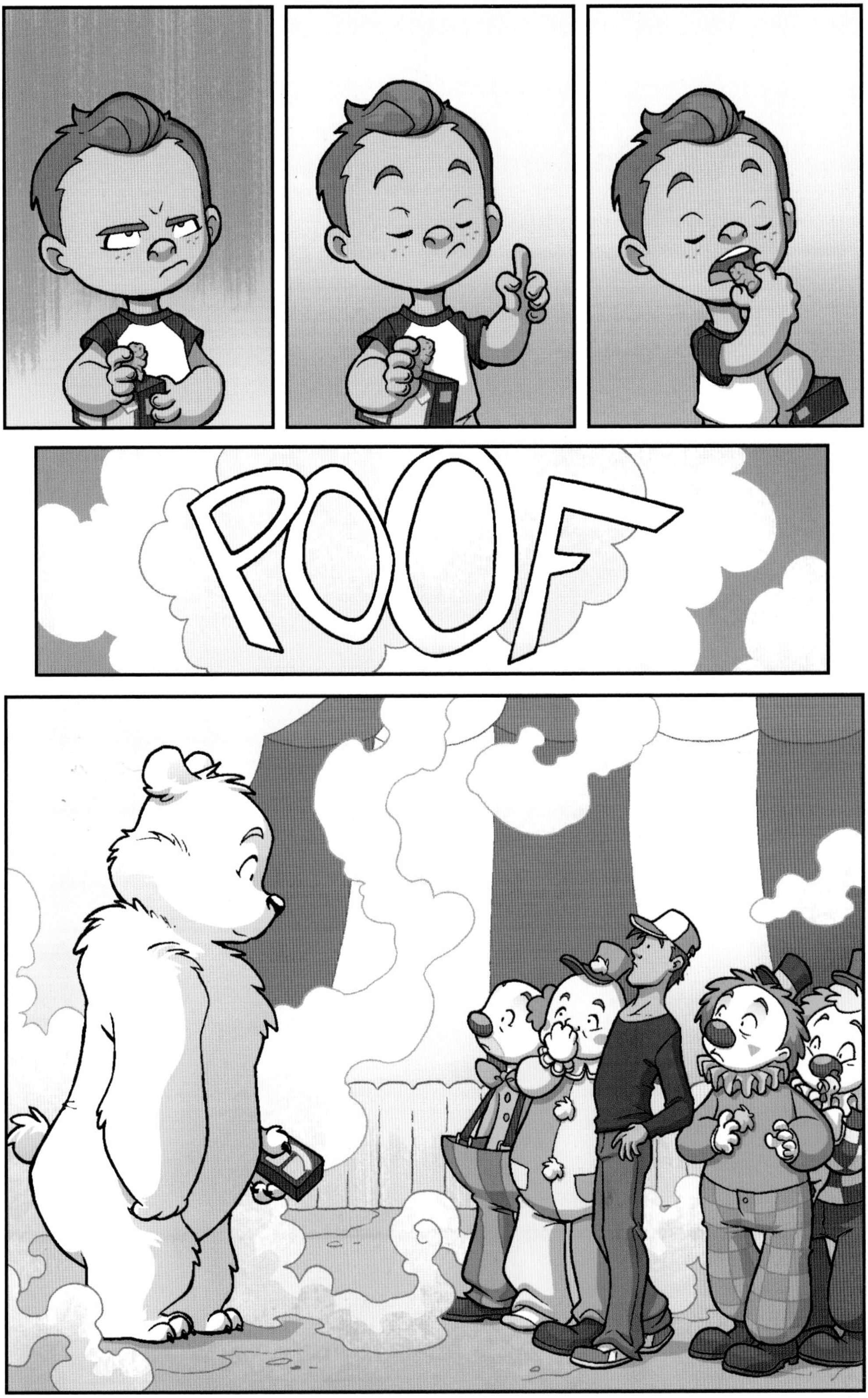
POOF

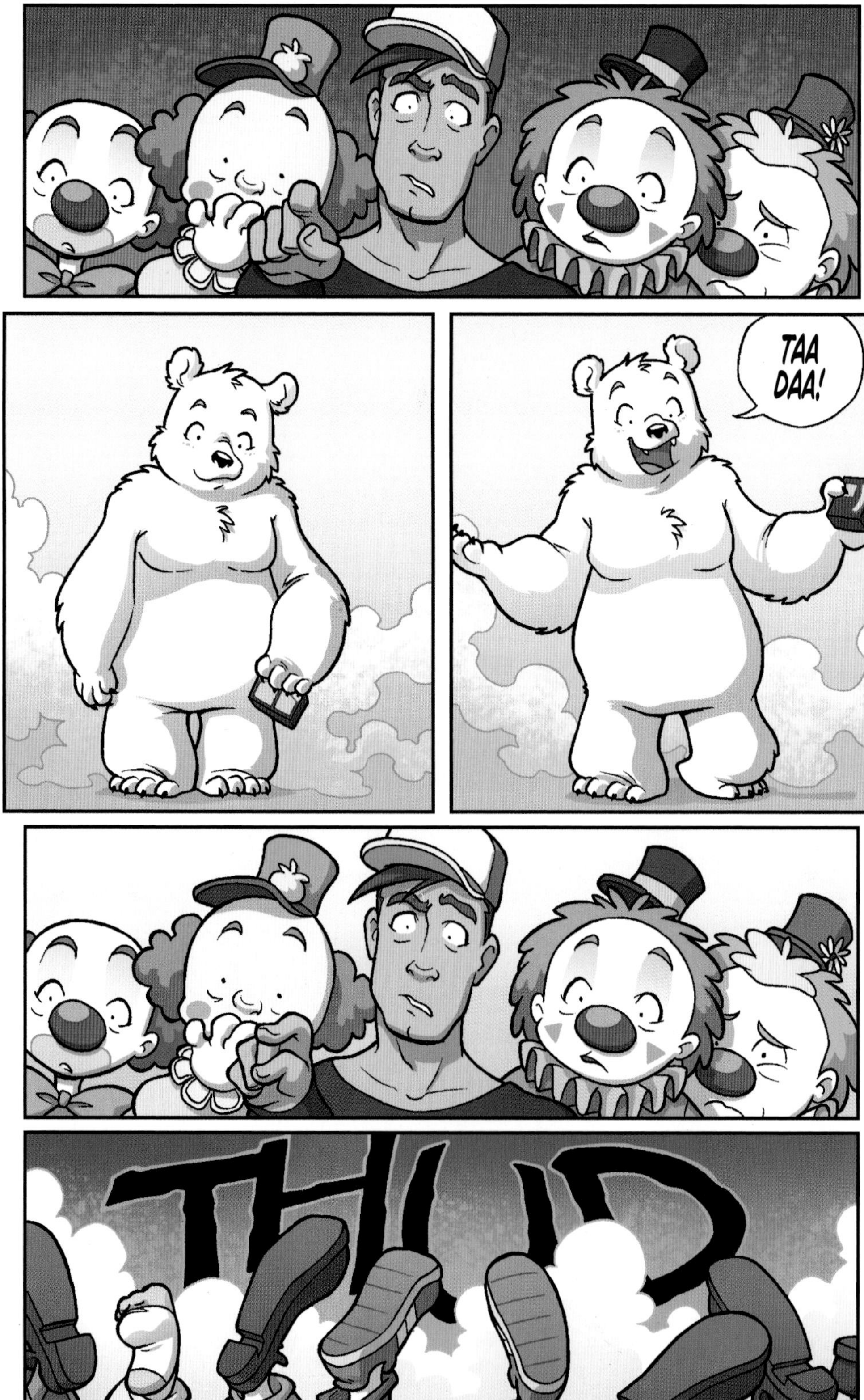
TAA
DAA!
THUD

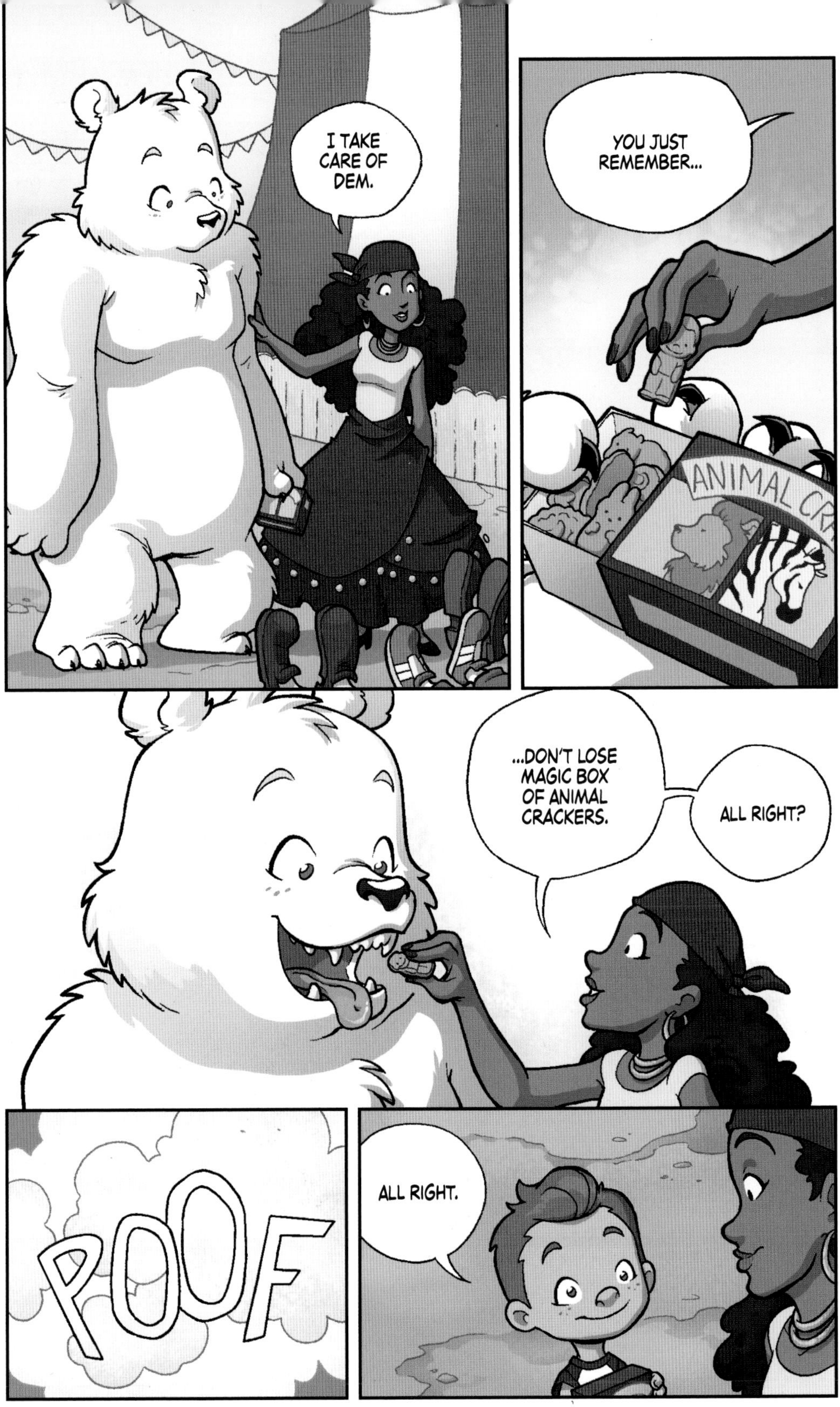
I TAKE CARE OF DEM.
YOU JUST REMEMBER...
ANIMAL CRA
...DON'T LOSE MAGIC BOX OF ANIMAL CRACKERS.
ALL RIGHT?
POOF
ALL RIGHT.

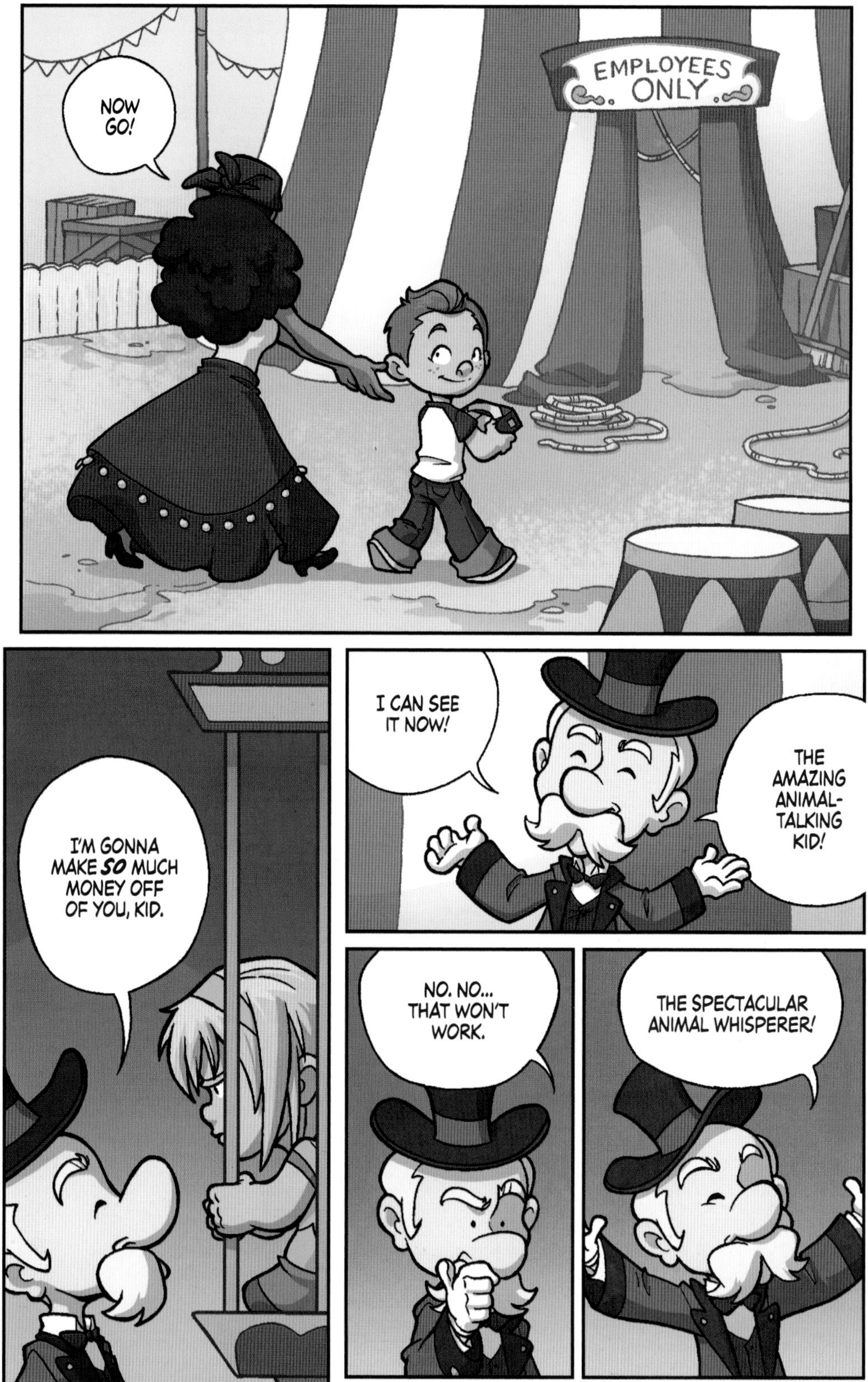
EMPLOYEES ONLY
NOW GO!
I'M GONNA MAKE *SO* MUCH MONEY OFF OF YOU, KID.
I CAN SEE IT NOW!
THE AMAZING ANIMAL-TALKING KID!
NO. NO... THAT WON'T WORK.
THE SPECTACULAR ANIMAL WHISPERER!

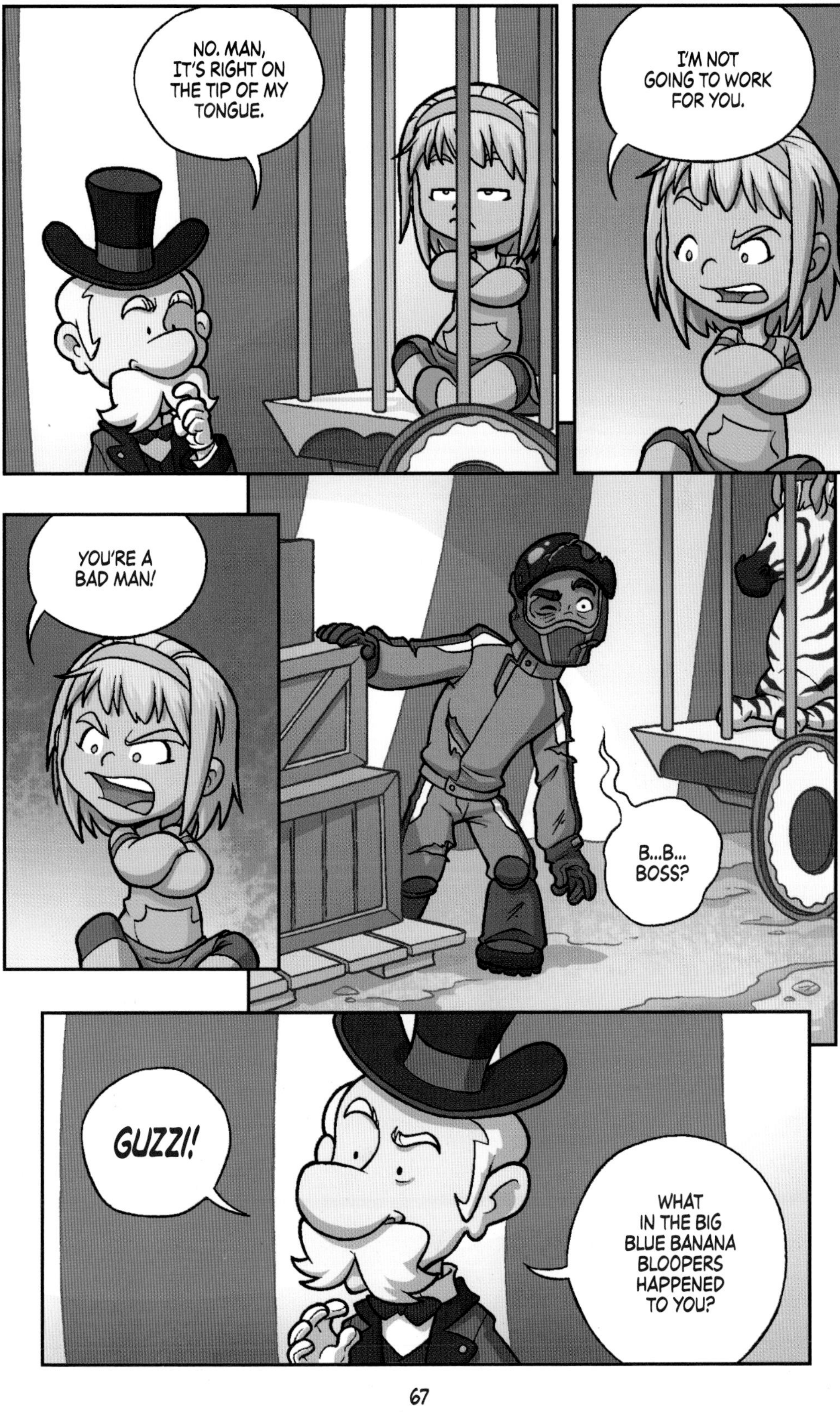
NO. MAN, IT'S RIGHT ON THE TIP OF MY TONGUE.
I'M NOT GOING TO WORK FOR YOU.
YOU'RE A BAD MAN!
B...B... BOSS?
GUZZI!
WHAT IN THE BIG BLUE BANANA BLOOPERS HAPPENED TO YOU?

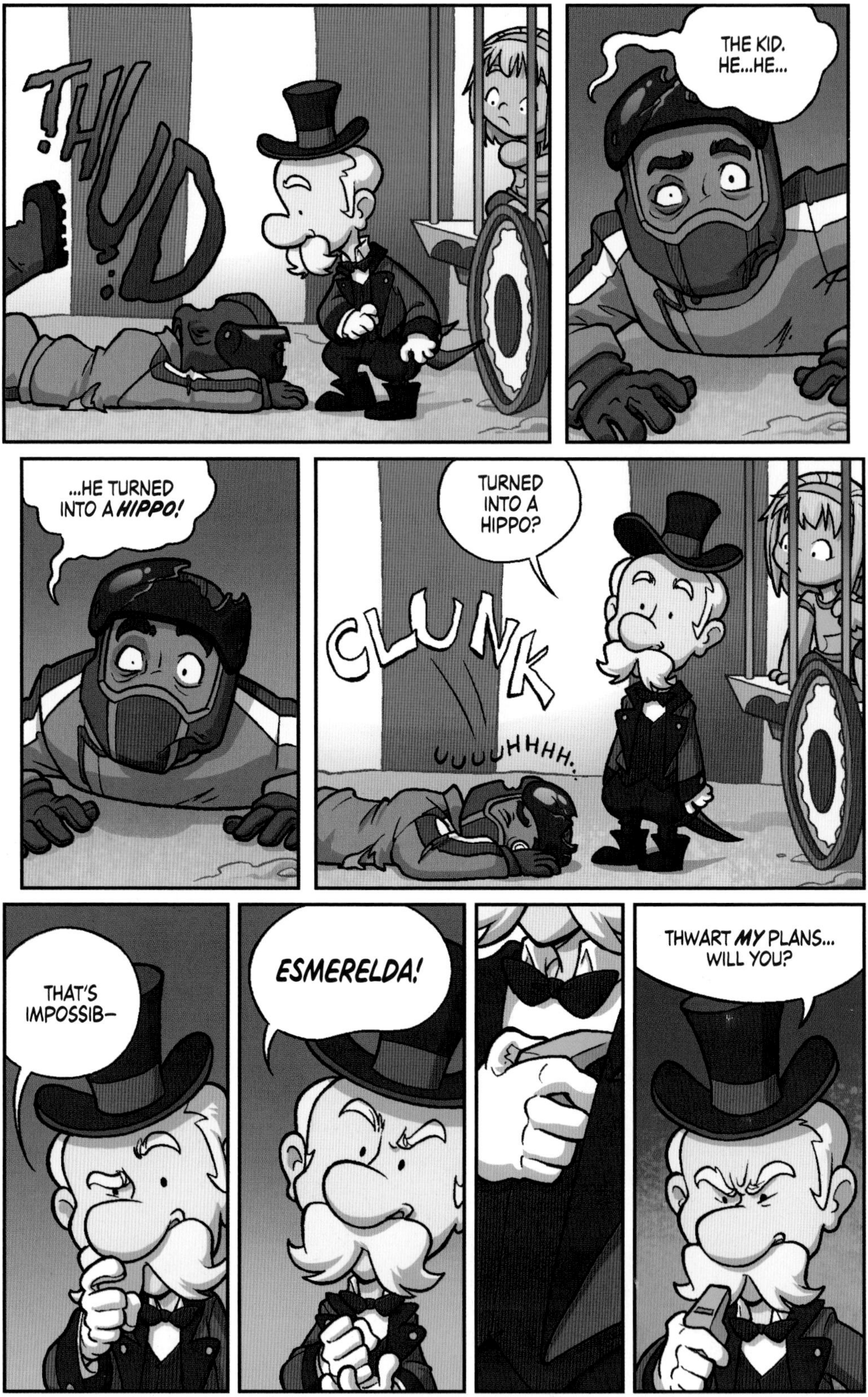
THUD
THE KID. HE...HE...
...HE TURNED INTO A HIPPO!
TURNED INTO A HIPPO?
CLUNK
UUUUHHHH...
THAT'S IMPOSSIB—
ESMERELDA!
THWART MY PLANS... WILL YOU?

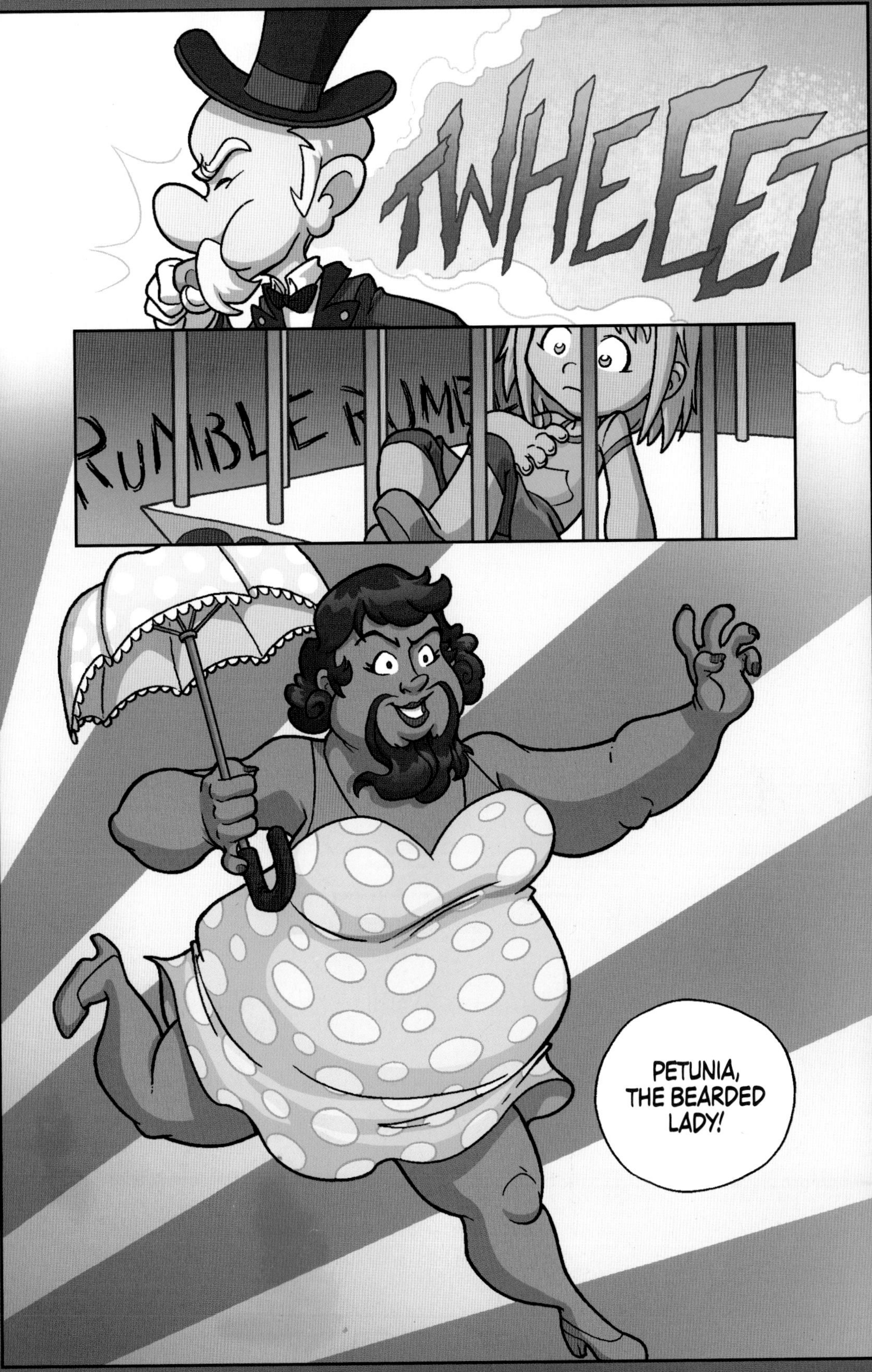
TWHEEET
RUMBLE RUMB
PETUNIA, THE BEARDED LADY!

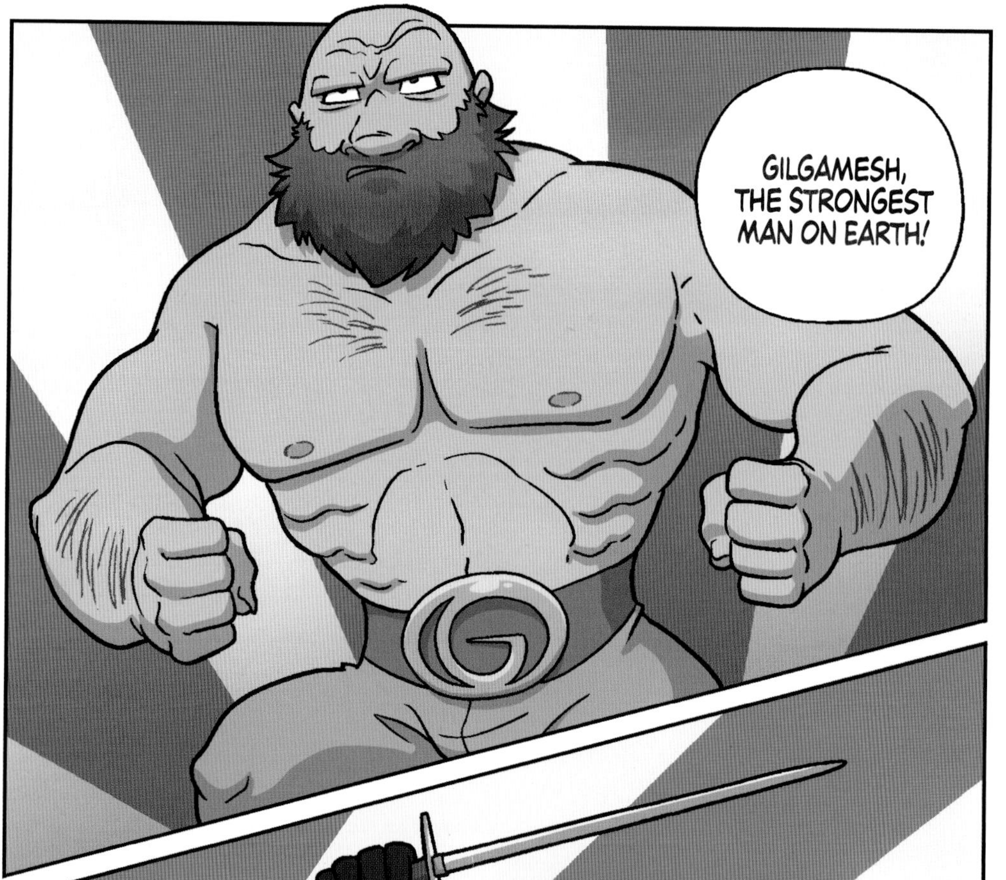
GILGAMESH, THE STRONGEST MAN ON EARTH!

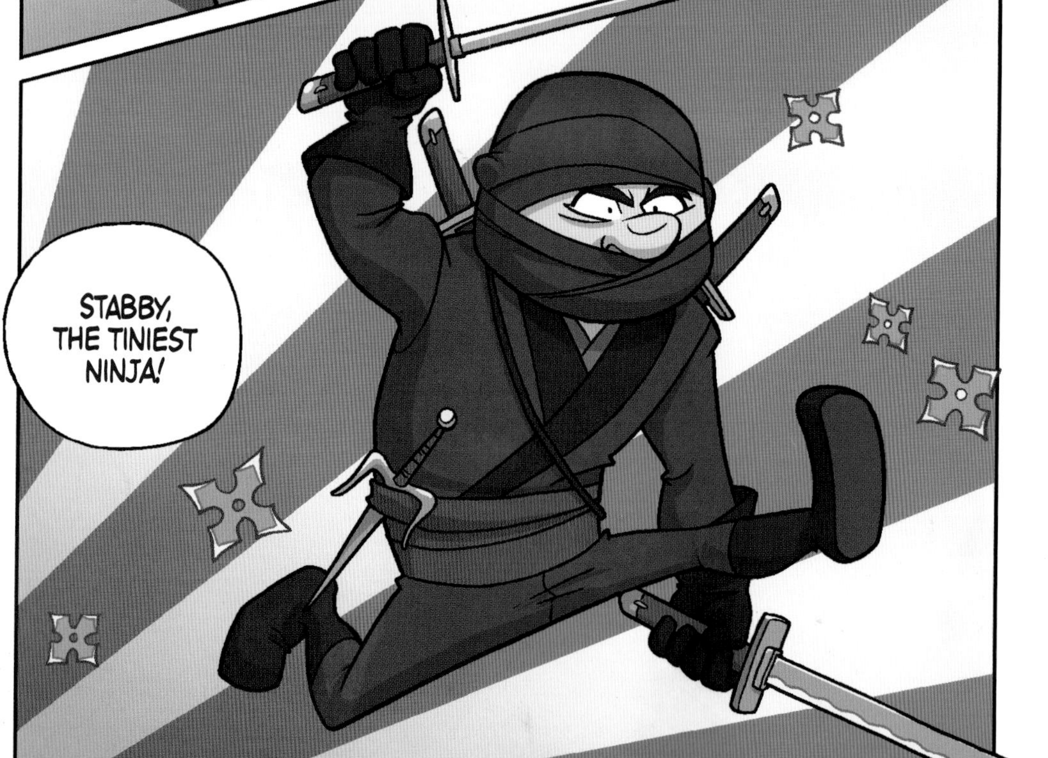
STABBY, THE TINIEST NINJA!

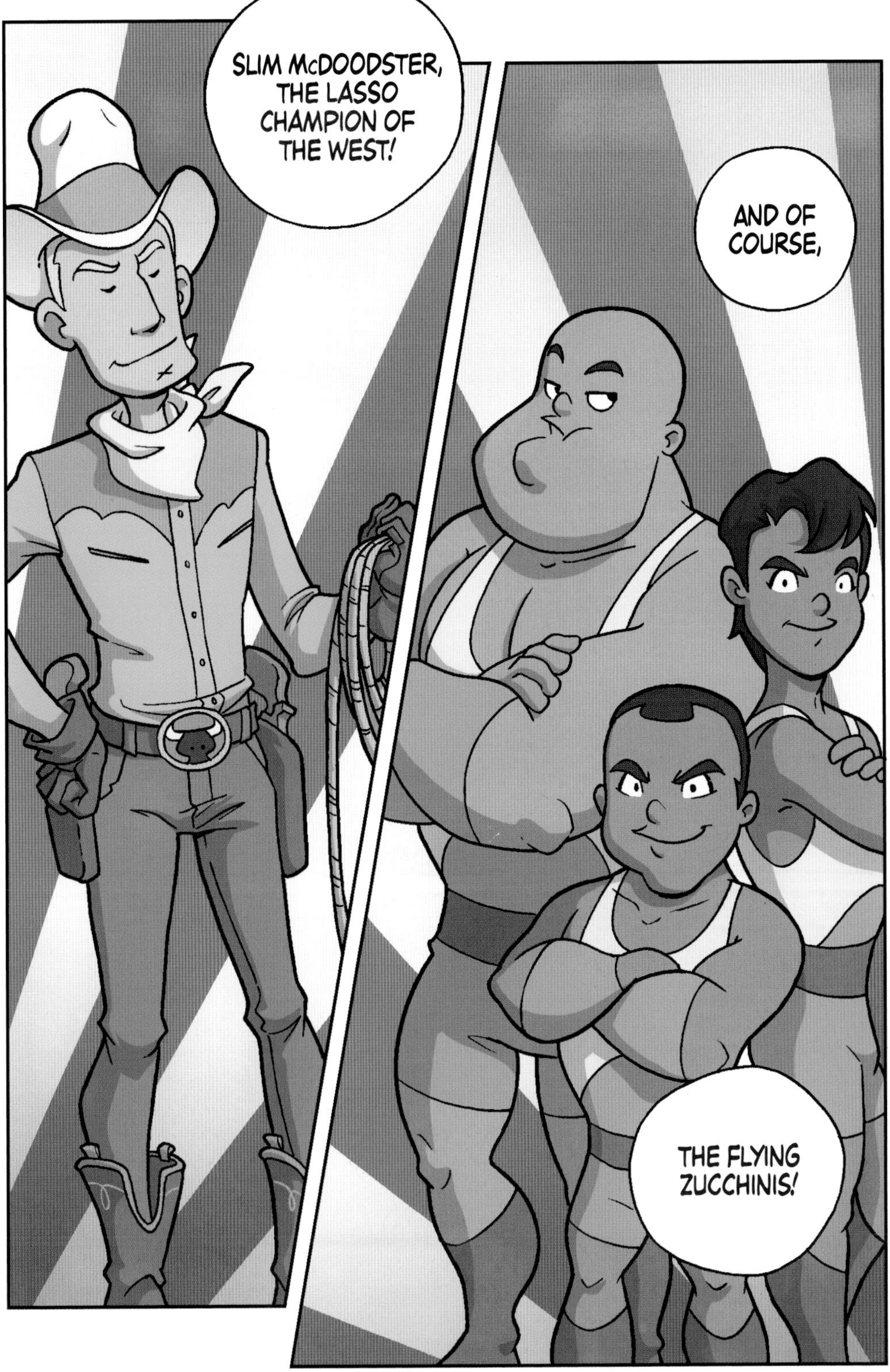
SLIM McDOODSTER, THE LASSO CHAMPION OF THE WEST!
AND OF COURSE,
THE FLYING ZUCCHINIS!

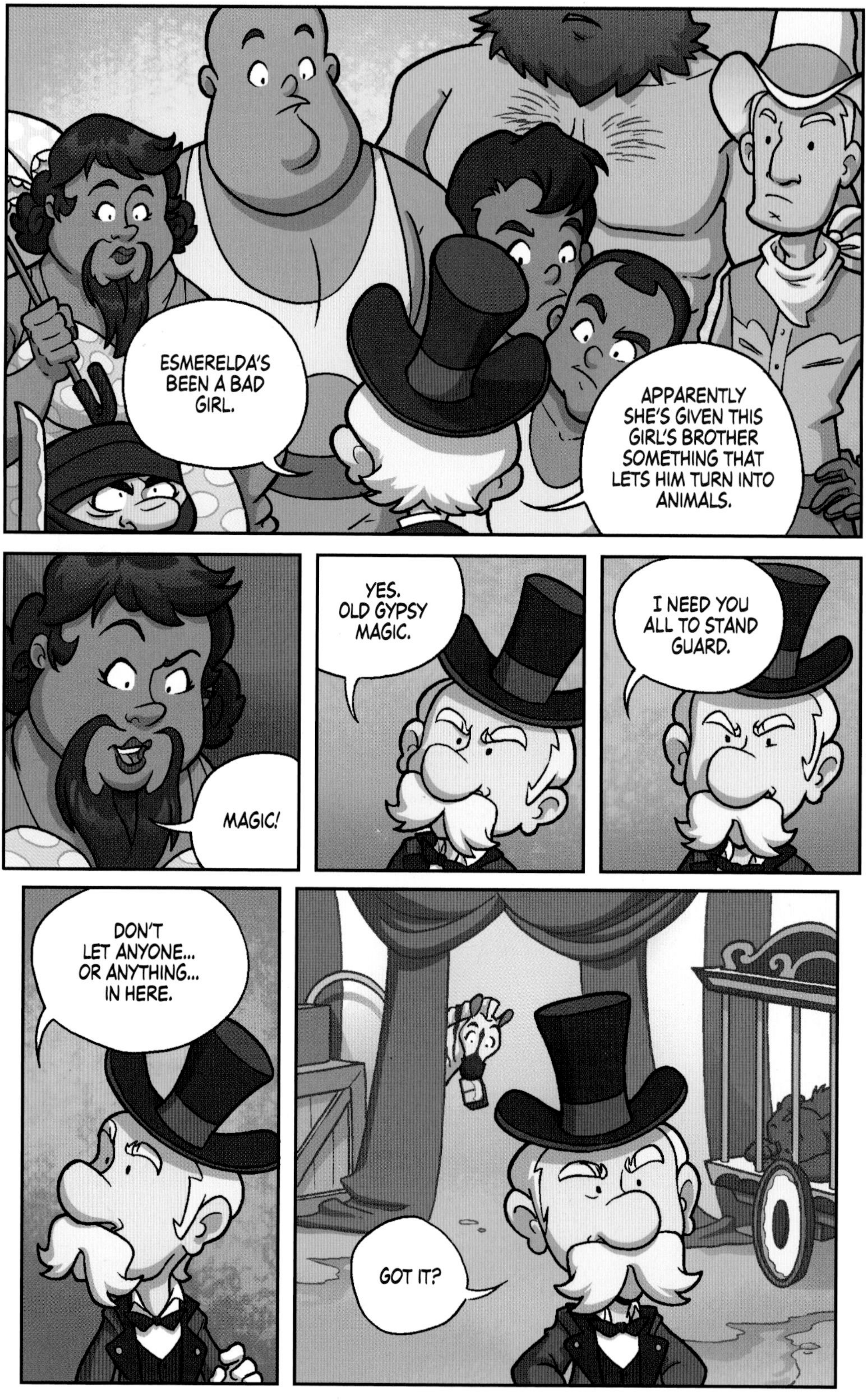

ESMERELDA'S BEEN A BAD GIRL.
APPARENTLY SHE'S GIVEN THIS GIRL'S BROTHER SOMETHING THAT LETS HIM TURN INTO ANIMALS.
MAGIC!
YES. OLD GYPSY MAGIC.
I NEED YOU ALL TO STAND GUARD.
DON'T LET ANYONE... OR ANYTHING... IN HERE.
GOT IT?

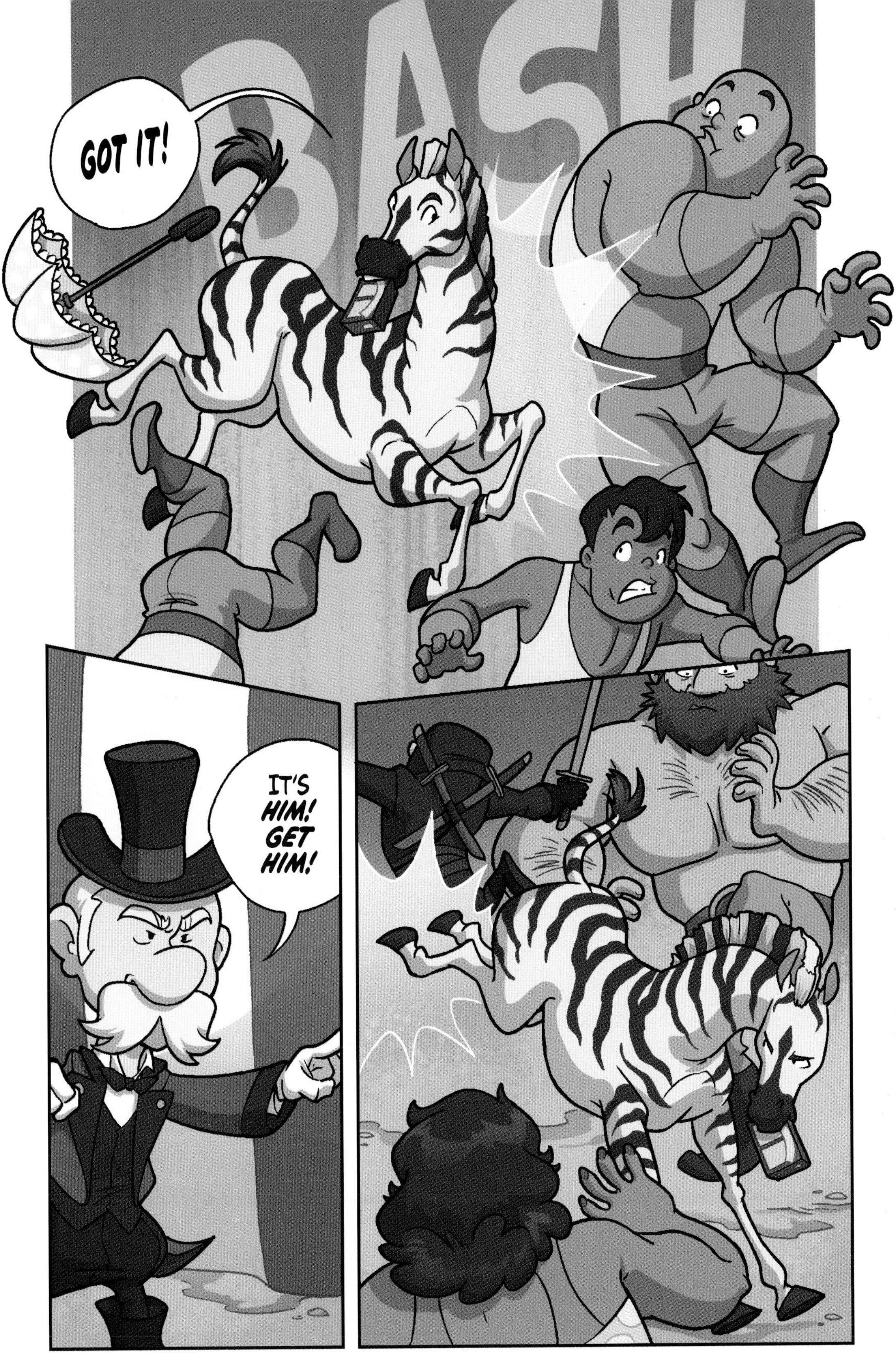
BASH
GOT IT!
IT'S HIM! GET HIM!

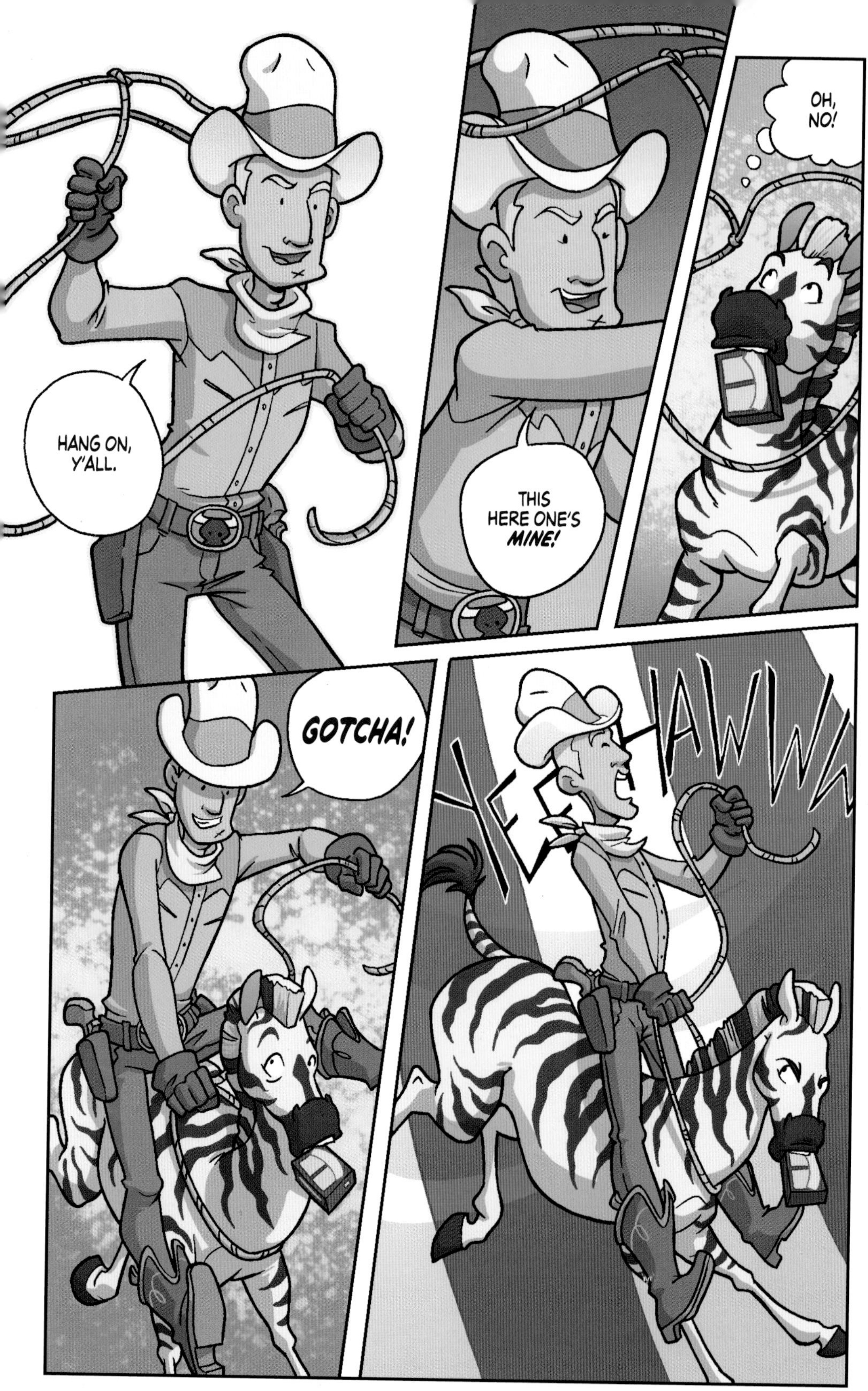
HANG ON, Y'ALL.
THIS HERE ONE'S *MINE!*
OH, NO!
GOTCHA!
YEE-HAWWW

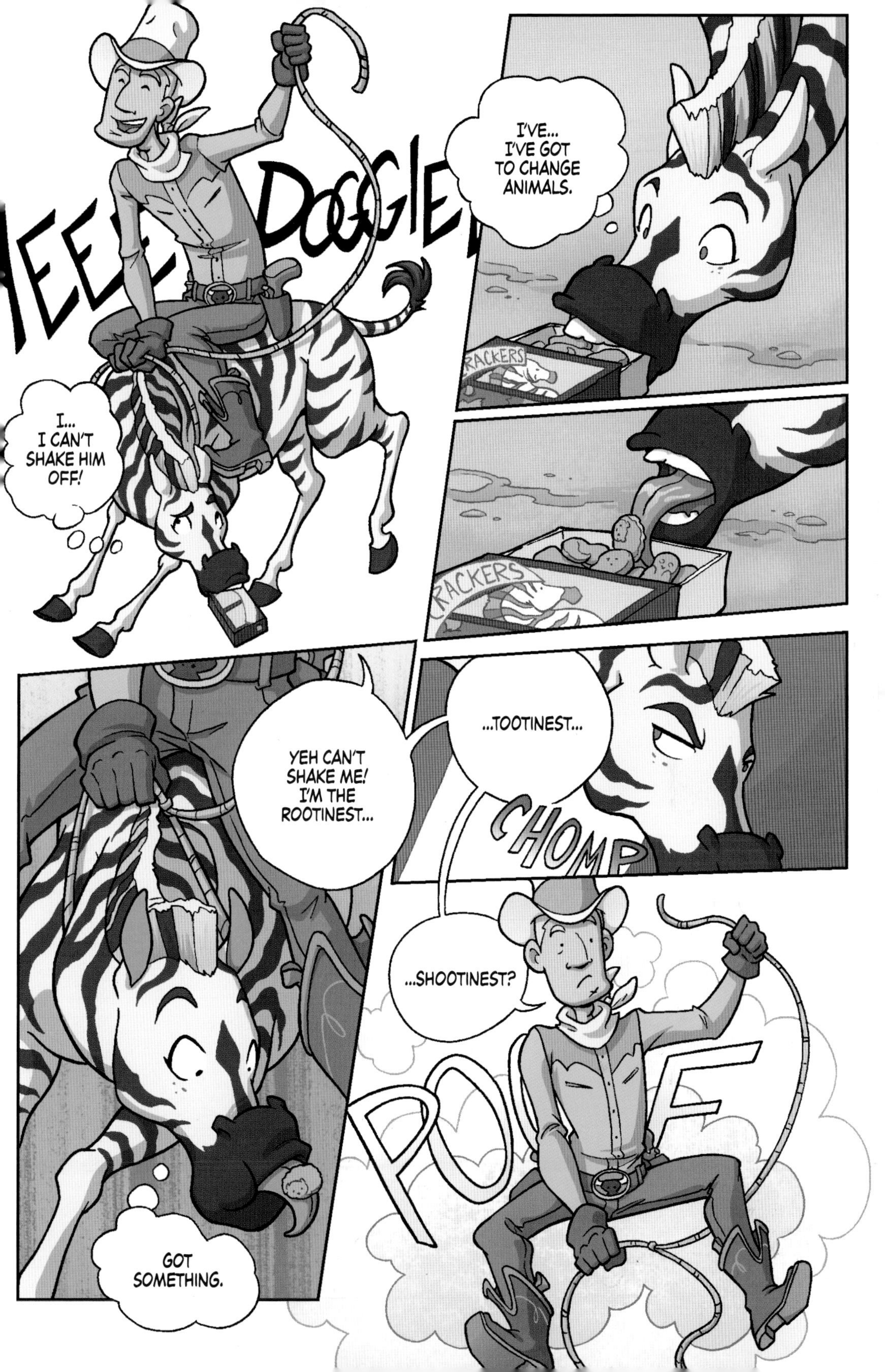
YEEEEE DOGGIE!
I... I CAN'T SHAKE HIM OFF!
I'VE... I'VE GOT TO CHANGE ANIMALS.
CRACKERS
CRACKERS
YEH CAN'T SHAKE ME! I'M THE ROOTINEST...
GOT SOMETHING.
...TOOTINEST...
CHOMP
...SHOOTINEST?
POOF

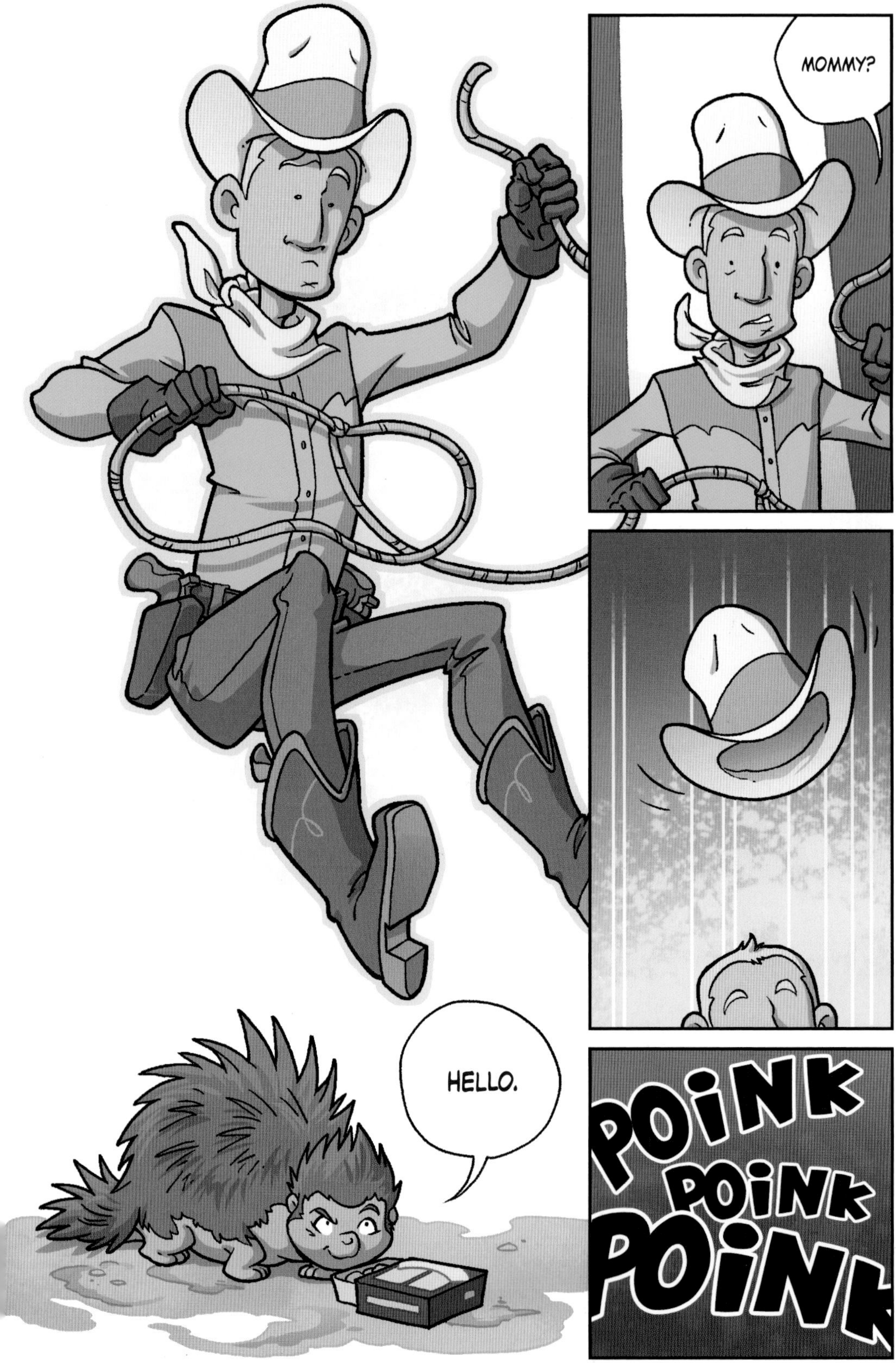
MOMMY?
HELLO.
POINK
POINK
POINK

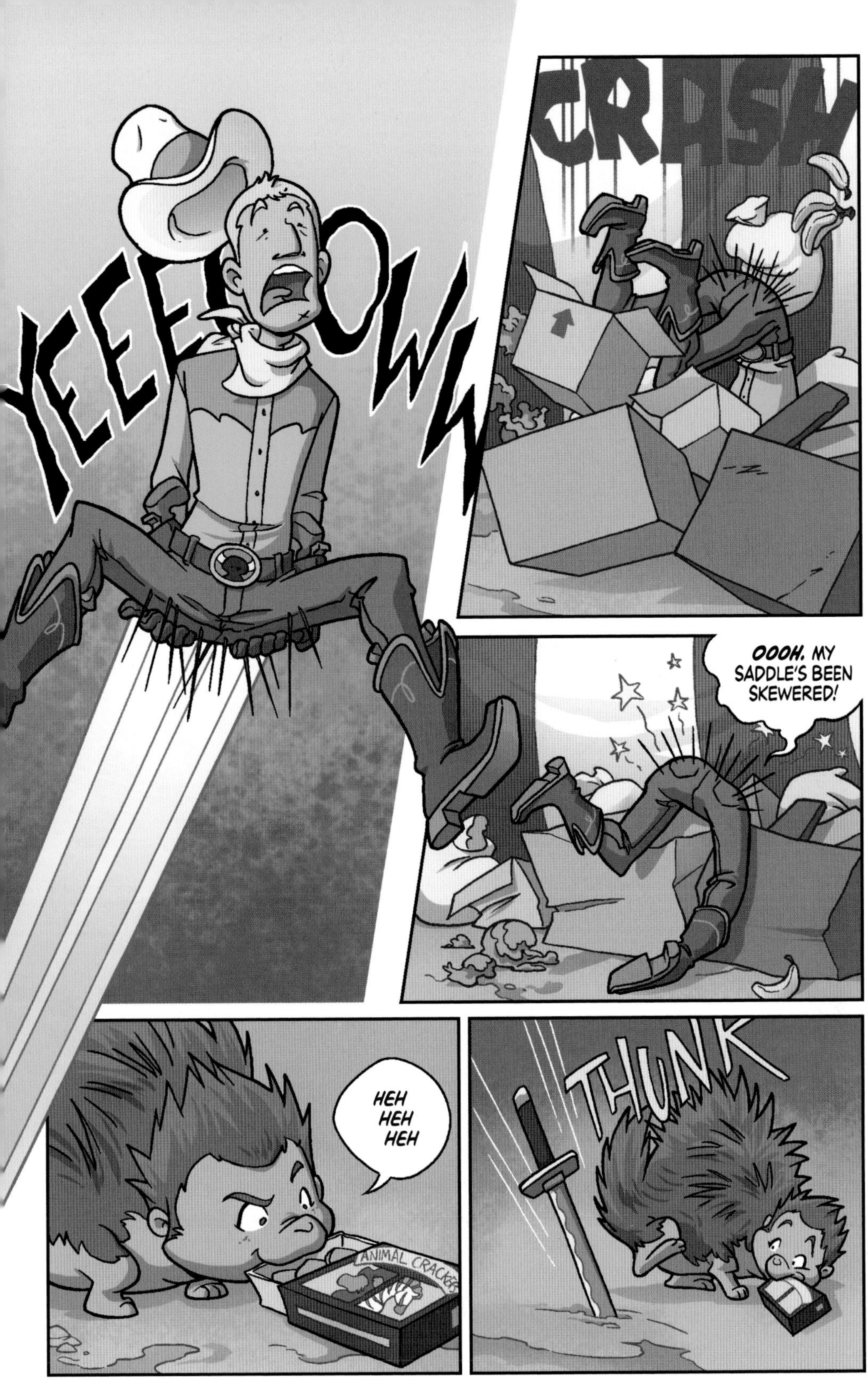
YEEEOWWW
CRASH
OOOH. MY SADDLE'S BEEN SKEWERED!
HEH HEH HEH
ANIMAL CRACKERS
THUNK

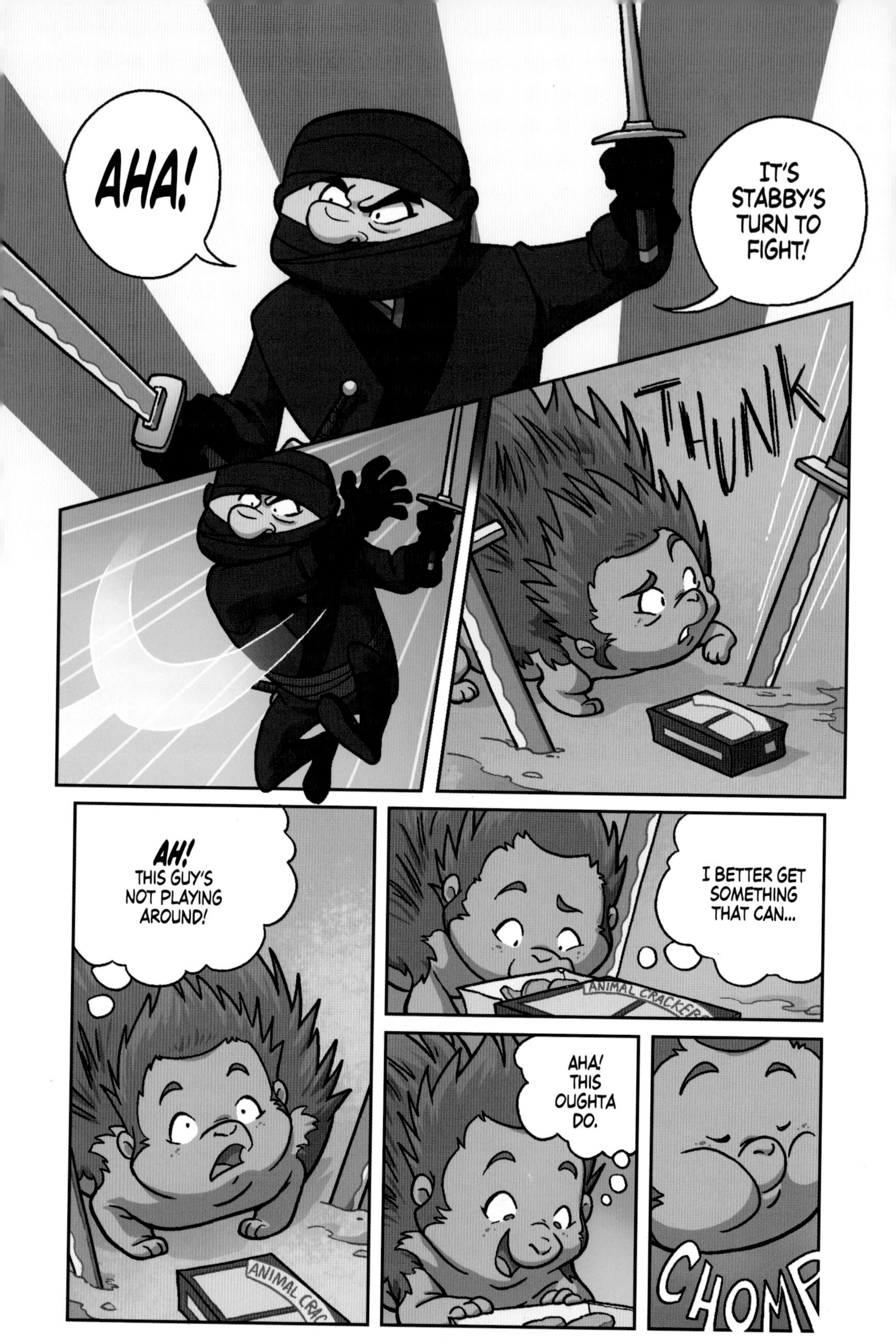
AHA!
IT'S STABBY'S TURN TO FIGHT!
THUNK
AH! THIS GUY'S NOT PLAYING AROUND!
I BETTER GET SOMETHING THAT CAN...
ANIMAL CRACKERS
ANIMAL CRAC
AHA! THIS OUGHTA DO.
CHOMP

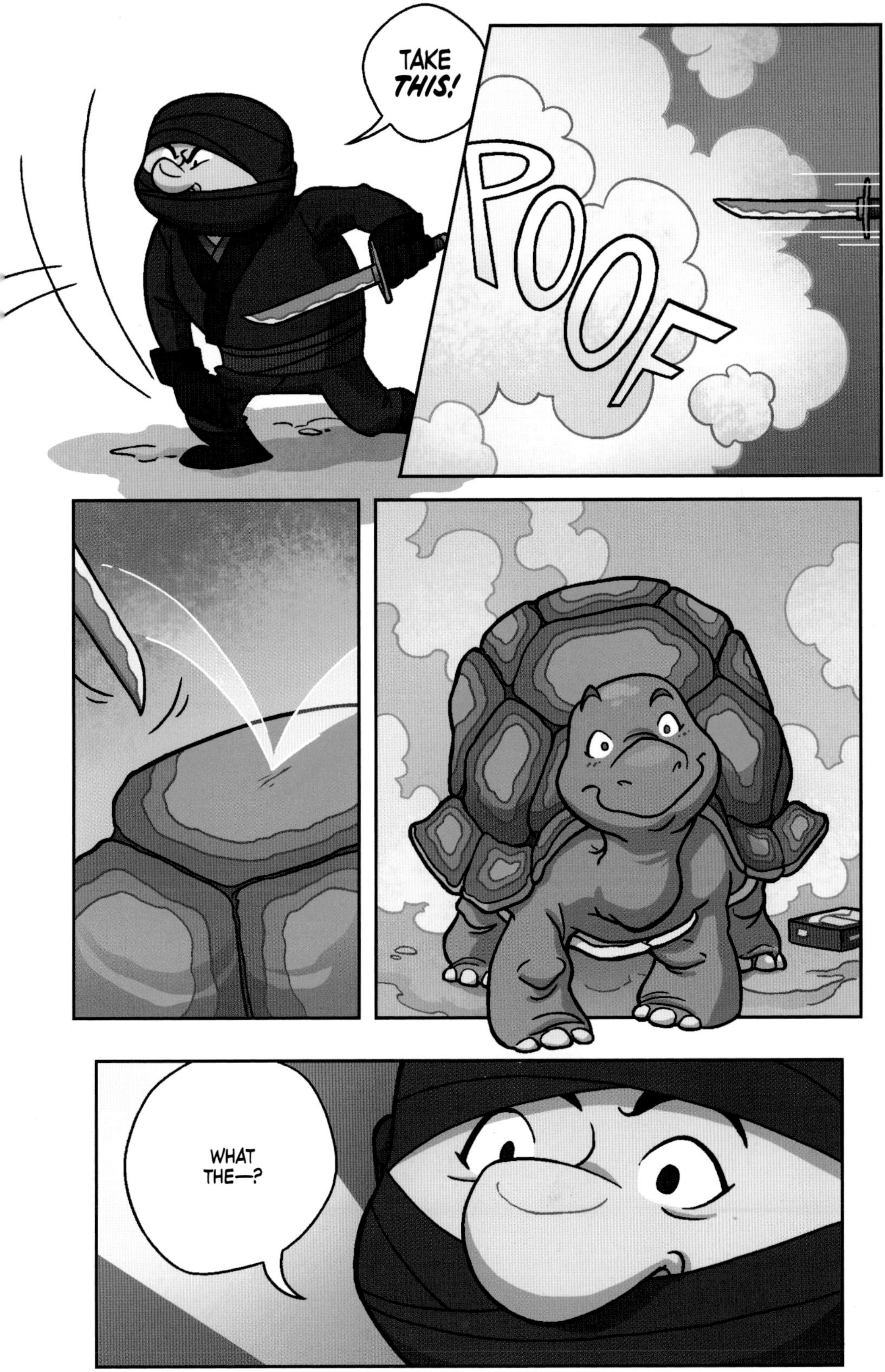
TAKE THIS!
POOF
WHAT THE—?

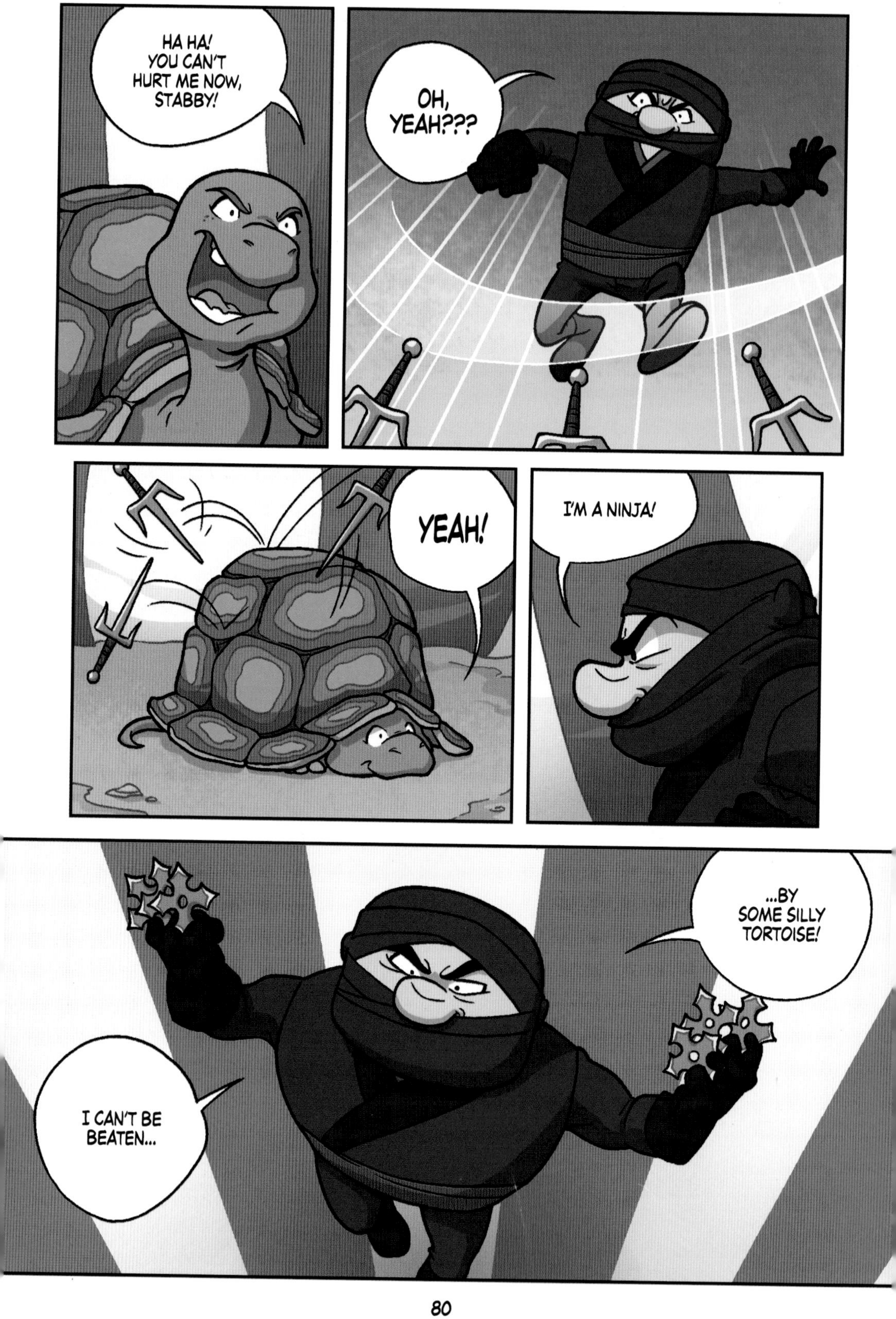
HA HA! YOU CAN'T HURT ME NOW, STABBY!
OH, YEAH???
YEAH!
I'M A NINJA!
I CAN'T BE BEATEN...
...BY SOME SILLY TORTOISE!

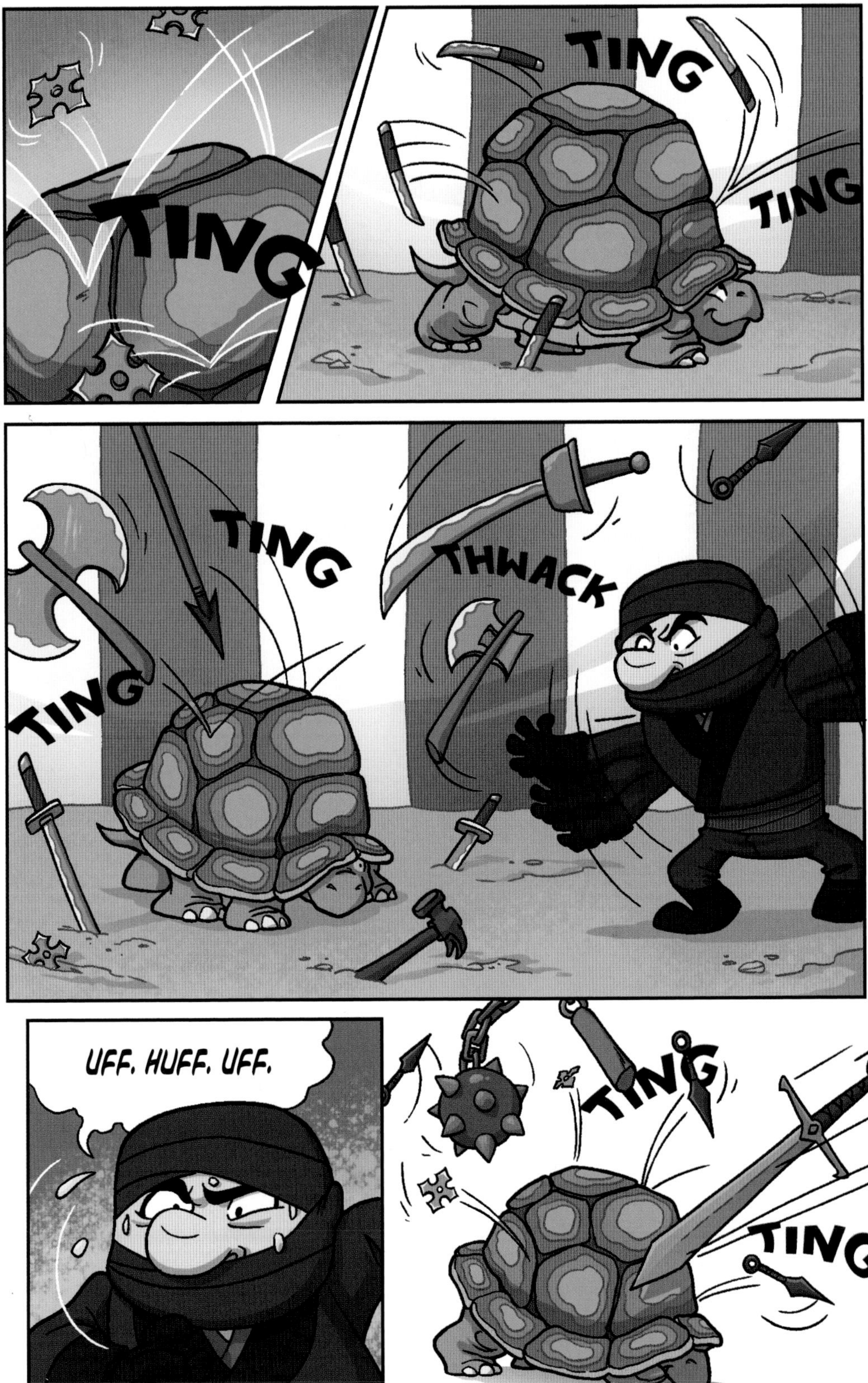
TING
TING
TING
TING
TING
THWACK
TING
UFF. HUFF. UFF.
TING
TING

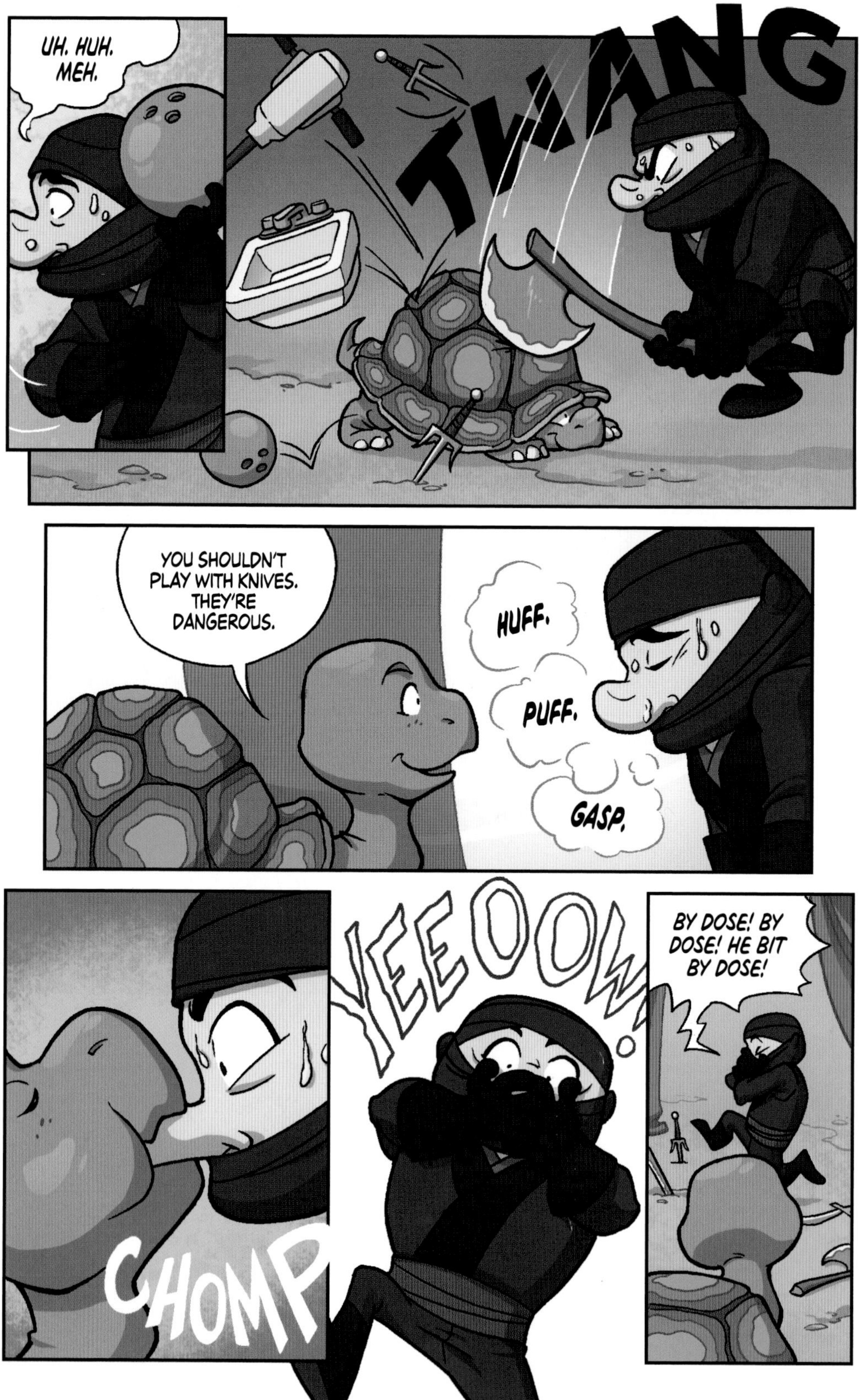
UH. HUH. MEH.
TWANG
YOU SHOULDN'T PLAY WITH KNIVES. THEY'RE DANGEROUS.
HUFF.
PUFF.
GASP.
CHOMP
YEEOOW!
BY DOSE! BY DOSE! HE BIT BY DOSE!

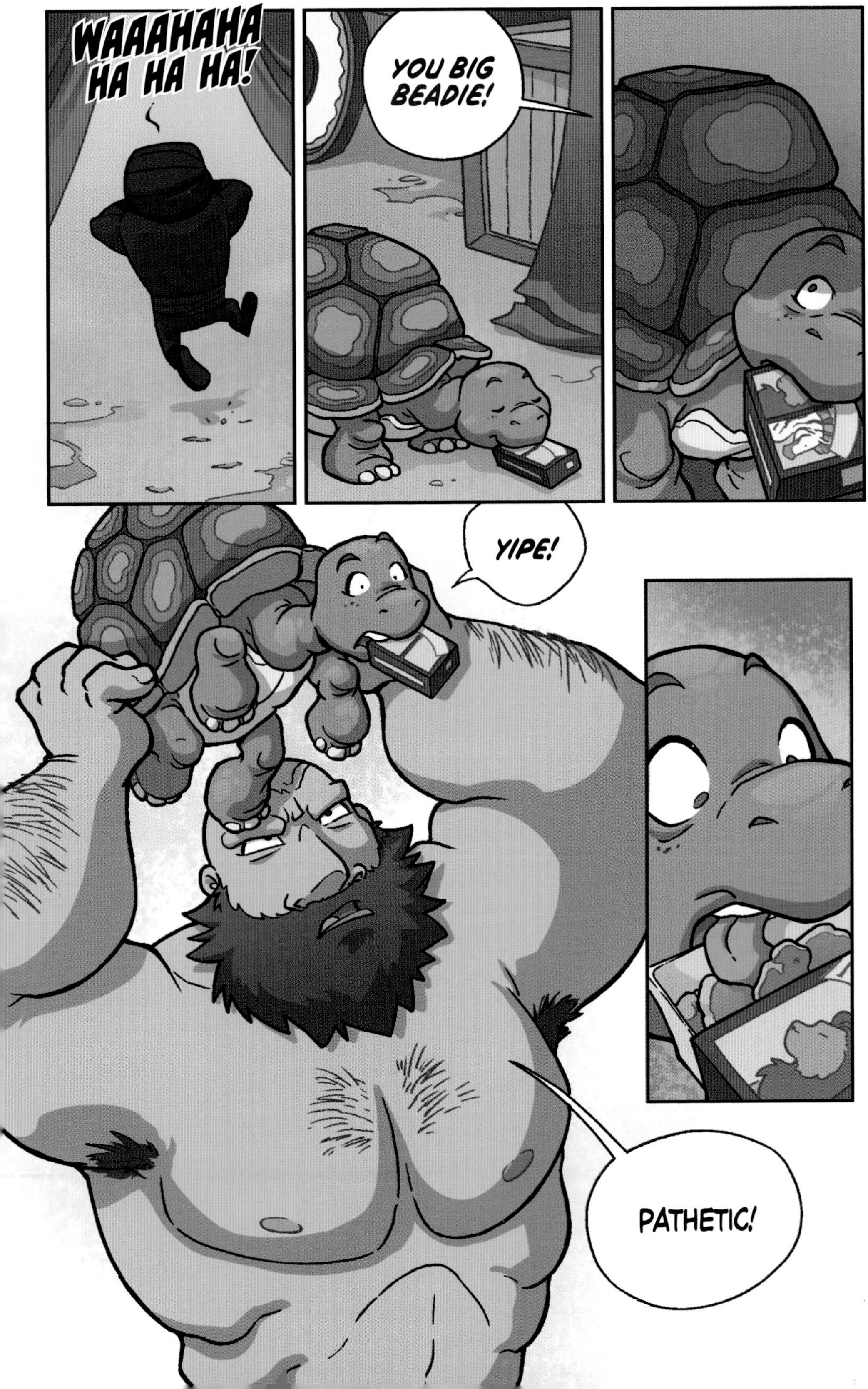
WAAAHAHA HA HA HA!
YOU BIG BEADIE!
YIPE!
PATHETIC!

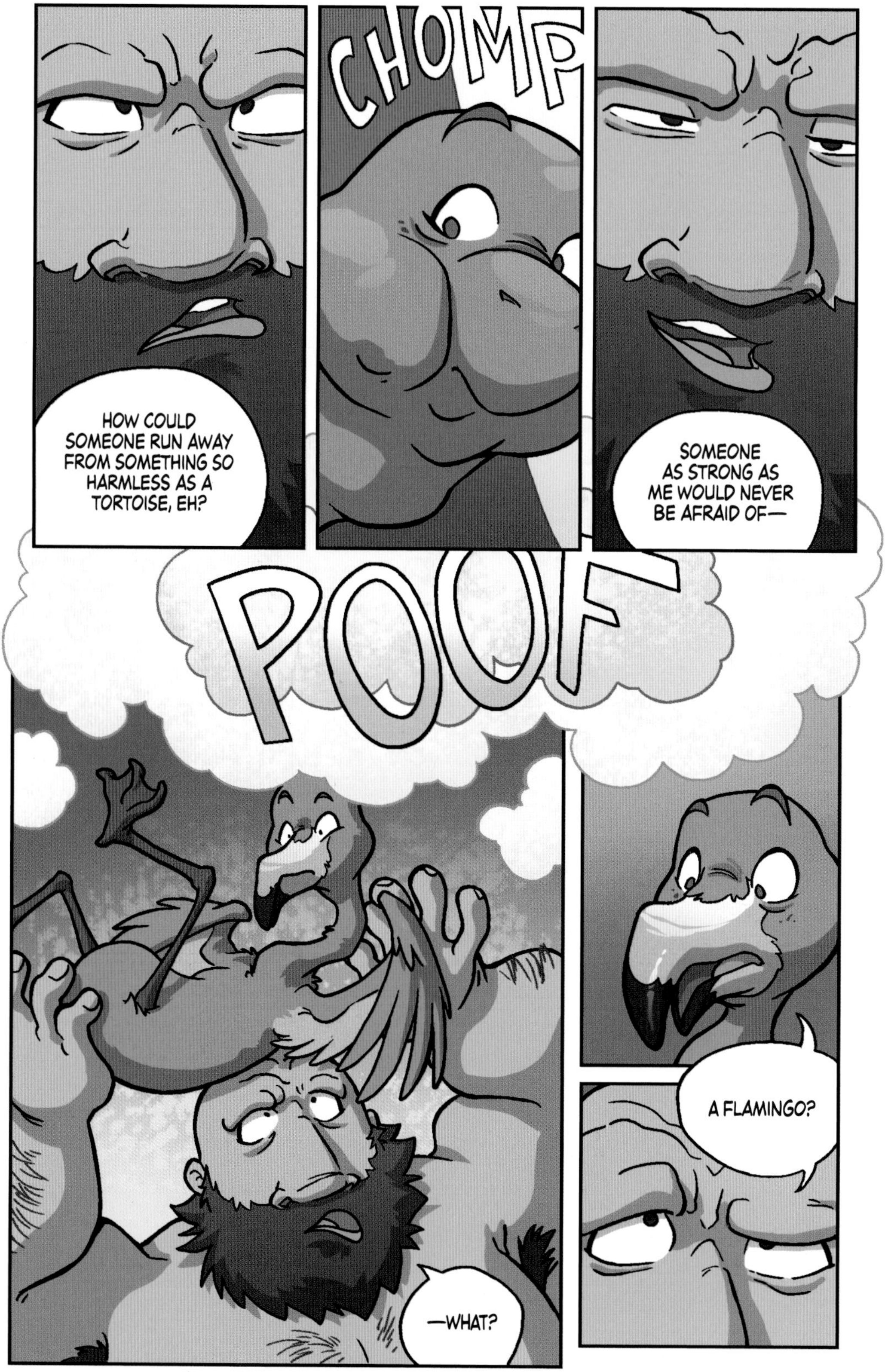
HOW COULD SOMEONE RUN AWAY FROM SOMETHING SO HARMLESS AS A TORTOISE, EH?
CHOMP
SOMEONE AS STRONG AS ME WOULD NEVER BE AFRAID OF—
POOF
—WHAT?
A FLAMINGO?

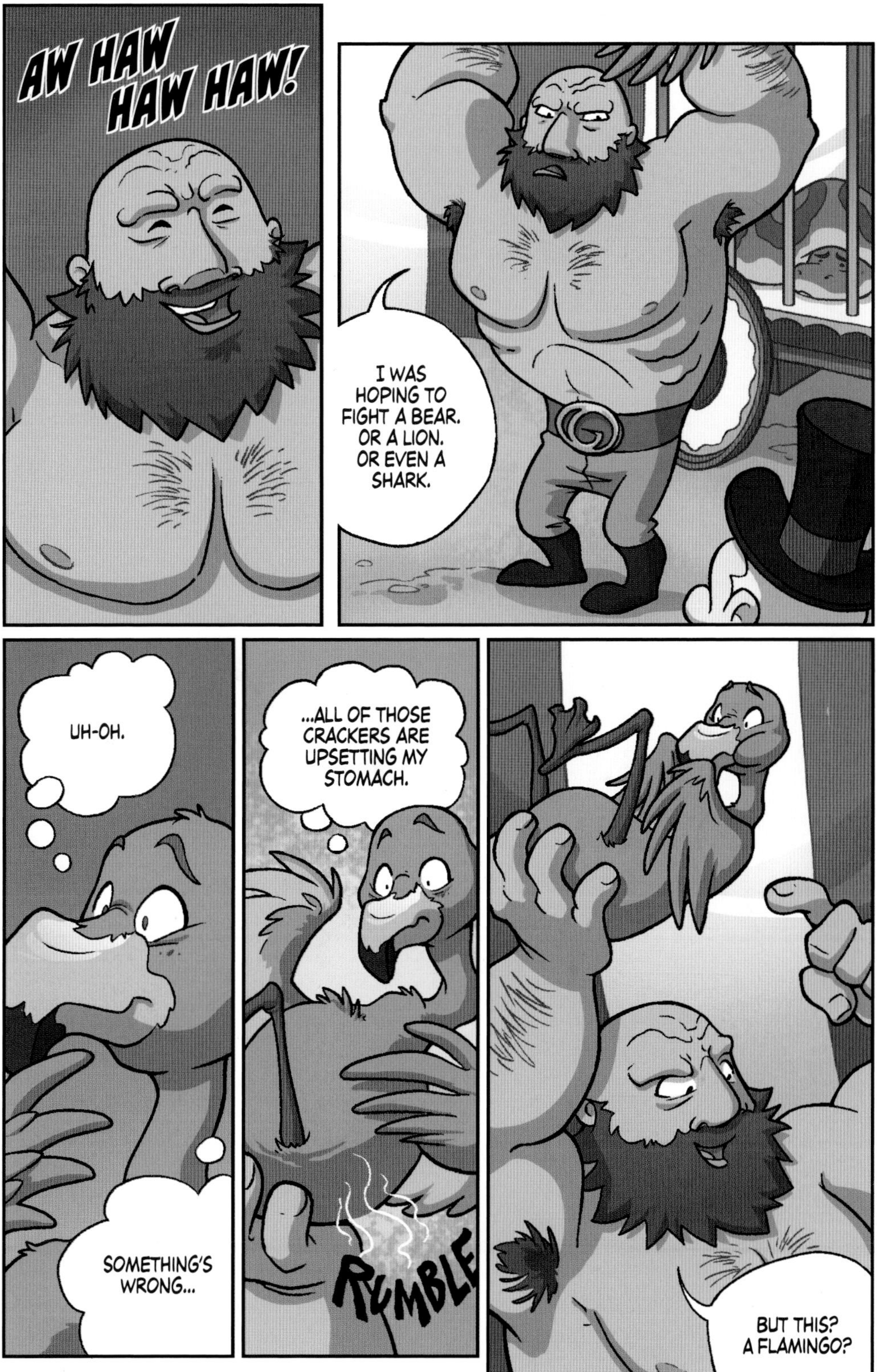
AW HAW HAW HAW!
I WAS HOPING TO FIGHT A BEAR. OR A LION. OR EVEN A SHARK.
UH-OH.
SOMETHING'S WRONG...
...ALL OF THOSE CRACKERS ARE UPSETTING MY STOMACH.
RUMBLE
BUT THIS? A FLAMINGO?

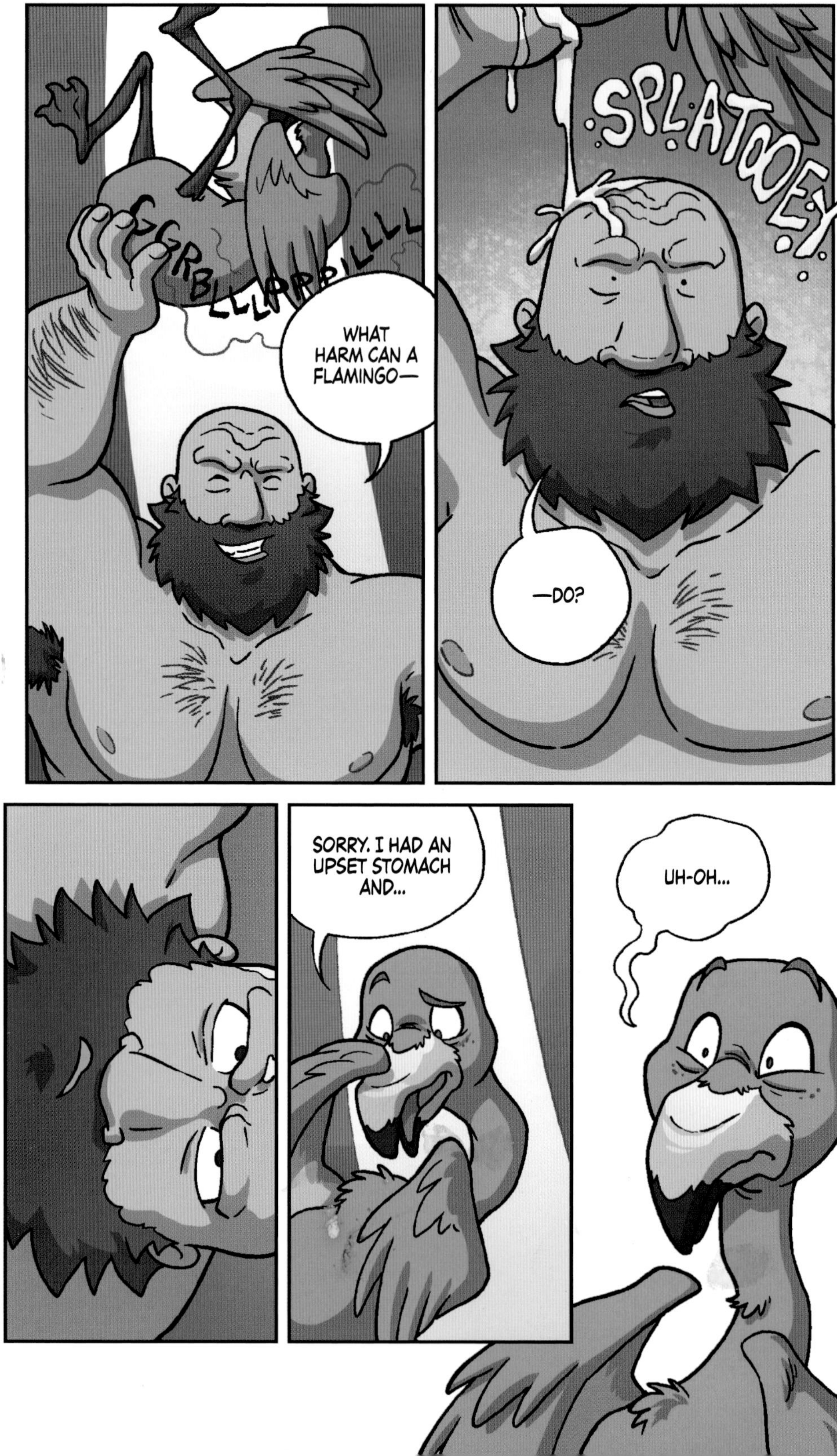
GGRBLLLLPPPILLLLL
WHAT HARM CAN A FLAMINGO—
SPLATOOEY
—DO?
SORRY. I HAD AN UPSET STOMACH AND...
UH-OH...

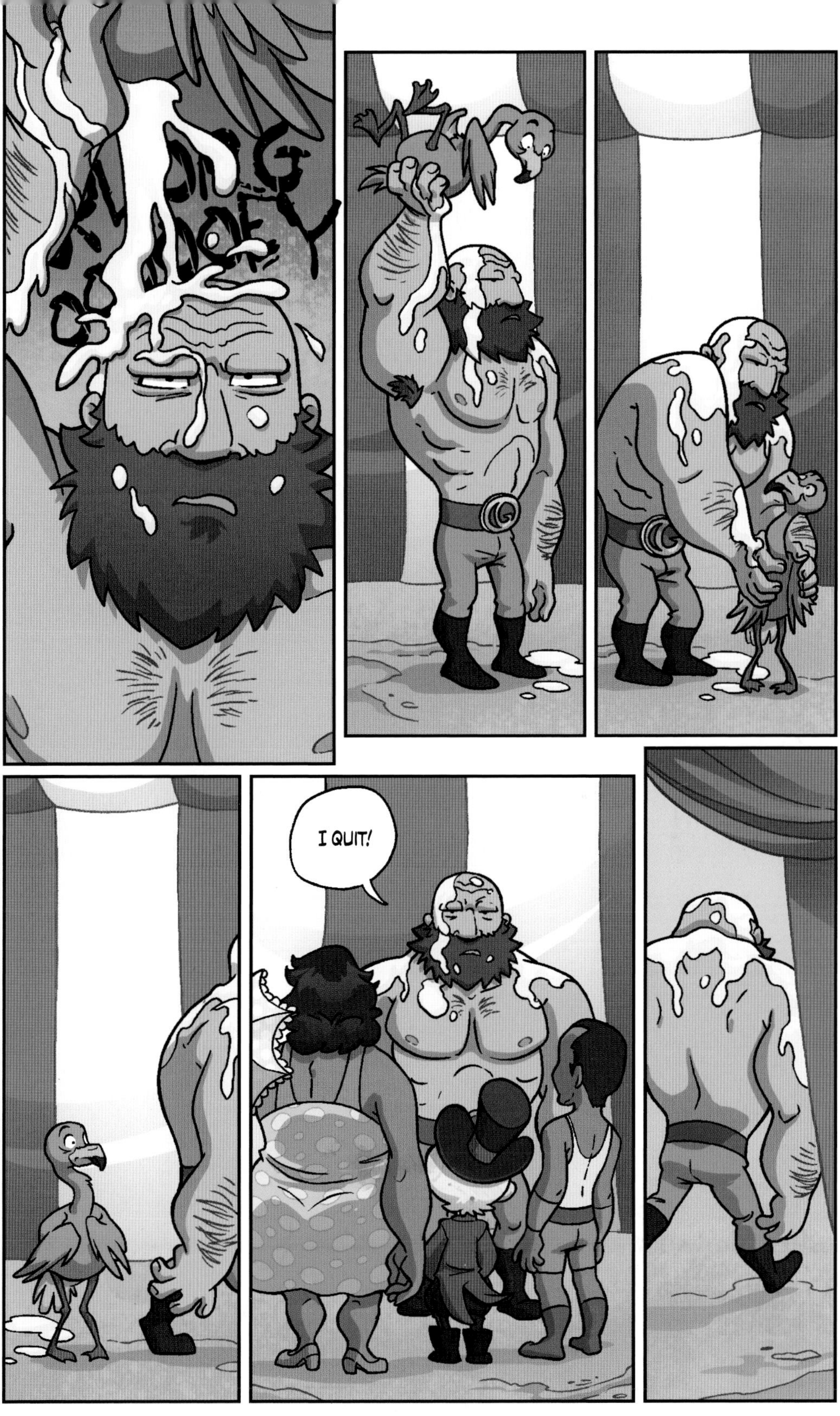
I QUIT!

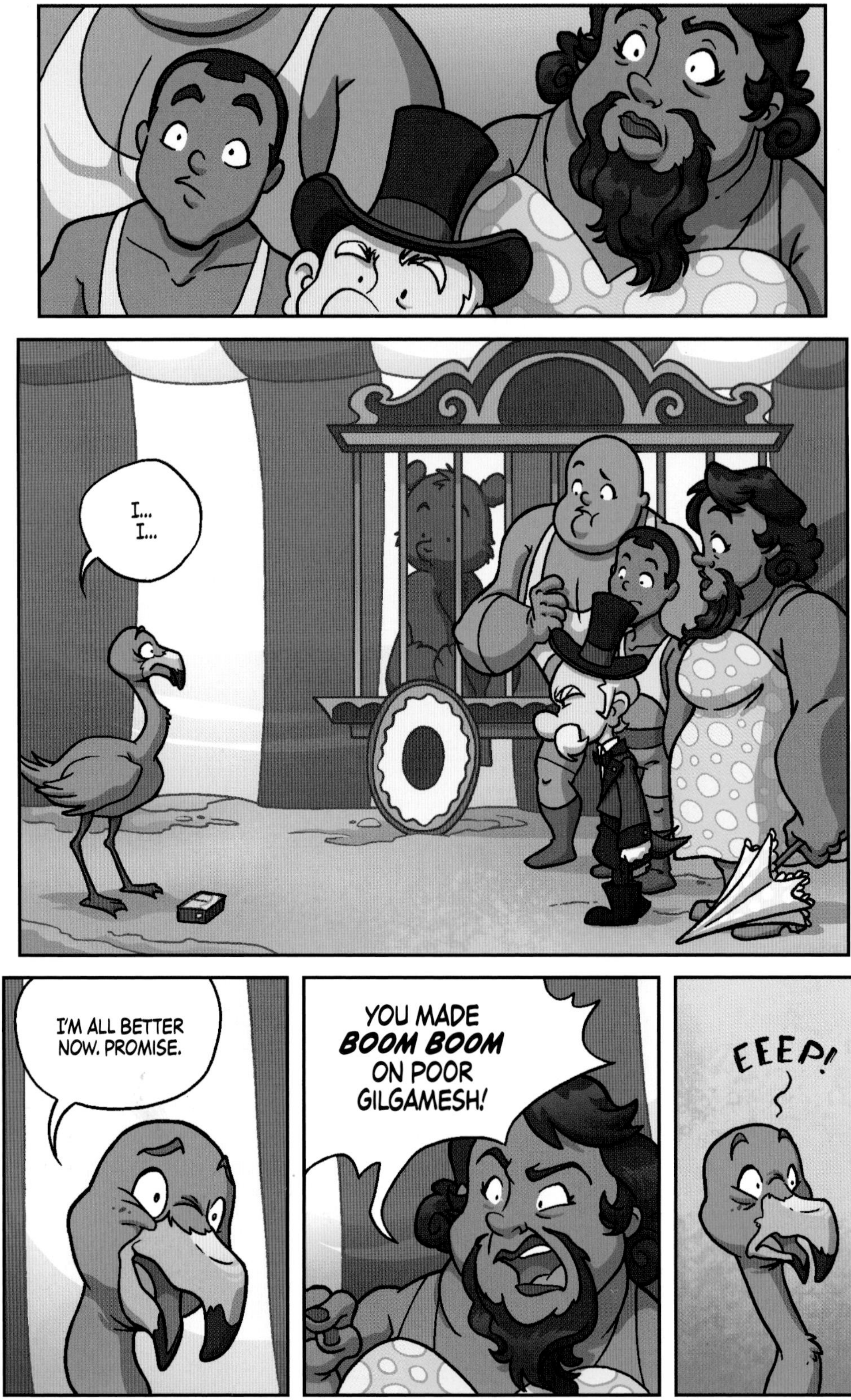
I...
I...
I'M ALL BETTER NOW. PROMISE.
YOU MADE BOOM BOOM ON POOR GILGAMESH!
EEEP!

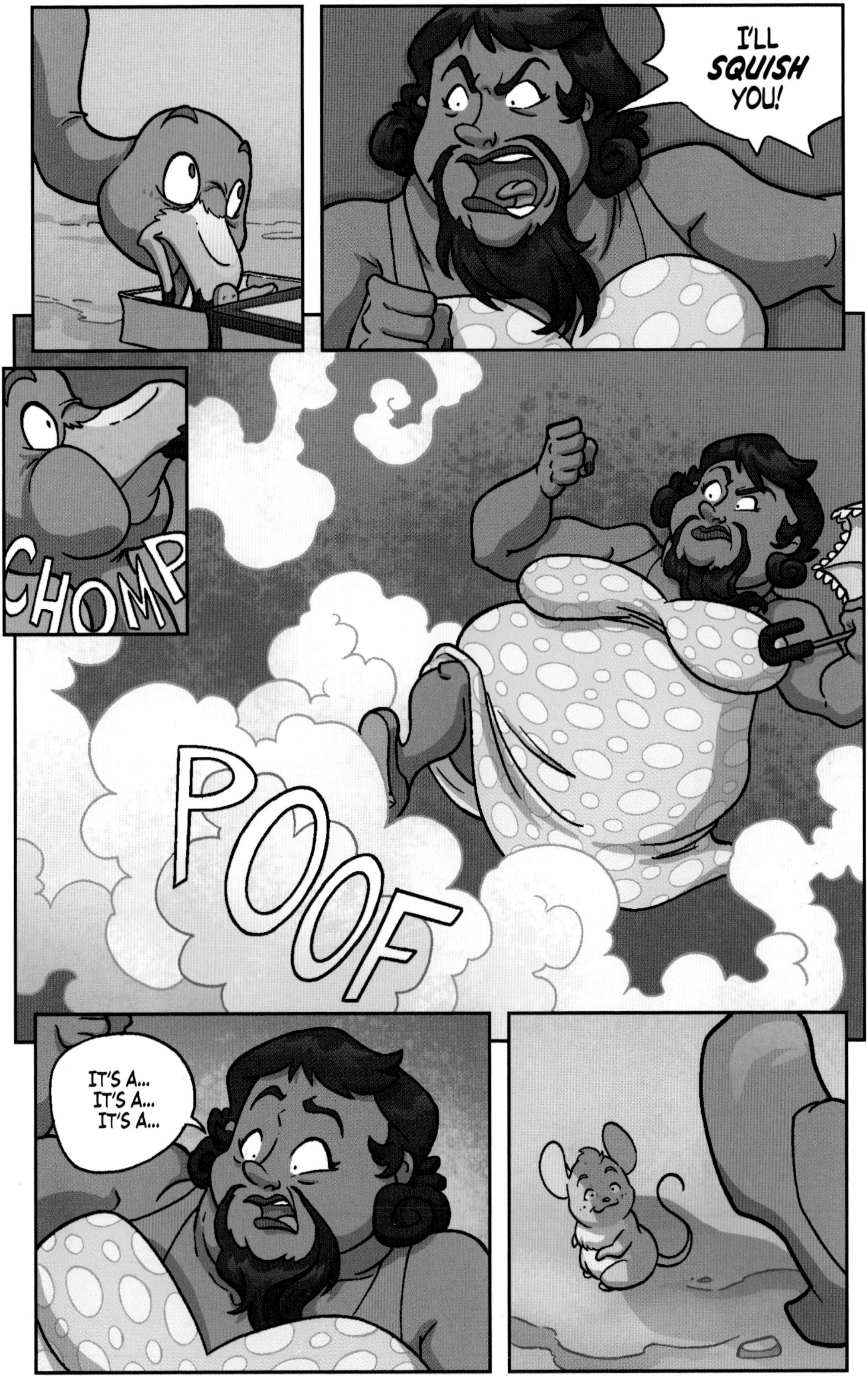
I'LL SQUISH YOU!
CHOMP
POOF
IT'S A... IT'S A... IT'S A...

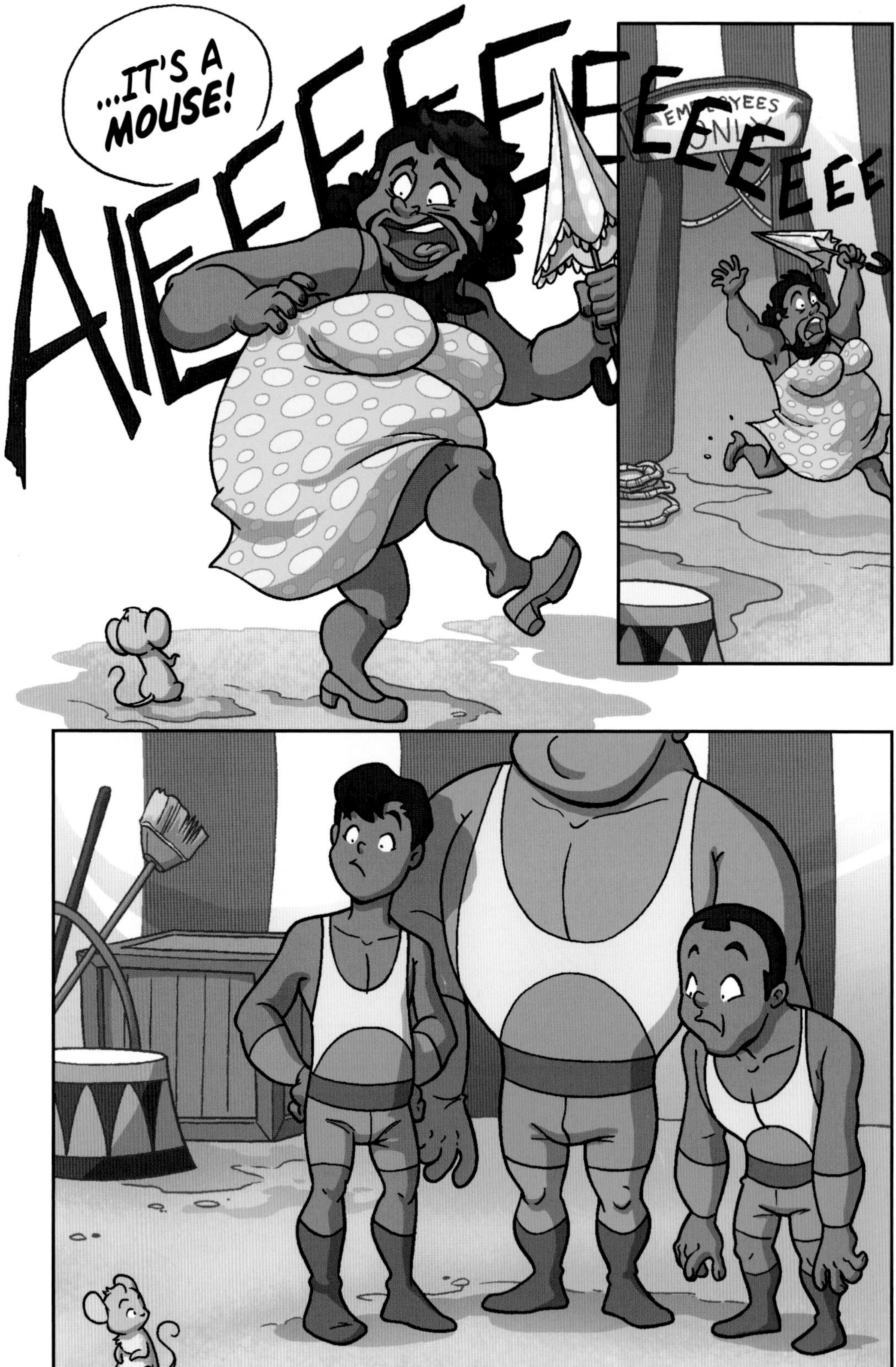
...IT'S A MOUSE!
AIEEEEEEEEEEEEEEEE

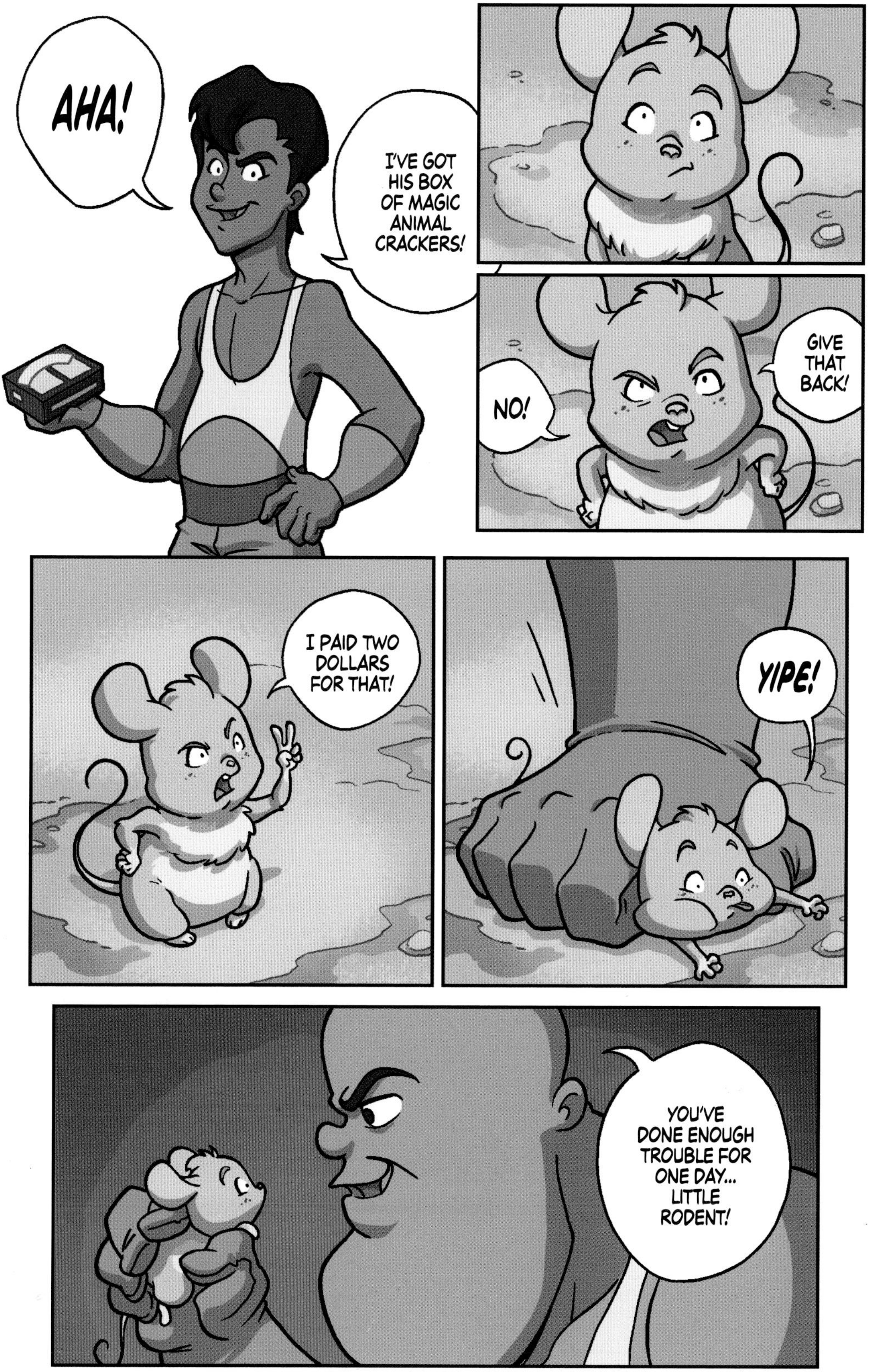
AHA!
I'VE GOT HIS BOX OF MAGIC ANIMAL CRACKERS!
GIVE THAT BACK!
NO!
I PAID TWO DOLLARS FOR THAT!
YIPE!
YOU'VE DONE ENOUGH TROUBLE FOR ONE DAY... LITTLE RODENT!

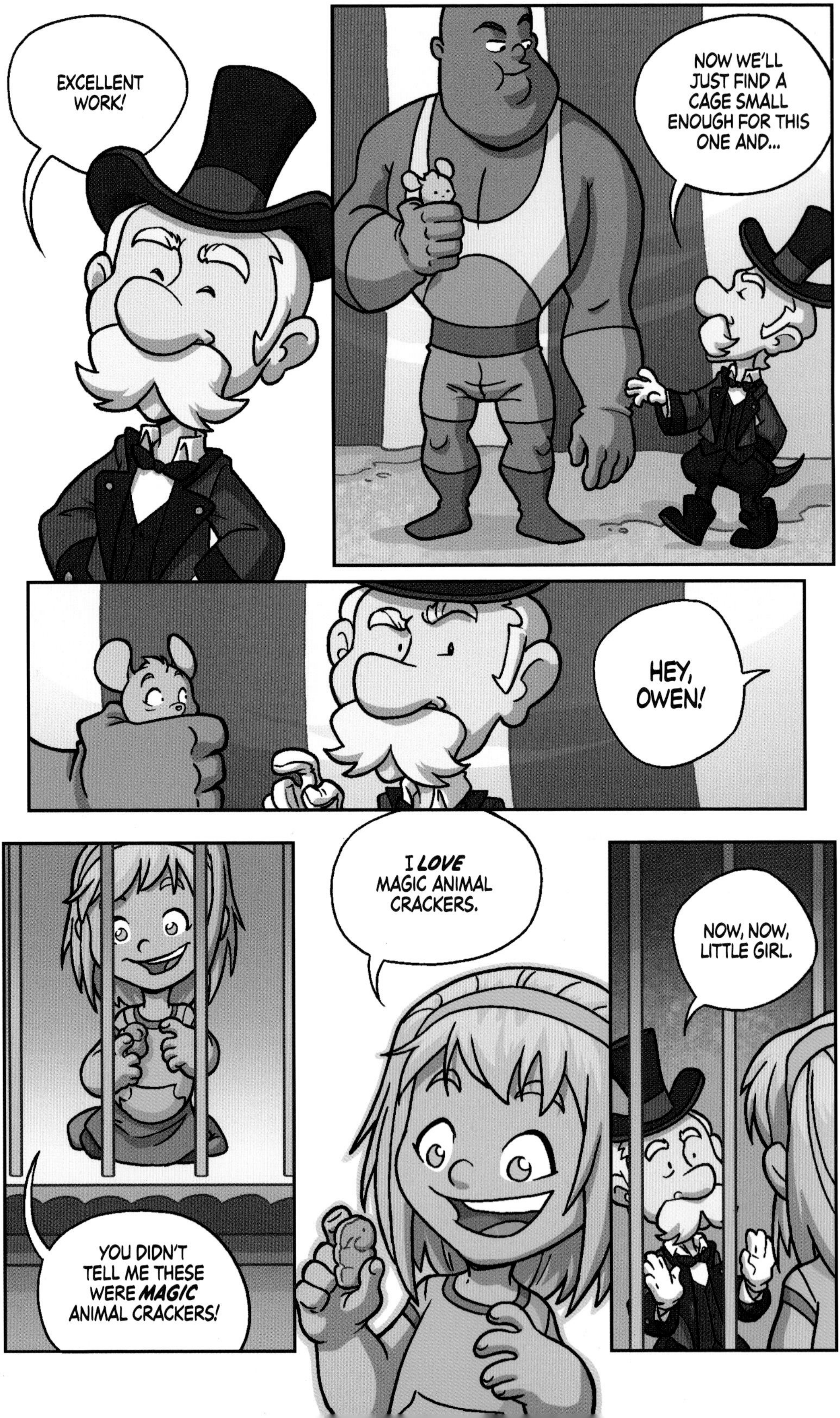
EXCELLENT WORK!
NOW WE'LL JUST FIND A CAGE SMALL ENOUGH FOR THIS ONE AND...
HEY, OWEN!
YOU DIDN'T TELL ME THESE WERE MAGIC ANIMAL CRACKERS!
I LOVE MAGIC ANIMAL CRACKERS.
NOW, NOW, LITTLE GIRL.

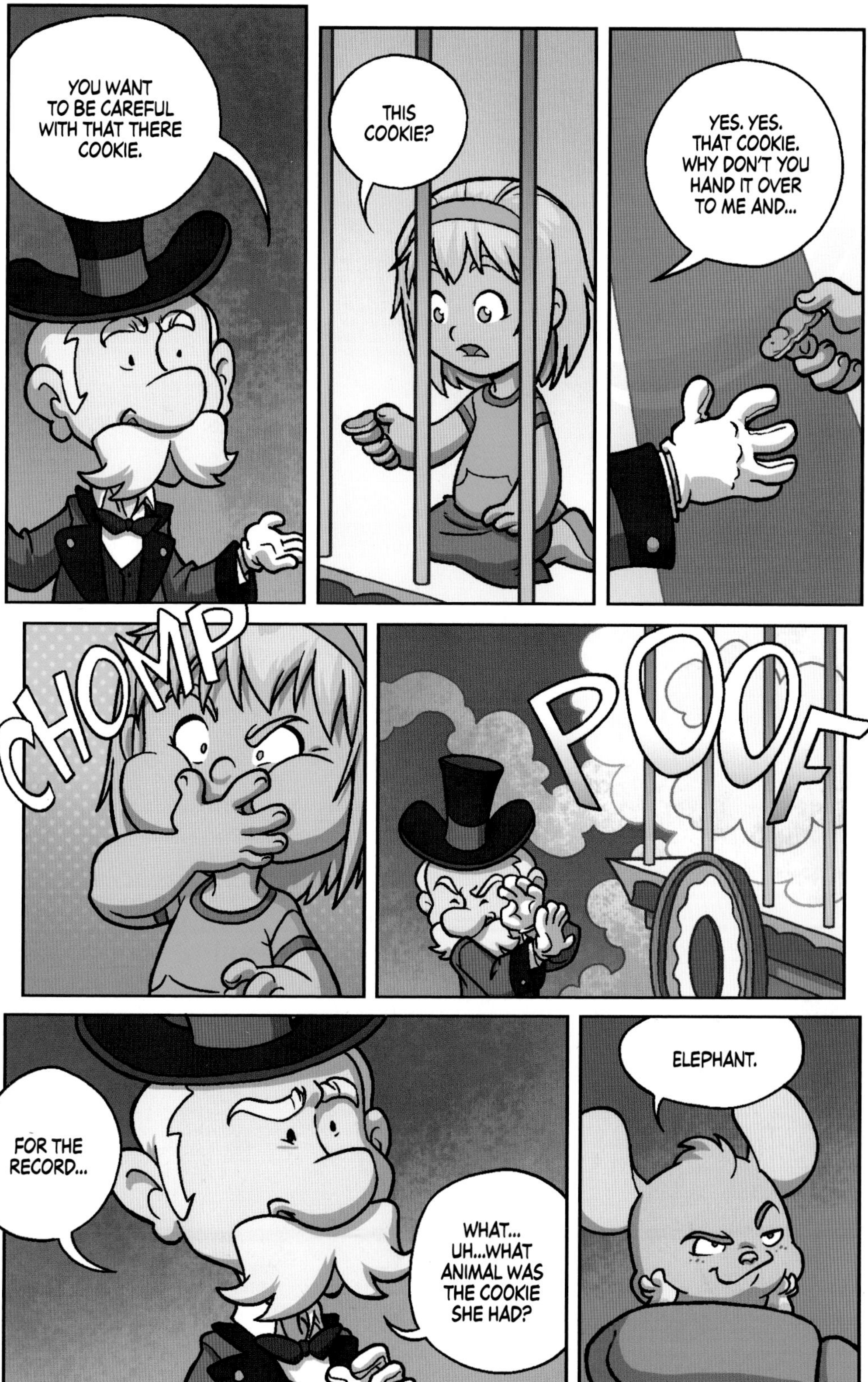
YOU WANT TO BE CAREFUL WITH THAT THERE COOKIE.
THIS COOKIE?
YES. YES. THAT COOKIE. WHY DON'T YOU HAND IT OVER TO ME AND...
CHOMP
POOF
FOR THE RECORD...
WHAT... UH...WHAT ANIMAL WAS THE COOKIE SHE HAD?
ELEPHANT.

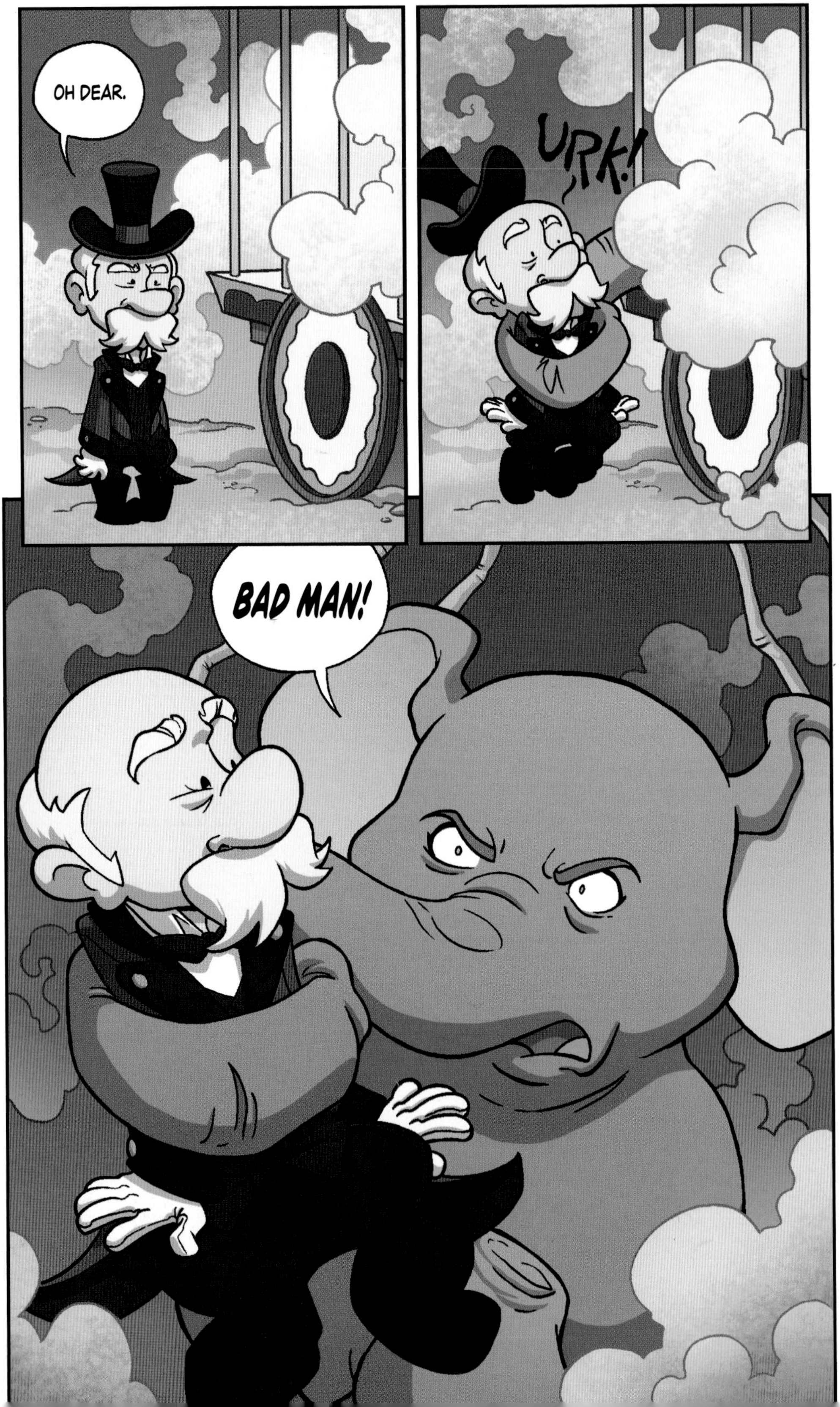
OH DEAR.
URK!
BAD MAN!

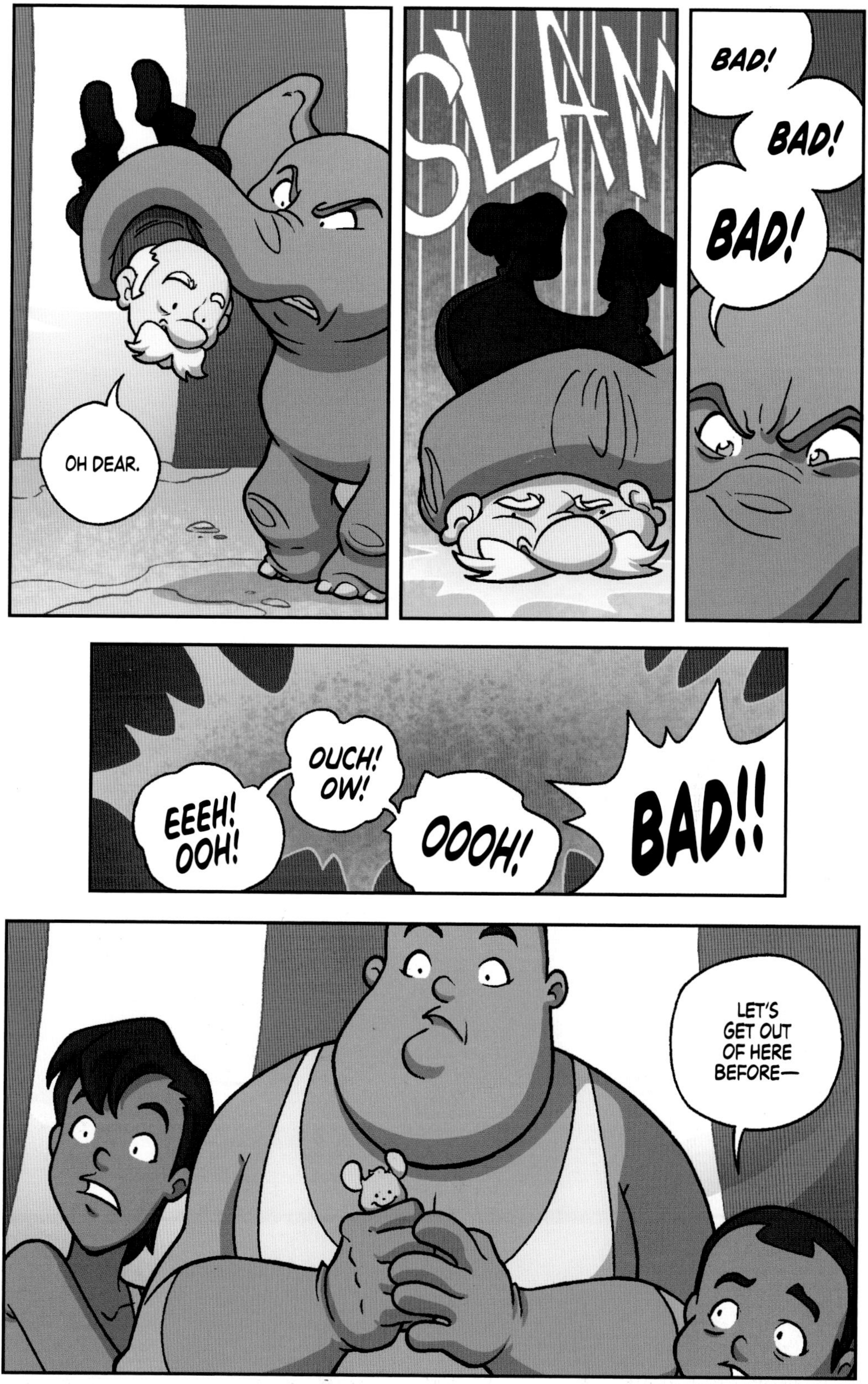
OH DEAR.
SLAM
BAD!
BAD!
BAD!
EEEH! OOH!
OUCH! OW!
OOOH!
BAD!!
LET'S GET OUT OF HERE BEFORE—

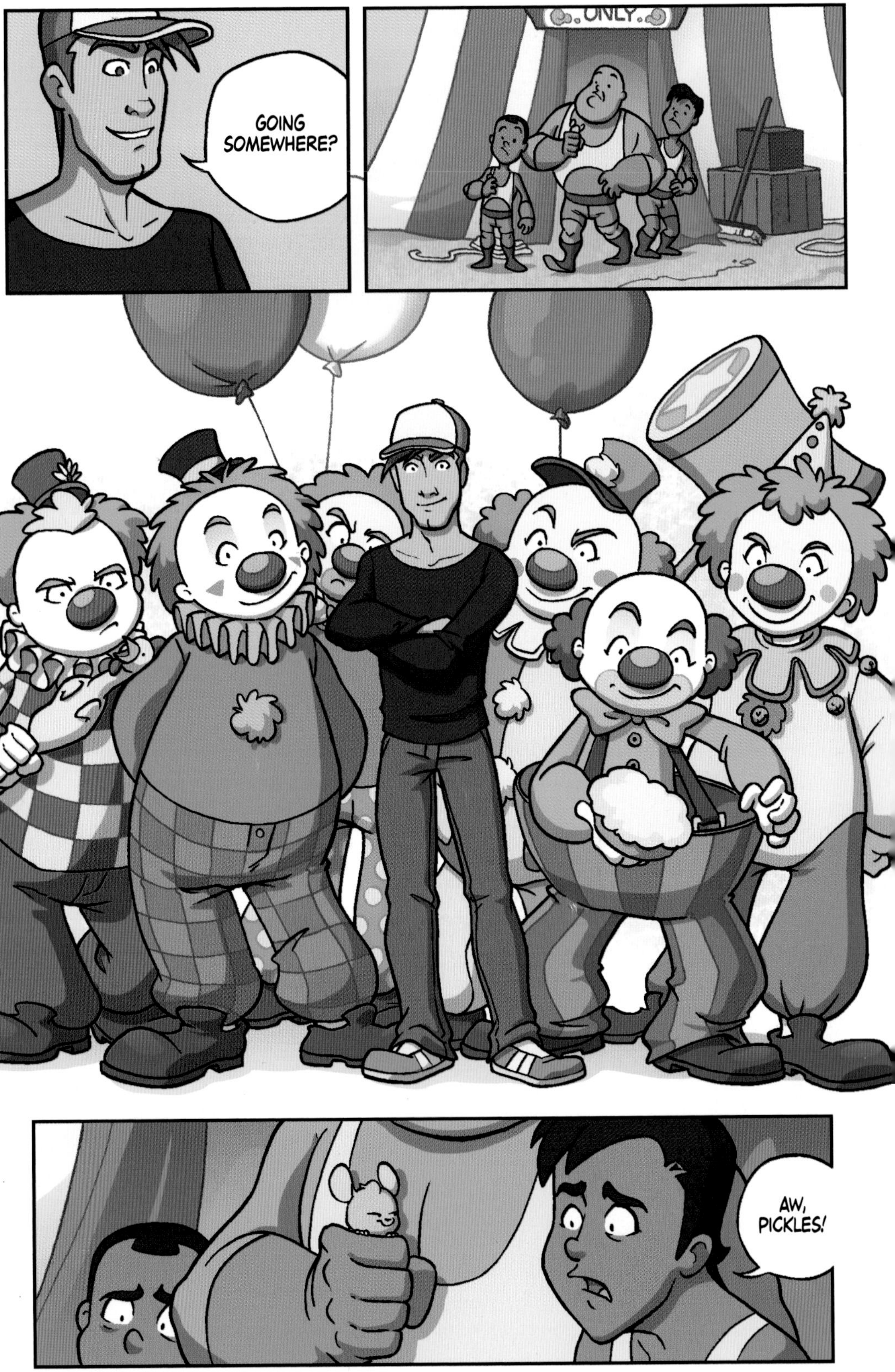
GOING SOMEWHERE?
ONLY
AW, PICKLES!

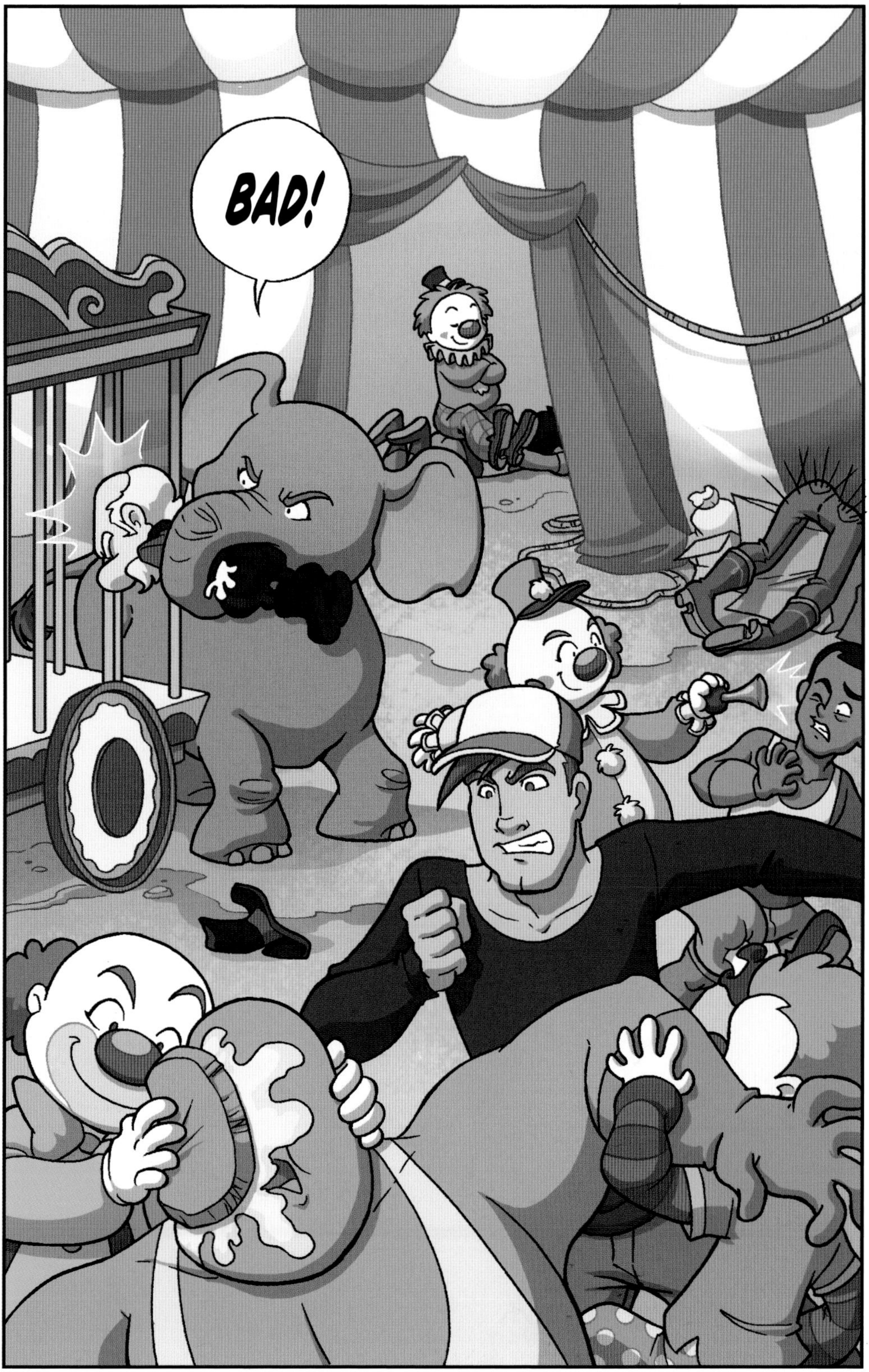
BAD!

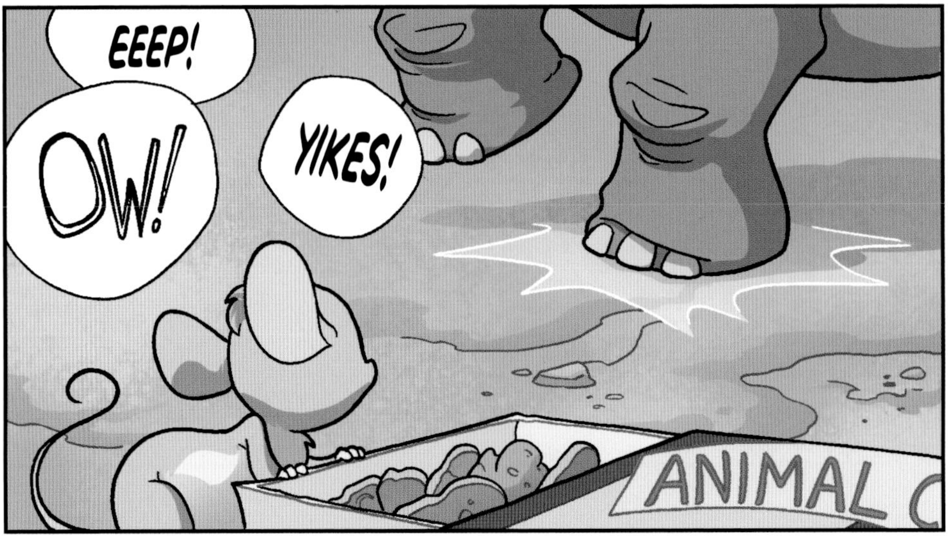
EEEP!
OW!
YIKES!
ANIMAL

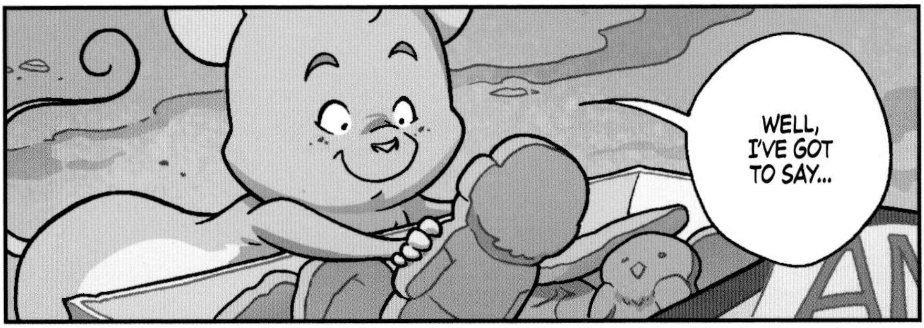
WELL, I'VE GOT TO SAY...

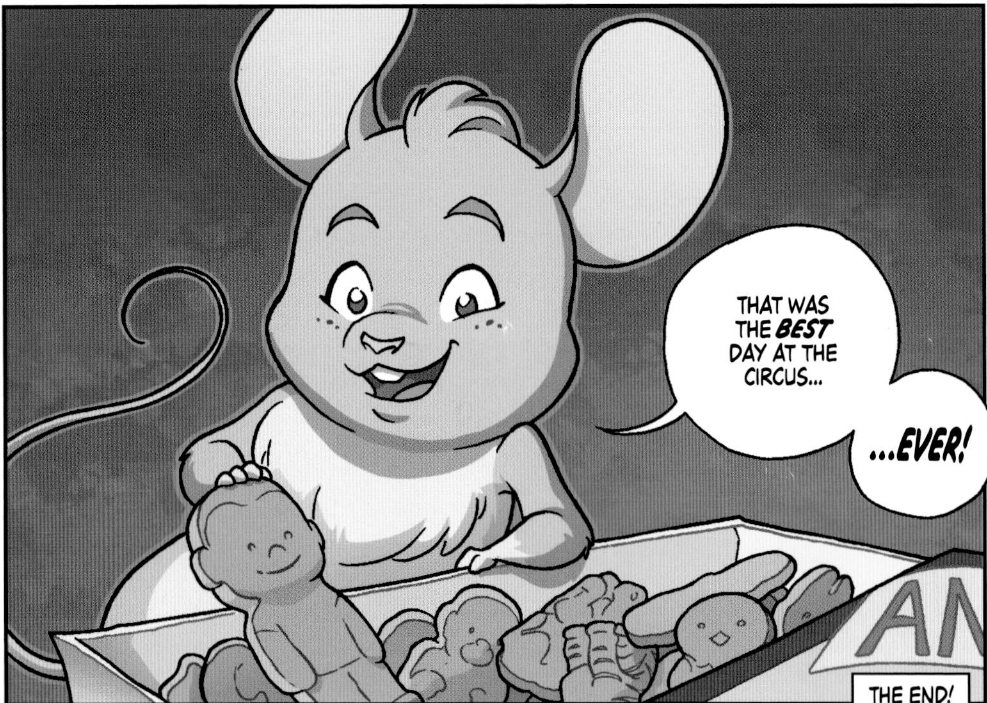
THAT WAS THE **BEST** DAY AT THE CIRCUS...
...EVER!
THE END!

THE ART OF ANIMAL CRACKERS

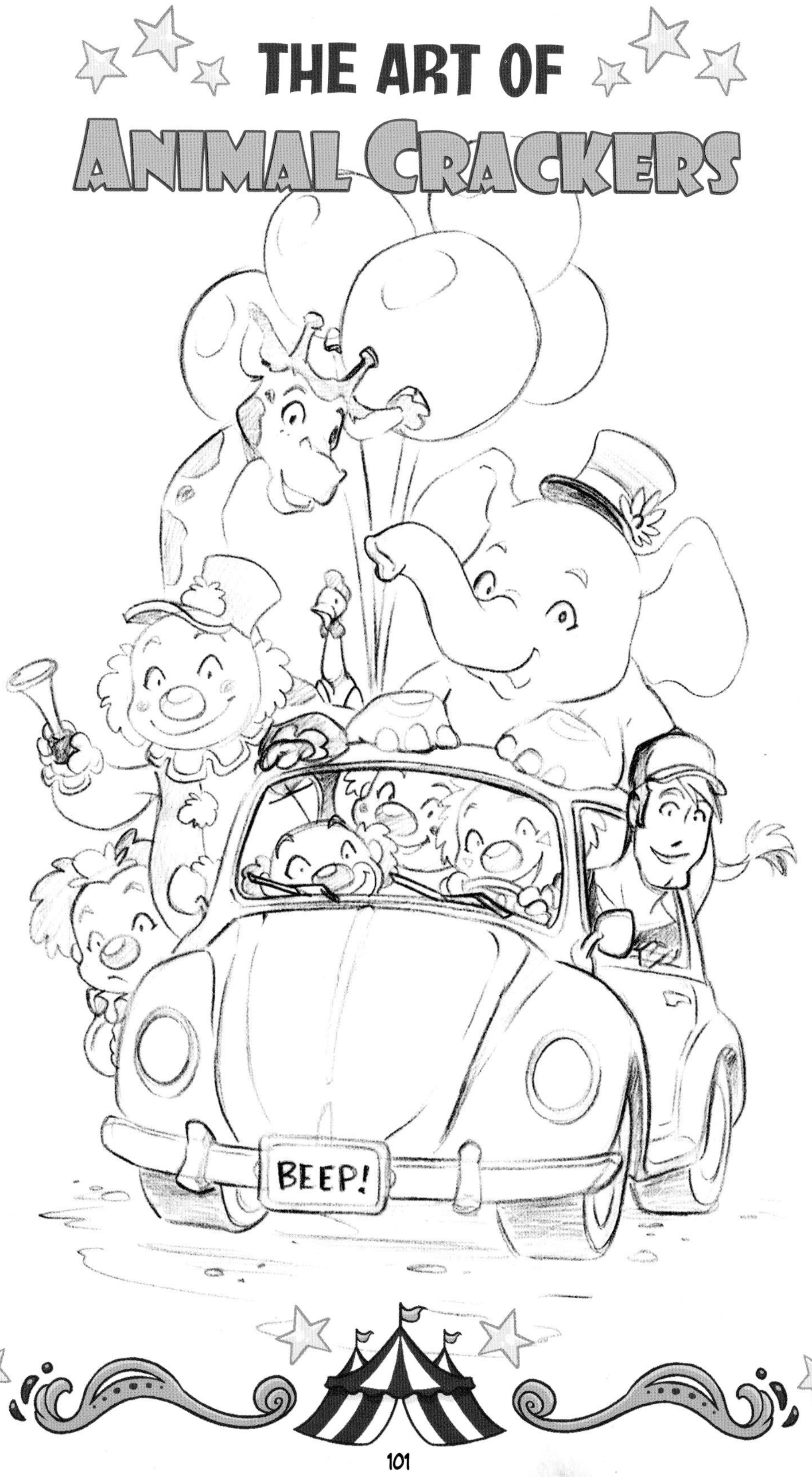

BEEP!

OWEN

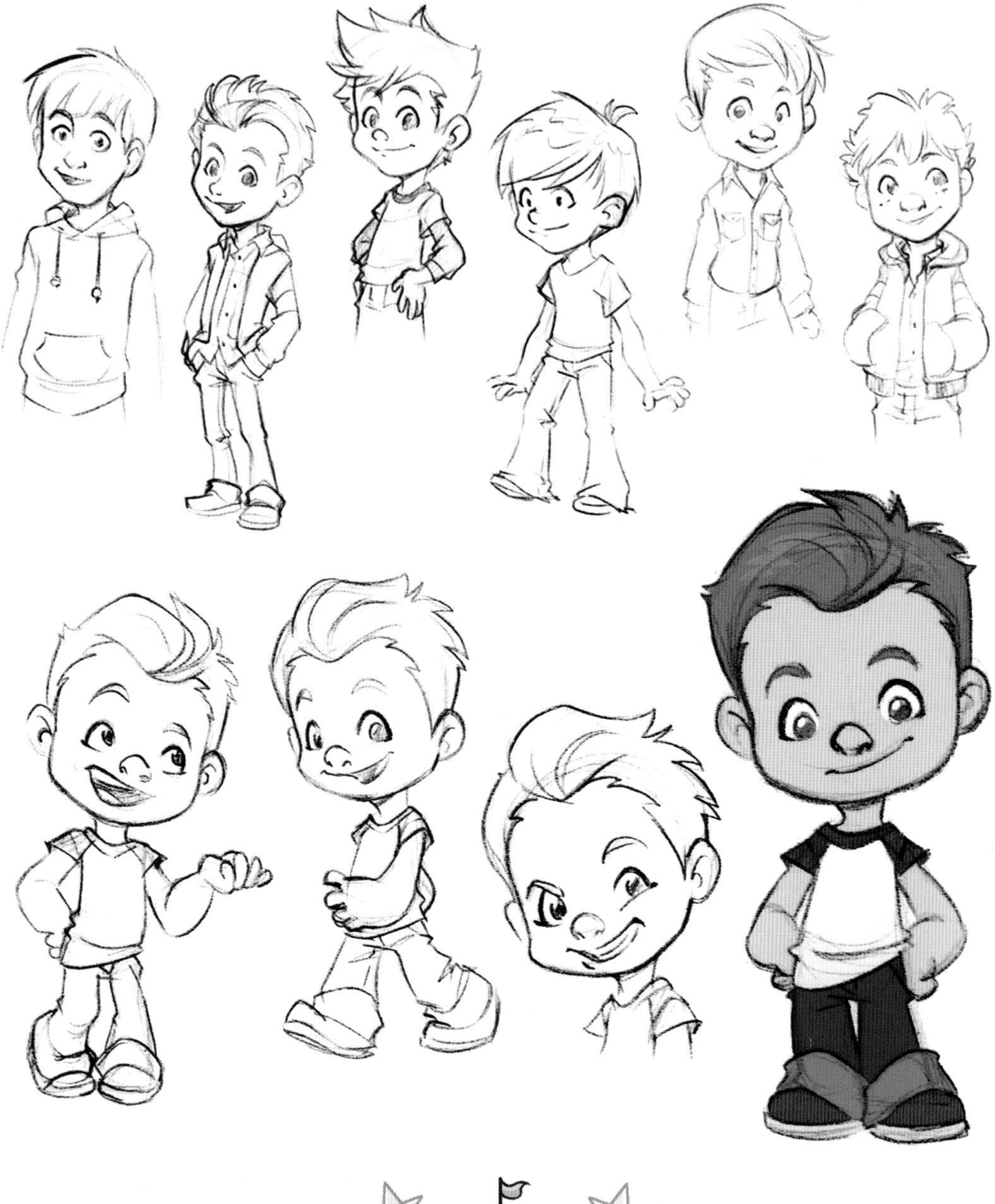

ZOE

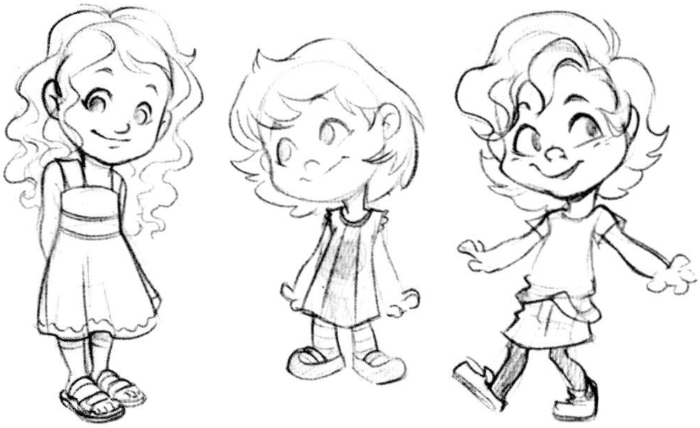

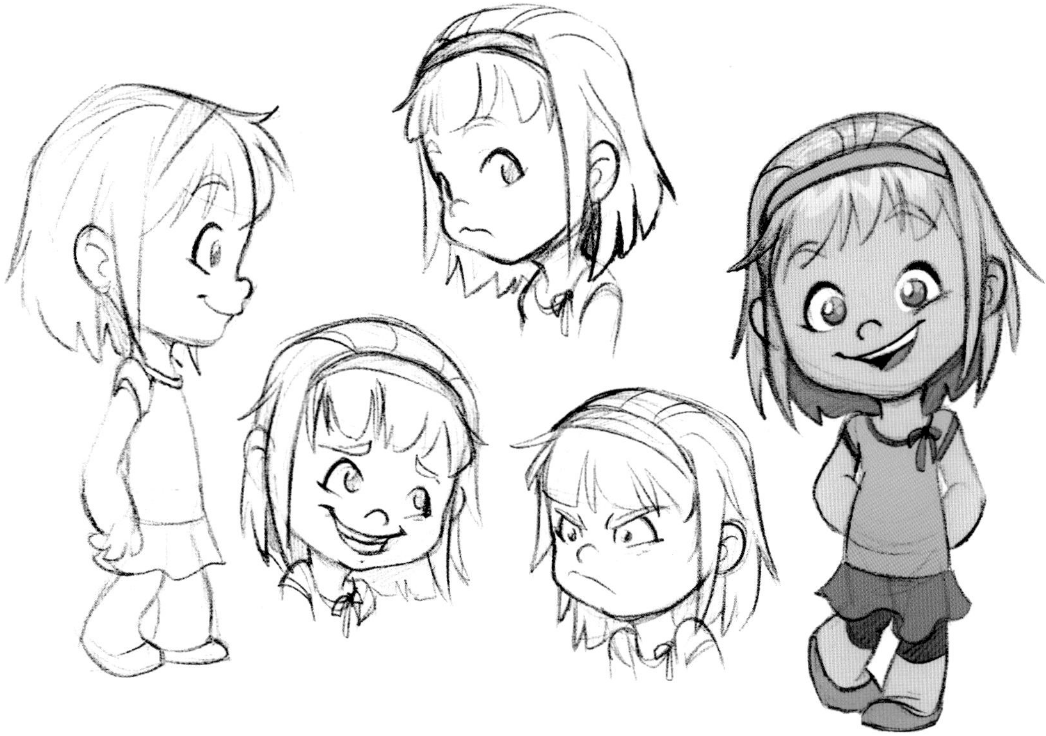

UNCLE DOUG

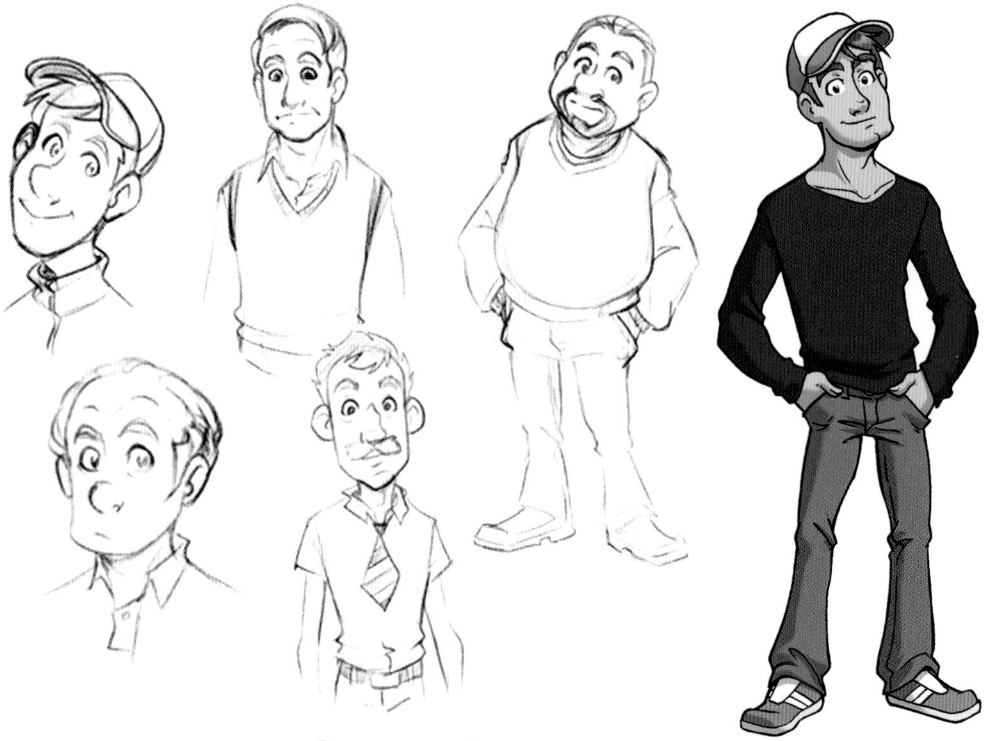

THE RINGMASTER

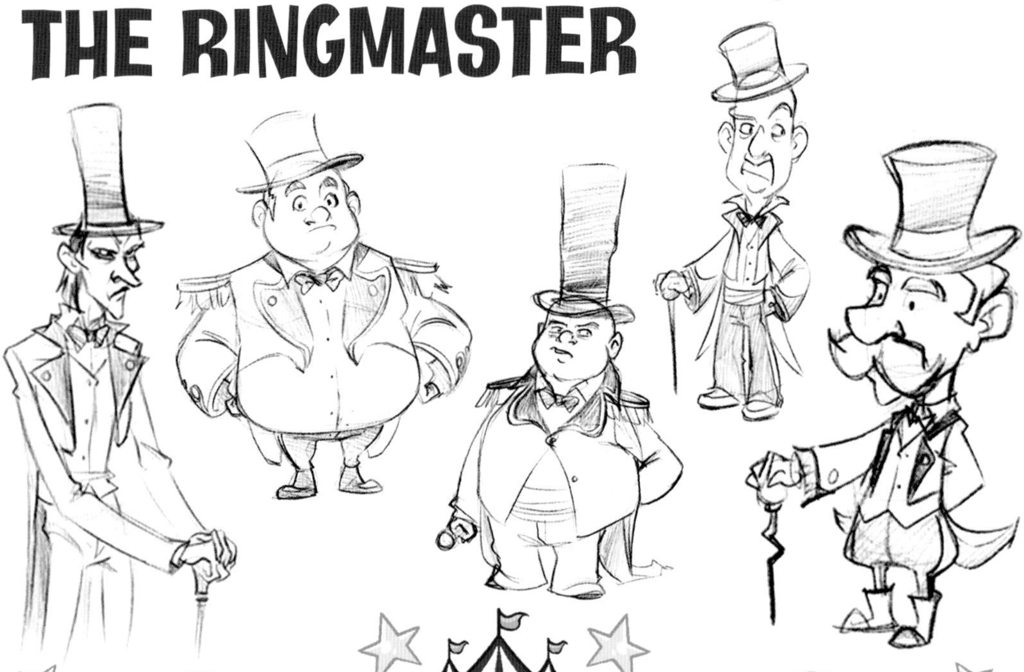

FAMILY

ANIMALS

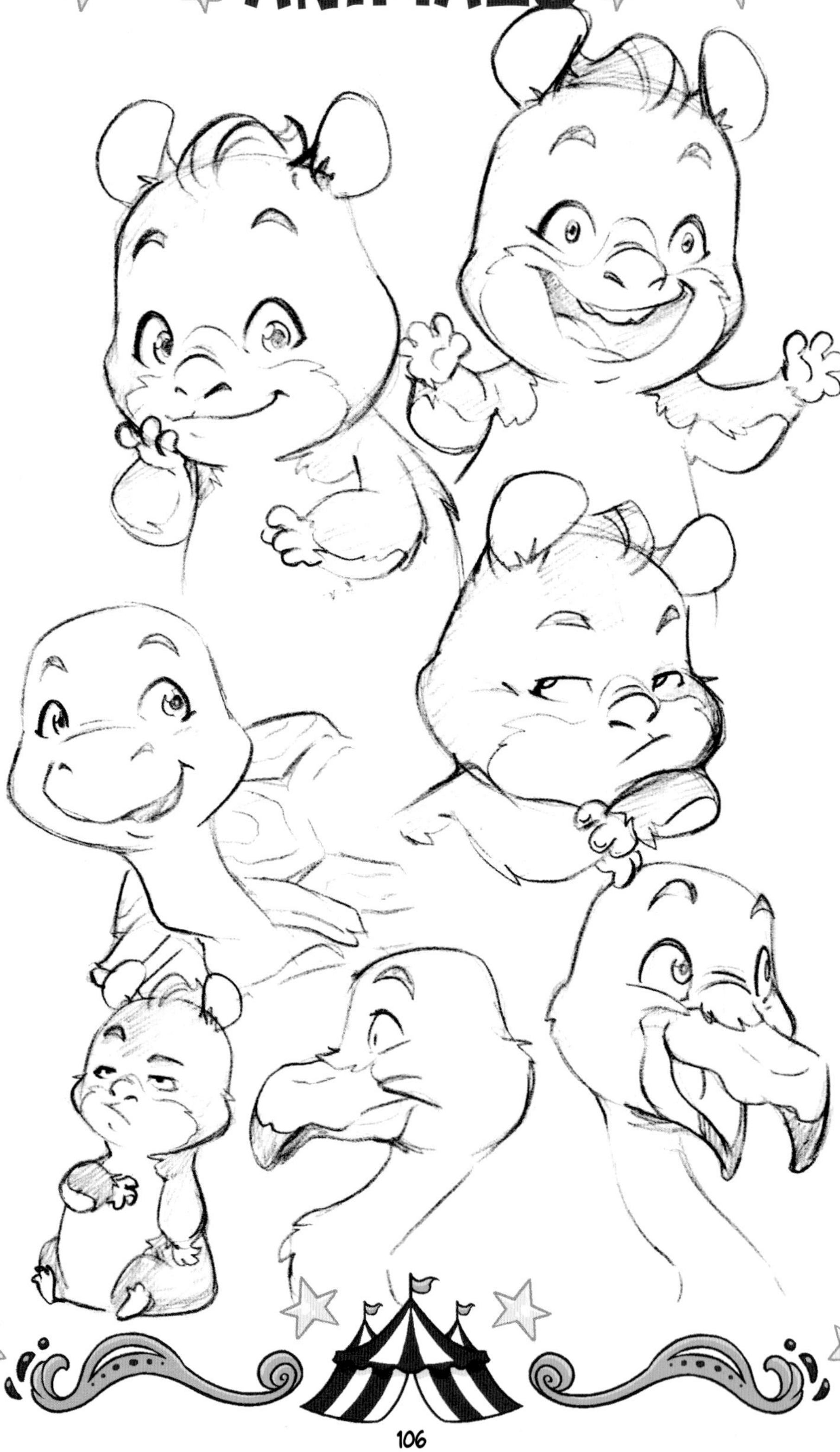

ANIMALS

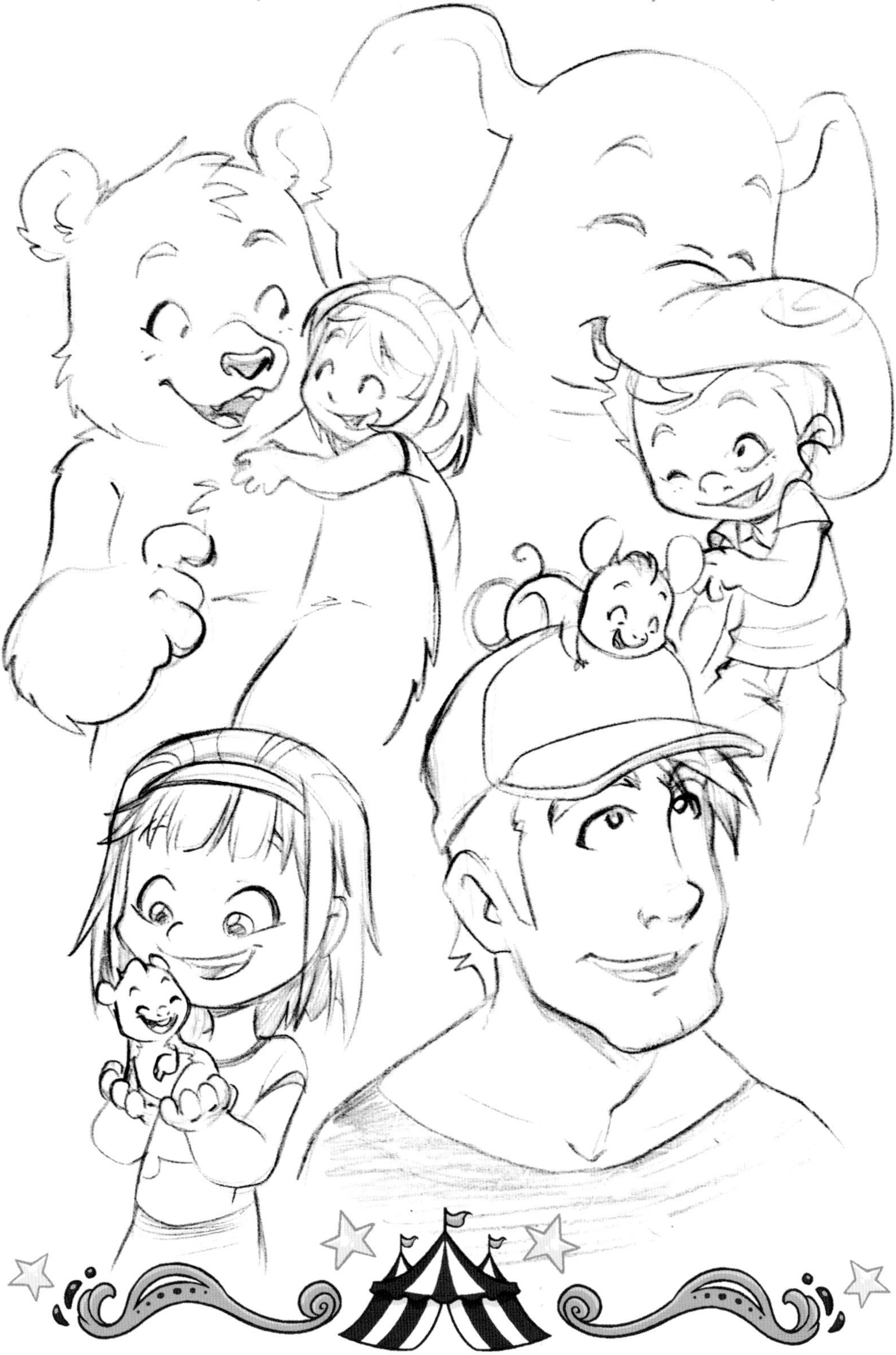

First Second

Text copyright © 2011 by Scott Christian Sava
Illustrations copyright © 2017 by Scott Christian Sava

Drawn with non-photo blue Col-Erase pencils, inked with Paper Mate Flair pens, and colored in Photoshop.

Published by First Second
First Second is an imprint of Roaring Brook Press,
a division of Holtzbrinck Publishing Holdings Limited Partnership
175 Fifth Avenue, New York, New York 10010

Library of Congress Control Number: 2016953278

ISBN 978-1-62672-935-3

Our books may be purchased in bulk for promotional, educational, or business use. Please
contact your local bookseller or the Macmillan Corporate and Premium Sales Department
at (800) 221-7945 ext. 5442 or by e-mail at MacmillanSpecialMarkets@macmillan.com.

FIRST EDITION

First edition 2017
Book design by John Green

Printed in China by Toppan Leefung Printing Ltd., Dongguan City, Guangdong Province
10 9 8 7 6 5 4 3 2 1

BY ART
WE LIVE